WARRIO...

Michelle Willingham

LIBRARIES NI
WITHDRAWN FROM STOCK

All rights reserved including the right of reproduction in whole or in part in any form. This edition is published by arrangement with Harlequin Books S.A.

This is a work of fiction. Names, characters, places, locations and incidents are purely fictional and bear no relationship to any real life individuals, living or dead, or to any actual places, business establishments, locations, events or incidents. Any resemblance is entirely coincidental.

This book is sold subject to the condition that it shall not, by way of trade or otherwise, be lent, resold, hired out or otherwise circulated without the prior consent of the publisher in any form of binding or cover other than that in which it is published and without a similar condition including this condition being imposed on the subsequent purchaser.

® and TM are trademarks owned and used by the trademark owner and/or its licensee. Trademarks marked with ® are registered with the United Kingdom Patent Office and/or the Office for Harmonisation in the Internal Market and in other countries.

Published in Great Britain 2015
by Mills & Boon, an imprint of Harlequin (UK) Limited,
Eton House, 18-24 Paradise Road, Richmond, Surrey, TW9 1SR

© 2015 Michelle Willingham

ISBN: 978-0-263-24822-7

Harlequin (UK) Limited's policy is to use papers that are natural, renewable and recyclable products and made from wood grown in sustainable forests. The logging and manufacturing processes conform to the legal environmental regulations of the country of origin.

Printed and bound in Spain
by CPI, Barcelona

RITA® Award finalist **Michelle Willingham** has written over twenty historical romances, novellas and short stories. Currently she lives in south-eastern Virginia with her husband and children. When she's not writing Michelle enjoys reading, baking and avoiding exercise at all costs. Visit her website at: michellewillingham.com

Visit the Author Profile page
at millsandboon.co.uk for more titles.

For Lori Yankoski, with thanks for being a good friend
and for sharing the gift of your music.

Chapter One

Ireland, 1172

Carice Faoilin was not afraid to die.

She had been sick for so long, she didn't know how it felt to be an ordinary woman any more. She didn't remember what it was to awaken without pain, to walk in the sunlight and enjoy each day as it was given. Most days, she stared at the walls, confined to her bed because she was too weak to move.

Until now.

In a matter of days, soldiers had invaded her home, demanding that she fulfil her delayed betrothal contract. She was ordered to accompany them to wed the High King of Éireann, Rory Ó Connor. The Ard-Righ had a brutal reputation, and few women wanted to wed him, herself included.

Perhaps she should have gone meekly, obeying the High King's orders as a woman should. But then, Carice had never been the obedient sort. She wouldn't have agreed to the betrothal, had her ambitious father given her a choice.

She was *not* going to lie back and offer herself up as the sacrificial lamb—even if this escape attempt killed her. And it very well might.

Each footstep felt leaden as she struggled to disappear into the dark forest. She'd chosen a long branch to use as a walking stick while she made her escape. A small voice inside her warned her, *You don't have the strength to reach shelter. You're going to die tonight.*

She silenced the voice. She had lived with the prospect of dying for so long, what did it matter any more? Worrying about it wouldn't change anything. Instead, she preferred to fight for every breath, living each day as if it were her last.

Although today might *be* her last day if she didn't find shelter soon.

With every step she took, the air seemed to grow colder. There was snow upon the breath of the wind, and Carice huddled within her cloak, leaning heavily upon the staff. Her feet were half-frozen, and her fingers were numb. She didn't know how long she'd been walking, but she prayed to find a warm place to sleep. *Please let there be shelter somewhere close by.*

Her prayer was answered when she reached the far side of the forest and ventured into an open field. Just near the horizon, the moon illuminated a fortress with a tall limestone wall surrounding it.

When she drew closer, she realised it was an abbey, not a fortress. Never had she visited this place, though it was only a few days' journey from Carrickmeath, her home. But tonight, it was her best hope for shelter.

I don't know if I can make it that far, her body reasoned. Every muscle in her body ached, she was starving, and the distance appeared vast.

If you don't keep going, you'll freeze, her brain reminded her. And death by freezing didn't sound very pleasant. She had to keep moving, especially since she'd made it this far.

Carice continued walking across the snowy meadow, counting the steps as she did. Though her legs were shaking from exertion, she forced herself to keep going. While she walked, she hoped that the monks who dwelled within the abbey would grant her a place to sleep and a warm fire. Or, at the very least, a place to collapse from exhaustion.

It was the promise of getting warm that kept her walking. Snowflakes began descending from the sky, the barest drifting flurries.

Just a little farther, she told herself. *Don't stop.*

When she reached the abbey, strangely, the gate was open. A crow cawed at her arrival swooping down to inspect her presence. Inside the grounds, the scent of smoke lingered like a harsh memory. A fire had ravaged the outbuildings, and the battered stone structures were charred and lay in ruins. Another building nearby was in better condition, but it, too, had visible damage, along with the nearby roundtower that was missing its roof.

'Is anyone here?' she called out.

There came no answer, no sound at all. She walked through the open space, her feet crunching within the wet snow. Near the cemetery, she spied four freshly dug graves. Snow covered the earthen mounds, and she crossed herself at the sight. A chill crossed over her spine as she wondered what had happened here. Were all the monks dead from the fire? Clearly, the abbey had been abandoned.

Carice walked up the stairs leading to the main sanctuary. There was no wooden door remaining, and inside, the chapel was dark and cold. At least it was better than remaining outside, she reasoned. The fire had not reached the inner sanctuary, for the scent of smoke diminished as soon as she walked inside the space. At one end, there was an altar with a larger chair beside it. Spider webs lined the corners of the walls, and a savoury aroma caught Carice's attention.

It was the faintest scent of food, like a roasted fowl. Someone *had* been here recently. She spied bones upon the floor and her stomach growled at the thought of a hot meal. It seemed that she could never satiate the endless hunger tormenting her. She pushed back the cravings and called out again, 'Is anyone here?'

But there was still no answer.

This time, she began exploring a narrow hallway at the back of the sanctuary that opened into a spiral staircase. She guessed that it likely led towards the abbot's private chambers. Since there had been food scraps left behind, then there might be someone sleeping above stairs.

Her skin prickled with a rise of nerves. It wasn't wise for a woman to approach a stranger, alone with no guard. But she had no alternative. Right now, her body was reaching the end of its strength. She needed to rest before she could continue her journey, for it was the only way she would survive what lay ahead.

Carice steadied herself before climbing the narrow stairs. After the sixth step, she had to sit for a moment to calm the dizziness. She listened hard for the sound of anyone, but only silence met her ears.

It will be all right, she told herself. If the abbot was here, surely he would find a place for her to sleep. And if he was not, then she would remain in his chambers until dawn. She reached deep inside her for the last of her strength. She crawled up the remaining stairs, struggling to reach the top. The stone floor was cold beneath her hands and feet, and she fought to stand once more.

Carice leaned heavily upon the wall, stumbling towards the first room. Inside the chamber, she spied a narrow bed with rumpled coverings upon it. The curtains were drawn back and hot coals lay upon the hearth, as if there had been a fire recently.

A trace of fear crept over her, but Carice was

too tired to care any more. If there was someone here who intended to harm her, there was nothing she could do about it. She lacked the strength to move.

Exhausted, she stumbled towards the bed, seeking its comfort. She huddled beneath the woollen coverlet, so grateful for a place to sleep. It didn't matter if someone had been here before her, or if they were still here. Nothing mattered except being warm and sheltered.

But as she drifted off, Carice sensed a presence in the room…almost as if someone was watching over her.

The woman sleeping on his bed was the most beautiful creature he'd ever seen. From the moment he'd heard her enter the abbey, Raine de Garenne had watched over her from the spiral stairs, remaining in the shadows while she had explored the sanctuary. He didn't know why she was here, but it was clear she was alone.

Fragile, too, like a snowflake upon his palm. She had collapsed after reaching his room, and now she was sharing the very bed he'd slept within.

Why had she intruded within this place? He remained standing in the shadows against the far wall until he was certain she was asleep. The room was growing colder since the peat fire he'd lit earlier was dying down.

He added more fuel to the hearth until the fire grew hot. The dim light illuminated her features better. Her long dark hair was not black as he'd imagined, but a warmer brown with hints of gold and red. It hung to her waist, and her skin was pale against the coverlet. How had she come to the abbey, and why was she alone? He couldn't imagine anyone leaving a woman like her unguarded, unless they had died trying to protect her.

His mood grew sombre as he thought of his own failings. *You should have died for Nicole and Elise*, his conscience taunted. *You should have sacrificed your life for theirs.* He was haunted by his sisters' fate even two years later. He'd believed he could get close to them and free them from captivity by joining King Henry's soldiers. Instead, he had been sent to fight with the Irish Sea separating them. He should have known that the king's men would never let him remain near his family.

But there was no means of unravelling the past, no reason to dwell upon the bitter memories now. Nothing would change his sisters' captivity until he carried out the king's orders. He would return to his commander just after dawn, and if he succeeded in his task, he might win their freedom.

Raine held fast to the thought, for it was the only shred of hope remaining.

Now, he questioned what to do about the woman. Raine pulled a chair beside the fire, considering his choices. She didn't belong in the abbey any more than he did. He rested his forearms upon his knees, and the amber fire-light revealed a long scar—a visible reminder of the battles he'd faced. Most of his scars and burned flesh were hidden beneath his chain mail armour, the cost of survival.

He stared into the fire, knowing he had no right to live. As a soldier, he'd stolen countless souls from the earth. He ought to feel guilty about their deaths, but he didn't. There was a stony sense of emptiness where his heart had once been. His sisters' lives depended upon his obedience. He was chained to this life of a Norman soldier that he didn't want, and he would continue to fight until he had earned back their freedom or he died. He had put aside any dreams he might have held for his own future, for he deserved this prison after failing to save his parents.

Mercenary, some had called him. A heartless murderer, the Irish would say. His soul was already damned, according to the priests, and he regretted nothing. As long as his sisters were alive and whole, none of it mattered.

Raine moved to stand beside the young woman, and her scent caught his attention. The air of innocence surrounded her, and her face was soft like a spring morning. It was doubtful that this woman had ever touched a weapon in her life.

He leaned down, reaching to touch a lock of her hair. It was not a heavy silk like other women he had known. No, it was fragile, like her—tangled and damp from the journey. As he studied her more closely, he realised how very thin she was, half-starved and frail. This was not a woman who had missed a meal or two. She was fighting for her life.

He'd seen folk who had starved to death before, men and women alike. And although he shouldn't care what happened to a stranger, he felt an invisible force drawing him closer. She needed someone to watch over her, someone to take care of her—the way he wanted someone to protect his sisters.

His mood darkened as he went to fetch her another blanket from the chest. He laid it over her, and she moved slightly, snuggling close within the blanket.

Dieu, how long had she been walking outside? He thought about awakening her but decided to let her sleep. She looked exhausted from her journey. He adjusted the blanket and touched her hair once again. His questions could wait until morning.

Raine lit a torch in the hearth and then left the room, closing the door to keep in the heat. He walked down the stairs and through the sanctuary. Although the worship space was untouched by fire, he could feel the presence of the holy men…and their screams haunted him still.

He blamed himself for their deaths, for being unable to save them. The devastating fire had claimed the lives of every man, and he'd been granted only a few days' leave to bury the bodies.

Raine walked outside to the kitchen, needing a distraction. He had eaten his own meal hours ago, and the truth was, he knew very little about cooking. Among the Norman soldiers, his food consisted of hunting meat and roasting it. However, the monks who had once lived here had root vegetables stored underground before they'd been attacked. He supposed he could find something for the woman to eat.

He paused, feeling like a thief. But dead men had no need of food, he reminded himself. There was no bread, but he found dried meat he didn't recognise, parsnips, and some walnuts. Would she like any of it? He wasn't certain, but it would have to suffice. Raine started to gather it up in a bundle, but then he stopped short.

What in the name of the Rood was he doing? Bringing her food and blankets as if she were a treasured guest? She was a stranger and an intruder. He ought to awaken her and demand to know why she was here. There was no reason to let her stay.

Raine seized the food and strode through the kitchens, slamming the door behind him. He didn't know this woman. He didn't know anything about her except that she was dangerously weak, and the sight of her stole his breath.

It was an undeniable fact that she would die if he turned her away. And the last thing he wanted was one more death on his conscience.

But he could save her.

Raine slowed his pace back to the *donjon*, letting out a low curse. He knew what would happen to a beautiful woman travelling alone, if he forced her to go. He bit back a curse at the thought.

She's not your responsibility. You must return to your commander and your duties.

He knew that. But when he entered the sanctuary and climbed the stairs bearing the bundle of food, he couldn't stop thinking about his sisters. They were alone in England, hostages of the king. Was anyone protecting them? Or were they at a stranger's mercy, like this woman was?

No, she was not his to protect. But neither would he abandon her. He had finished burying the holy men, and before he returned to his commander and the other soldiers, he could bring her to safety. At least then he would know that she had come to no harm.

Raine pushed the door open, and the chamber was warm and inviting. The peat fire glowed upon the hearth, casting shadows within the room. A simple cross hung upon one wall, and beside the hearth was a wooden chair. The woman was sleeping within his bed, her breathing deep and even. He moved silently, setting

the food down on a low table before returning
to the shadows.

Raine knew he should be resentful that this
woman had stolen his bed. Instead he felt…
grateful that he could give her a place to sleep.
There was the sense that he could watch her
sleep, all night long, and he would enjoy the
peace upon her face.

She stirred a moment, and he remained
against the far wall out of the light. But a moment later, she sat up in the bed. Her long brown
hair hung over her shoulders, and her eyes
opened. They were a clear blue, like a summer
sky. A sudden wariness crossed over him, for
she was easily the most beautiful woman he'd
ever seen.

Which meant that her presence would be
missed, and men would pursue her.

'I know you're there,' she said quietly. 'You
built the fire up while I was sleeping.'

She spoke in Irish, and for once, he was
thankful that he'd learned their language. He
understood her, although he had difficulty
speaking beyond a handful of words. Though
he had lived in Éireann for more than two
years, he said nothing, not wanting to frighten
her. And yet, he had a hundred questions he

wanted to ask this woman. Who she was…why she was here.

After a time, she asked, 'Do you intend to harm me?' There was weariness in her voice as if she hardly cared anymore.

'No,' he said. 'You are safe.' He said nothing else, letting her draw whatever conclusions she would—though his armour made it clear that he was not a monk.

'You are a Norman soldier,' she predicted, studying his appearance.

'*Je suis.*' There was no reason to deny it, particularly when her gaze had settled upon the conical helm he had set aside.

She let out a slow breath and surprised him by switching into his own language. 'Will you come into the light, so that I may see you?'

He didn't want her to see his face. Let her think of him as one of hundreds of nameless soldiers, men easily forgotten. If she never saw him, it would be easier for him to fade from her memory. He wanted no one to remember him, no one to know who he was. It was the only way he could protect himself from being recognised—especially if he succeeded in the task his commander had set before him.

'I will remain here,' he answered in his own

language. 'You may sleep in peace, and I will watch over you for the night.'

She stiffened at that. 'And what is it you're wanting from me in return?'

He had no expectations of her, but simply answered, 'Tell me your name.'

She seemed to relax at his request, recognising that he had no intention of harming her. 'I am Carice Faoilin, of Carrickmeath. And you?'

'I am Raine de Garenne.' The name would mean nothing to her, he was certain.

She pulled the coverlet higher and asked, 'Are you alone here?'

'I am.' At least for now. It was likely that other priests and holy men might come to view the damage when they received word of the fire. By then, he intended to be gone.

'Why? Where are the rest of your men?'

'I will join them in the morning. I stopped here only for a short while.' But he would not tell her all of his reasons.

Instead he said, 'There is food and drink, should you want them. I bid you *adieu*.' He kept his hood over his head to shield his appearance from her, departing the room before she could ask more questions.

* * *

The next morning, Carice awakened in a strange bed. The sheets held the unfamiliar scent of a man's body. It was like being entangled with someone else, though she knew she had slept alone. And although bits of memory returned, making her realise where she was, she felt an intimacy with the man whose bed she had shared.

Raine had kept his word not to harm her, and she had slept soundly, feeling safer than she had in years—which made no sense at all. Slowly, she sat up, holding the bed coverlet close. It was always difficult to stay warm, and she was never comfortable any more—not really.

But strangely, the night of rest had renewed her strength. She eased her legs to the side of the bed and saw the food and drink waiting near the fire. There was also a basin of water upon the floor near the hearth. Curious, she eased out of bed and walked slowly towards the waiting chair. She sank down upon it and then reached out to the basin of water. Steam rose on the surface, and she realised then, that he'd heated it for her.

Her heart stumbled at that. When she touched the water, the heat made her sigh with pleasure.

How had he known when she would awaken? She eased off her stockings on impulse and placed her freezing feet into the warmed water.

Bliss sank through her, and she smiled as the heat overtook her. Though she knew nothing about Raine de Garenne, he had sensed her needs and cared for her in a way she'd never anticipated.

The food was meagre, only a bit of dried meat, walnuts, and raw parsnips. But she recognised the offering for what it was—the best he had to give. She ate the meat and walnuts, and was deeply grateful when her stomach did not ache at the food.

At Carrickmeath, the constant nausea and stomach difficulties had been neverending. Only after she'd left, had her aches diminished. It had made her wonder if someone had been trying to poison her in her father's house. She couldn't understand why, if that were true. There was no reason for anyone to harm her— she had no power at all within the tribe. Although she was betrothed to the High King, her death would accomplish nothing.

But since she'd left, each day had become a little easier. At least now when she ate, she didn't feel as if knives were carving up her insides. Perhaps it was the taste of freedom that made food more tolerable.

Carice had just reached for the parsnip, when her door opened. In the daylight, she got a better glimpse of Raine, though he was still wearing the hood to hide his features. He was a tall man, broad-shouldered like a fighter. He wore chain mail armour with a leather corselet and a long sword hung sheathed at his waist. Under one arm, he carried his conical helm.

Why did he continue to hide his face? She was curious about this man and the mysteries surrounding him.

'Thank you for the warm water. And for the food,' she said, speaking the Norman tongue. 'I am sorry. I should have saved you some, but I fear there's only a parsnip—' She held up the white root vegetable apologetically, but he dismissed her offer.

'It was meant for you,' he countered. 'I've already eaten.' He crossed his arms over his chest, staring at her.

It made her uncomfortable, and Carice asked, 'Won't you sit, then?'

And remove your hood so that I may see your face, she thought to herself. He was clearly hiding his identity, though she could not guess why.

'Where are your escorts?' he asked. 'Who was guarding you?'

She removed her feet from the basin of water and dried them with the hem of her gown before replacing her shoes. 'No one. I was running away.'

'From whom?'

Carice sent him a half-smile. 'My father was escorting me to my wedding. I am betrothed to the High King of Éireann.' She remarked, 'I suppose you'll want to turn me over to them for a reward. They would pay handsomely for my safe return.' Most men would be eager to hand her over for the promise of silver or gold. But she rather hoped that he would leave her alone.

Raine paused a moment before his hand moved to the hilt of his sword. 'It's more likely that your father would kill me, believing I was the one who took you.'

His candour revealed a man of intelligence. 'That is indeed possible.' She straightened the hem of her gown and stood up from the chair. 'If you would help me to disappear where they'll never find me, I could compensate you for your assistance.'

He didn't move as she took a step closer. Then another.

'Please consider it,' she said softly, reaching towards his hood.

His hands seized her wrists, drawing them downward. His grip was firm, almost bruising. 'I have other duties more important than you, *chérie*.'

Carice drew back, startled by his refusal. 'I don't doubt that. But I was only asking for your help.'

She tried to pull away, but he held her wrists fast, as if he had more to say. His silence made it clear that he wasn't going to help her escape. Her nerves took control, and she continued talking too fast.

'Trahern MacEgan was supposed to help me leave last night, but he never arrived. I had no choice but to run, while we were still far away from Tara.'

Raine gave no response. Slowly, his thumbs edged the pulse point of her wrists, the heat of his touch burning through her. Why did he continue to hold her hands? Carice stilled, and the caress moved through her like a wave of yearning.

Her heartbeat quickened, and his fingers laced with hers. Never had any man touched her in this way, and her mind envisioned his hands moving over her bare flesh. Upon his forearms, she saw the evidence of scarring, the healed wounds of battle. Perhaps his face held the same. Was that why he would not reveal himself?

She took an unsteady breath, and said, 'I don't know if anyone will come for me or not.'

'I know of the MacEgans,' Raine said at last. 'I will look for Trahern and bring him back if he is nearby. But soon, you must leave.' He let go of her hands, and the heat of his palms remained upon her skin.

Her heart was pounding, and she turned her back. 'What if you cannot find him? Am I to go on alone?'

'My duties lie elsewhere. I cannot accompany you.'

There was another reason; she could sense it. 'What duties?' she demanded. 'There are no other soldiers here. You are alone.'

'For now,' he acceded. 'But I am under the command of King Henry,' he said. There was a hint of darkness in his tone, and he added, 'His Grace has given me his orders, and those I must obey.'

In a crumbling abbey? Although he had no reason to lie to her, his words made little sense.

Her thoughts drifted back to the fresh graves she had seen. Had he been ordered to burn the abbey and kill the monks? Was that why he'd been sent here? She swallowed hard, not wanting to believe it. 'A king would have no interest in a place like this.'

His posture stiffened, and she took a step backwards. 'You know not King Henry's orders, *chérie*. And you do not know me.'

He was trying to frighten her, she was certain. And perhaps he was a ruthless fighter and the king's man. But then…he had brought her food and warmed water. These were not the actions of a cruel man. She sensed that he was here for a very different reason.

'You are right,' she agreed. 'But you showed me kindness, for which I am grateful.' She nodded towards the hearth where the basin of water remained.

Again, he held his silence for a time. Carice didn't know what to say, but she didn't truly want to know what had happened in this place—or Raine's part in it. She took a step towards the hearth, and the motion unsettled her. Despite the food she'd eaten, the effects of her illness began to set in.

Her ears rang as the dizziness swept over

her. She rested her palm against the wall, try-ing to take steady breaths. *Please, not now.* Not when she had come so far. The tide of weak-ness washed over her, stealing away her vision.

'What is it?' he asked quietly.

She turned to Raine, but his hooded features blurred. The room spun, and her hand slipped against the wall.

She cursed herself, knowing she wasn't going to make it to the bed. A moment later, her knees collapsed, sending the world into blackness.

Raine barely caught the young woman before she fainted. One moment Carice was speaking, and the next, she dropped like a stone. He car-ried her over to the bed, bothered by how light she was. His mouth set into a line as he lowered her to the mattress. Despite his demand for her to leave, she was incapable of making any jour-ney, as weak as she was. And unless he left her behind, he wasn't going to meet his commander on the morrow.

Her face was the colour of snow, and he didn't know the nature of her illness. He poured a cup of wine for her and waited for her to re-gain consciousness. It took a moment, but when her eyes fluttered open, he saw the fear in them.

'I'm sorry,' she said softly. 'I wasn't feeling well.'

'You need to return to your family,' he said, 'where they can take better care of you.'

'Where I'll be sent to wed a man old enough to be my father.' She shook her head. 'I've no wish for that.'

'It's what marriages are,' he told her. 'Nothing more than an alliance.'

'I am going to die, Raine. My time grows short, and I do not wish to spend my last months wedded to a monster.'

The urge to deny it came to his lips, but he could see the fragility in her body. The weariness there was more than exhaustion from a journey.

'I have been ill for years now,' she said. 'And each day is worse than the next.' She shook her head slowly. 'Surely you can understand that I would prefer to die as a free woman.' A wistful look crossed her face. 'The day will come when I cannot bear to live in this pain any longer. And then it will end.'

'Is it a wasting sickness, then?' He had seen men and women die in such ways before.

A twisted smile came over her. 'In a manner of speaking. I can hardly eat without becoming sick.' She leaned back and stretched her arm over her head. It brought the curve of her breasts to his attention. *Oui,* she was thin. But he wondered what she would look like if her body were filled out with plumpness.

'Is it always this way?' Undoubtedly her illness had caused her to collapse. But he had never heard of a wasting sickness that involved food—unless it was poison of some kind.

'Usually it's worse,' she admitted. 'But this meal was small, and sometimes that helps.' She closed her eyes for a moment. 'You may as well remove your hood, you know. I saw your face when you were leaning down over me.'

He ignored her, for it might have been a ploy. 'It is better if you do not see my face.' Though she might not have a memory of him, it seemed wiser to remain shadowed—especially when he'd been ordered to kill her betrothed husband, the High King of Éireann.

'I would still know you, even if I hadn't glimpsed your face.'

Her response surprised him, and he couldn't help but ask, 'How?'

'Because of your voice,' she murmured. 'I would know you from the moment you spoke.' Her eyes opened then. 'Your voice is deep and low, almost wild.'

He was unnerved by what she'd said. Her words cast a spell over him, drawing him nearer. No woman had ever had this effect, stirring his senses in the way she did. He wanted to rest his hand on either side of her shoulders, leaning in to kiss her, learning the shape of her mouth.

Instead, he said gruffly, 'Rest now. I will return later.'

He needed to hunt, to bring back food for both of them. And while he was away, he could search for the MacEgan man she had spoken of.

A grimness settled over him, for he had met the MacEgans in battle before. Later, their king, Patrick MacEgan, had married a Norman bride. While there might be peace between their people now, Raine knew to never underestimate the power of Irish loyalty.

'If anyone comes, bolt the door,' he warned. He didn't like leaving her defenceless, but there was no choice. He had to bring back more food to nourish Lady Carice, despite the risks. Though her illness had likely caused her to faint, he also didn't believe she'd eaten enough.

After he departed the chamber, he went down the stairs and returned outside. As he cast a look back at the ruins, a sense of guilt passed over him. He felt responsible for the brethren who had lived within these walls. The abbot and the holy men were innocent, blameless for what had happened. The raiders had been seeking holy treasures, and they had set the abbey on fire during the attack.

The moment he'd witnessed the flames against the night sky, he should have ridden hard to reach the men instead of alerting his commander. The delay had meant the difference between life and death.

Raine stopped before one of the graves, brushing the snow from the simple wooden cross he'd made. For a moment, he rested his hand upon the wood, feeling the rise of anger. He'd been too late. Although he'd tried to help the monks escape, their quarters had been consumed by flames and he'd nearly burned to death himself. Had it not been for one of the brethren dragging him out of the fire, he would not have survived. And then that monk had died, too.

The raw ache flooded through him. He hadn't been able to save these men any more than his sisters—and he could sense the ghosts of their disapproval haunting his conscience.

The air was cold, and it was near to Imbolc, the Irish feast of Saint Brighid. Raine returned to the stables to prepare a horse. He wondered if his commander, Sir Darren de Carleigh, would send men to bring him back. It had taken a great deal of convincing for the man to grant him leave. He suspected that Darren had only allowed it because he recognised the need to bury the bodies—and because it was a means of doing penance.

The two days Raine had spent here alone had given him a false sense of peace. His soul was already damned, but at least he could give the monks a proper burial. He glanced back at the chapel, wondering what to do about Lady Carice. Her very presence had tangled up his plans—but not in the way she imagined. His conscience warned that he should leave her alone…but there was no doubt she could be of use to him.

He took a bow and arrows, then rode out into the forest, moving deeper into the stillness. The morning air was cool, and there were no sounds at all—not even birds. Their lack of noise made him wary. The shadows of the trees hung over him, while golden light skimmed the tops of the bare branches. Raine drew his horse to a stop and dismounted. Nocking an arrow to his bow, he paused, searching for the source of the tension. Frost rimmed the dry leaves, and he moved with stealth.

There. He spied a small group of men on the far side of the wood. Perhaps a dozen intruders, most on horseback. He didn't know if they were searching for Carice, but he intended to find out why they were here. Silently, he gave his horse a light push, sending the animal out of the woods and back to the abbey. Then he moved in closer, climbing a tree to get a better glimpse of them.

One was carrying the High King's banner, and he saw another older man whose face appeared grim. The Irish soldiers broke off into smaller groups, searching the forest—most likely for Carice.

She'd wanted her freedom and had fought with all of her strength to flee these men and reach the sanctuary of the abbey. If he wanted to be rid of her, all he had to do was bring them to her.

Yet, that wasn't at all what he wanted. He didn't know why a possessive urge had come over him, but he could not allow her to fall into the hands of these men. He had failed, time and again, to save innocent people from being harmed. Carice would face punishment for daring to run, and he didn't want that to happen.

This time, he would succeed in protecting an innocent life.

An insidious voice within him prompted, *Or you could use her to get close to the High King.*

He shut down the thought, for his own purposes didn't matter. What mattered was protecting the lady from being recaptured—for if those men reached the abbey, they would find her within moments.

Unless he intervened.

The best way to keep her free of these men was to hide all traces of her. Raine climbed down from the tree, hurrying back to the outskirts. They would find his tracks and follow him, but he had an advantage. He knew the abbey well, after spending days here. He also knew of the secret passageways between the walls, for the abbot had left one of them open. Most of the alcoves were so narrow, his shoulders brushed against both sides of the walls— but no one would find them.

When Raine reached the clearing, he found his horse and swung up, riding hard for the abbey. The only thing that mattered now was protecting *her*.

And in this, he would not fail.

Chapter Two

Carice awoke to the sound of her chamber door being thrown open. Raine de Garenne stood there, his hood down at last. Why? He'd gone to such lengths to conceal himself that she'd begun to think he was scarred or disfigured in some way. Instead, he was one of the most handsome men she'd ever seen.

His dark golden hair was cut short against his head, his face clean-shaven. His eyes were a deep green, his mouth a firm slash. There was a quiet sense of determination about him, an air of command that gave her confidence. She had lied before when she'd claimed she had seen his face. But now that she saw him, she felt a rush of self-consciousness.

Before Carice could say anything, he dumped sand upon the fire, extinguishing it immediately. Then he crossed over to the bed and pulled back the coverlet. 'Come with me,' he commanded, lifting her into his arms.

'Where? What is happening?' Her pulse quickened with fear as he strode towards the wall.

'The High King's men have come for you. And I suspect your father is with them.'

Dear God. Then they had tracked her here, as she'd feared. If they found her, they would force her to continue towards Tara, the dwelling of the Ard-Righ. She couldn't bear the thought.

But Raine's strength was comforting, and she rested her cheek against his chest, feeling the cool links of the chain mail armour he wore. It was a tangible reminder that he was a soldier, a man fully capable of guarding her.

He led her to the back corner, where a simple cross hung upon the wall. After setting her down, he seized the cross and pushed hard. A chunk of stones the size of a window moved inward, revealing an opening just large enough for her to climb inside.

She wanted to ask questions about how he'd known of such a place, but Raine's swiftness revealed the need to remain silent. He lifted her into the space, and she found herself within a narrow corridor hidden behind the wall.

He stood upon the bed and swung one leg, then the other, into the opening, before setting the stone and cross back into place. Darkness enveloped them, and she kept both palms upon either wall, trying to ignore the cold. Her body shuddered, her teeth chattering.

'Your hood,' she started to ask, but he drew his arm around her waist and touched a finger to her lips.

'I need you to trust me.' He spoke in a low whisper against her ear. She supposed that was the reason why he had revealed his identity. Though she didn't understand why he had wanted to remain hidden, now it seemed those plans had changed.

She obeyed his command, moving in closer to draw warmth from his body. He stiffened when she put both of her arms around his waist. She was so tired, so weak, but this was the only way to stop herself from trembling.

He brought her closer, surrounding her in an embrace. The moment her body was pressed against his, it was like an awakening. She grew aware of his hard, muscled body and the masculine scent of him. His strong arms made her feel protected, and it dissipated the fear.

The heat of his body was welcome, and she snuggled in close. His mouth rested against her hair, and she felt a subtle shift in the way he was holding her. It was as if he were conscious of the way they fit against one another. She stood between his legs, and against her body, she felt the sudden rise of his arousal.

Carice knew she ought to move away. It was a natural reaction of a man to desire a woman—especially when their bodies were so close. But instead of being afraid, she found that she was responding to his touch. She rested her cheek against his chest, tucking her head beneath his chin. This man could have harmed her many times over, yet he'd not laid a hand upon her, except to guard and protect.

Curiosity wove a web of interest, and she grew more aware of him. It was a good feeling to be in a man's arms. And though he was a stranger, she liked what she'd seen. Most maidens would be shy and awkward in such close proximity. But her own opinions had changed over the years.

No longer did she care about what was expected of her. She'd grown so weak, and the knowledge of her impending death gave her a courage that she'd never anticipated. This man had kindled an unexpected need, and she wanted to know more.

The chamber door suddenly flew open, and she gripped him tightly, out of shock. Men entered the room, and she heard her father's voice.

'I want her found. This is the closest shelter to our camp, and she must have been here.'

'She might have,' one of the men remarked. 'But if she did, she's gone now.'

In the darkness, Carice sensed Raine's tension. He was listening to every word, his hands tight around her waist. Whether or not he would admit it to himself, his sudden choice to hide them was the action of a man who would not hand her over to her father. She breathed a sigh of relief, feeling so grateful for his protection.

He stroked back her hair, still holding her close. And the longer he held her, the more she wanted to explore these unknown feelings. She had never been in a man's embrace, for her father had threatened all the men of the tribe. They would not dare to defy Brian Faoilin or touch his daughter.

But this was her life now, and she could make her own choices. In the darkness, she reached up to Raine's face, touching his cheek. She explored the smooth surface, fascinated by him. He caught her hand and drew her fingers back to her lips in a silent warning to be still and silent.

The risk of being discovered was far too high. She knew that—and yet, she was tempted to seize a moment to herself. He was only going to push her away as soon as they were out of hiding. She wanted to embrace every last chance to live, even if it was pushing beyond what was right. Raine would never understand her need to reach out for all the moments remaining.

This man intrigued her, for he was a living contradiction. He was both fierce and benevolent, like a warrior priest. And though he claimed to be a Norman loyal to King Henry, she knew he was a man of secrets.

His skin was warm beneath her fingertips, his face revealing hard planes. A sudden heat rushed through her as she explored his features. During her life, she'd never had the opportunity to be courted by a man, and even her illness had shut her away from the world. Her father had isolated her until it seemed that only the hand of Death was waiting in her future.

Perhaps it was the lack of time that made

her act with boldness. Or perhaps it was her sudden sense of unfairness. There was a handsome man beside her, one who attracted her in ways she didn't understand. Being so near to him was forbidden…and undeniably exciting. Why shouldn't she seize the opportunity that was before her?

Her pulse was racing, and the proximity of his body against hers was a very different kind of risk.

He leaned down and against her lips, he murmured, 'Don't move.' The heat of his breath and the danger of discovery only heightened the blood racing through her. She was aware of every line of his body, of his warm hands around her, and the feeling of his hips pressed to her own.

Her imagination revelled in what it would be like to be kissed by this man. His mouth was so close to hers…and if she lifted her lips, they would be upon his.

Carice gave in to impulse and stood on tiptoe, brushing her mouth against him. She wanted to know what a real kiss was, even if it was given by a stranger. But the moment she kissed him, he went motionless. Instead of taking her offering, he grew rigid like a block of stone.

Heat rushed to her cheeks, when she realised the mistake she'd made. She wanted to tell him that it had only been a whim, hardly more than a means of satisfying her curiosity. But she could not dare to speak a word, not with her father's men still inside the chamber.

There was a rigid tension within Raine, and she understood that she had overstepped her bounds. His hands tightened upon her waist in a silent warning. Unfortunately, she could not move away from him, because of the tiny space within the walls.

The voices in the chamber grew quieter, and eventually she heard the door close while the soldiers searched the remainder of the abbey.

'Why did you do that?' he demanded in a low whisper. The feeling of his mouth against her ear brought a rush of gooseflesh over her skin.

He was right—it had been nothing but a mistake. There were no excuses for what she'd done, and he wouldn't understand her reasons. But even so, she answered honestly, 'I wanted to know what it would be like to kiss a man. You were near, and I acted on impulse. I wasn't thinking clearly.'

'We could have been found by those men,' he whispered harshly. 'Or was that what you wanted?' He touched his finger to her chin in silent chastisement.

She winced, embarrassed by what she had done. All she could say was, 'Have you never acted without thinking?'

'No.'

And she suspected that was true. This man was iron-willed, a strong soldier accustomed to making battle plans. His commanding presence suggested that he expected all orders to be obeyed.

She tried to extricate herself from his body, but he stopped her. Against her ear, he murmured, 'We cannot leave yet. They may still be nearby.'

Carice said nothing, but turned her back to him. At least then he would know she hadn't truly meant to bother him.

The tension lingered, making her feel ashamed of what she'd done. If he had stolen a kiss from her, she might have had the same reaction. It was no wonder he hadn't kissed her back.

Liar, her mind chided. *If he had kissed you first, you would have enjoyed every moment.* She pressed both hands to her cheeks, wondering what was the matter with her. Standing with him in the dark was giving her a strange sense of recklessness. But then again, when you knew your life would likely end before the year was out, there was no reason to be coy or shy. She couldn't bear the thought of the High King being the only man to ever kiss her. The chains of her betrothal were suffocating, and she fought against them with every breath.

Raine's hand brushed against hers, and he threaded his fingers as he held her palm. His gesture confused her, for it was almost an apology. She squeezed his hand in return, wishing she could go back and ask permission before she'd assaulted his mouth.

His thumb began to stroke the edge of her hand in a silent caress. It confused her, because wasn't he angry with her right now? She closed her eyes, though his touch echoed within other places in her body. She tried to focus on the freezing cold stone walls or on how weary she was.

Not the man who was quietly undoing her senses.

But then, he took her hand and brought it to his neck. Beneath her fingertips she felt the warmth of his bare skin, and she couldn't resist the urge to put her other hand up, bringing them back into an embrace.

He leaned in, and against her lips, he whispered, 'We are naught but strangers, Lady Carice.'

They were. And perhaps that was why she wanted to kiss him. It would mean nothing, and after they parted ways, she would have a memory of what it was like to kiss a man.

She kept her voice hushed and murmured, 'That is why it will not matter to either of us.'

His hand cupped her face, and she felt the forbidden heat that was there. She brought her hand back to his face, feeling the smoothness of his skin. Upon his throat, there was a faint trace of bristle, as if he'd missed shaving there.

And then he did lean in, kissing her softly. It was hardly there at all, and she felt a sense of disappointment. He was holding back, treating her as if she were made of glass. She could almost imagine his silent question: *Was that what you wanted?*

No, it wasn't. Several times, she had seen men and women engaged in trysts. On some nights after they celebrated feasts, she would sometimes find couples stealing time together. But there had never been anyone for her. And then she'd grown so ill, she hadn't been able to leave her chamber.

The kiss had been an idle wish born of longing and loneliness. She found Raine de Garenne quite handsome…and she knew that there would never be anything more between them, beyond a day or two spent in his presence.

His hands moved over her face, framing it. For whatever unknown reason, his touch was now a silent question. He was waiting for something, and she knew not what. In answer, she tightened her arms around his neck. Both of them were aware that these moments were unwise, and if she were caught in the arms of a Norman, her father would murder Raine where he stood.

She didn't care.

Carice had no time to react before his mouth descended upon hers. The kiss was hot, melting away her awareness of the outside world. Her lips merged into his, and she tasted a hint of mead upon his breath. His tongue entered her mouth, and her knees gave out at the unrelenting sensations. He caught her, pressing her back against the frigid wall. But as his mouth consumed hers, she felt none of the cold—only a desire that was transforming from a kiss into a frenzied need.

'No one will take you against your will,' he murmured against her mouth before he claimed it again. 'Not while I'm here.'

He was behaving like a ruthless bastard. Raine knew it, and yet, he didn't want to stop kissing this woman. Despite her frail body, there was a fire within her. He tasted her yearning for a different life, and *she* had kissed him first. Though it might seem that she was a woman of loose virtue, somehow he didn't believe it. Her gesture spoke of a woman who wanted to claim every last moment of life before she went to her grave.

It was unnerving, and yet, he was entranced by her sweetness. She aroused him with the barest touch, and his wicked mind imagined touching her boldly, marking her innocent skin. But he would not force her into more—not as weak as she was.

Raine broke the kiss and listened intently. There was no sound of her father's men, and when he peered through a tiny crevice, he could see no one. He supposed it was unwise to reveal his face to her, but he'd spoken the truth when he'd said he needed her to trust him. It was unlikely that they would see one another again, and if he saved her life, she would not believe he was guilty of killing the High King.

'Do you think it's safe?' Carice whispered. Her voice was breathless, and her hand touched his. 'Are my father's men gone?'

'Stay here while I look.' He pressed her back into the shadows while he pulled the stone door open, climbing into the chamber.

The moment he entered the room, he drew his sword, listening hard. Carice obeyed his orders, remaining hidden within the wall.

When there appeared to be no danger, he moved towards the door, waiting. Though it was likely that the men had continued their search elsewhere, he knew better than to believe that the threat had vanished. He rested his hand against the door, keeping his sword poised. Seconds ticked by, and he threw open the door, only to find an armed soldier standing guard.

Raine shoved the man back against the wall, his sword at his throat. 'Why are you here?' He spoke in his native language, not caring if the man understood him or not.

The soldier's face went white, but he stam-

mered a reply in the Norman tongue. 'The—
the chief of the Faoilin clan is searching for his
d-daughter.'

'Do I look like the sort of man who would
allow a woman to trespass here?' He pressed
his blade against the man's throat, leaving a
trace of blood.

The soldier's hands were shaking, and Raine
told him, 'Leave your weapons behind and go.
And if I see you or any of the other men return,
you won't breathe again.' Never once did he
speak in the Irish language, for he wanted the
man to believe he was an enemy.

He released the soldier, and the man hurried
down the stairs. Raine followed him, keeping
his weapon drawn. The chapel was empty, and
he crossed the space, watching as the man retreated. It soon became clear that the guard was
the only one left behind, for a single horse was
tethered. He guessed that the man had stayed to
learn whether or not Carice had hidden herself.

Which she had, but thankfully, the woman
had not emerged from her place within the wall.

Raine watched while the man rode away,
and he wondered what he should do about the
Lady Carice. He had been commanded to kill
the High King—Henry had demanded it as the

price of his sisters' freedom. It would cause chaos in the midst of Éireann, making the provincial kings rise up against one another. And it would allow Henry to gain full control of this land, creating order where there was none.

Carice Faoilin could allow him to get even closer to the High King, giving him a reason to be at Tara. Why should he not deliver the missing bride to her betrothed husband? Especially if Raine intended to kill the man anyway? Carice would not have to wed Rory Ó Connor—not if he carried out the man's death sentence.

And yet, she had already fled her father in an effort to avoid the marriage. If he tried to bring her to Tara, she would only run away from him as well. Or if Trahern MacEgan arrived, she would go willingly with the man she had already asked to save her. Raine turned over the idea in his mind, wondering if he should use her or let her go.

She kissed you, his conscience reminded him. What sort of man would betray a woman who had willingly touched him? Only a bastard whose soul was already damned. He hardened his heart, knowing that it was better if she hated him. He was a killer, not a man worthy of redemption.

Yet, he didn't want to let her go. Not only was she the most beautiful woman he'd ever seen, but she had awakened a protective instinct within him. He wanted to guard her innocence, to see those sky blue eyes look upon him with gratefulness. She was unable to defend herself, and he wanted to slaughter any man who dared to threaten her.

There was no logical reason for his possessive urges, save her touch. It had conjured a fire inside him, stoking the need to caress her, to make her burn in the same way he did. The taste of her lips had aroused needs he'd buried for months. And if he took her with him, he could spend more time in her company.

After he was certain the soldier had gone, Raine returned to the sanctuary. Shadows clung to the stone walls, and he stared at the simple altar, remembering the men who had died in the fire. He could almost sense their chastisement for the thoughts he was considering. For a moment, he rested his palm upon the wall, hoping the men's souls had found peace.

Slowly, he ascended the winding stairs and pushed open the heavy wooden door. He expected to find Carice seated before the fire or resting upon the bed. But she was not there.

He walked towards the opening in the wall and peered inside. She was seated on the floor with her knees drawn up, and her body was shivering violently.

'It's safe to come out,' he told her, offering his hand. But she didn't take it.

His suspicions tightened, and he stepped into the opening. When Carice didn't move, he reached down and lifted her into his arms. *Dieu,* she was so light. And despite the gown and cloak she wore, her skin was like ice.

'I was c-cold,' she said. 'And I didn't have the strength to climb out. I am sorry for it.' She was trembling, and he brought her over to the bed, tucking her beneath the coverlet. 'I heard you talking to someone. Who was it?'

'One of your father's men.' He reached for her hand and began rubbing at it, trying to bring warmth back into her skin. 'I sent him away.'

She closed her eyes and murmured, 'I am sorry for disturbing you here. I will leave as soon as I can.'

No, he wasn't going to let her go. Not yet.

'You need to rest first,' he said. 'Try to warm yourself.'

She nodded, burrowing tightly beneath the coverlet. He sat beside her, wondering if she would even survive the journey to Tara. There was no doubt that she could never wed the High King of Ireland. Why would Rory uphold the betrothal when she was so ill? Either the Ard-Rígh was unaware of her weakness, or he didn't care. It was possible that Carice's father held a lot of influence among the chiefs.

And yet, there was no denying her beauty, in spite of the illness. Her face was lovely, while her eyes were the colour of sapphires. Although her hair hung limply against her shoulders, it held all the mysterious shades of brown and red, like polished wood.

'I can't seem to get warm,' she admitted, biting her lower lip. 'My feet are freezing.'

He knew the fastest way to warm her was to lie beside her, curling his body against hers. But he didn't want her to see him as a threat. She needed to feel safe with him, to trust him.

Before you take her to a wedding she doesn't want. Before you betray her.

He silenced the voice of his conscience and reached beneath the coverlet to find her feet. With his hands, he began to massage the skin, bringing warmth to it.

Her eyes locked onto his with gratitude. Raine knew he ought not to touch her in this way, but she held him captive with her gaze. She stared at him as if she remembered every moment of their forbidden kiss. As if she wanted him to stay with her.

This woman was dangerous in a way he'd never anticipated. And the longer he spent at her side, the more she might bind him to her.

Abruptly, he covered her feet and stood. 'Rest now. I'll find more blankets.'

It was an excuse to leave her, for he had not yet decided what to do. An honourable man would bring her to safety at Laochre Castle with the MacEgans. Raine could leave her there with no regrets.

But he wasn't honourable. He was a soldier, ordered to spill the blood of men, whatever the cost. He would have struck down her father's guard without a second thought, except that he wanted the soldier to inform the chief that they should not return.

He shouldn't care that Carice was a fragile beauty whose kiss had tempted him. She was a pawn in a game that he had no choice but to play. Henry held his sisters captive, and their lives depended on Raine's obedience.

Kill the High King, and they would have their freedom. One life taken and two lives given.

He knew well what it was to be a pawn, used for another man's ruthless commands. But when it was done, he would have his own freedom.

And so would Carice.

Her body felt as if it were frozen in a block of ice. Carice could hardly feel her hands and feet, and despite the layers of blankets, it wasn't enough.

Raine hadn't returned in hours, and she was beginning to wonder if he had left the abbey. He was a man of contradictions. One moment he kissed her like a starving man, and the next, he disappeared, as if he no longer wanted to be near her.

Soon enough, she heard his footsteps approaching, and the door swung open. Snow dotted his hair and cloak while in his hand, he carried a wrapped bundle of food. 'Eat, and then rest again. We leave tomorrow at nightfall.'

She hesitated, for there was a hint of unrest in his voice. 'We? I thought you were searching for Trahern MacEgan to bring me to Laochre.'

'I did not find him,' he answered, 'and you lack the strength to travel alone.'

Carice knew that was true, but why had he suddenly changed his mind? Earlier, he'd seemed insistent that she leave him behind. Had her impulsive kiss affected him in such a way that he was now wanting to help her?

She rested her palm against her cheek, studying him. His face was like stone, utterly impassive. No, it didn't seem that he was feeling in any way protective. Instead, there was impatience in his mood, as if he wanted to leave now. Or perhaps he was wanting to be rid of her.

'What changed your mind?' she asked bluntly. 'You didn't want to help me before.'

He sat down and unwrapped the food. 'Eat something before you rest. You'll need your strength for the journey.'

'You didn't answer my question.' She tried to sit up, and he reached back to help her.

'Does it matter why?'

The cool tone of his voice bothered her, for he behaved as if she was a burden he didn't want. 'If you are too busy with your duties for King Henry, you needn't trouble yourself on my behalf. I can go alone.'

His expression shifted. 'You couldn't last more than a mile, *chérie*.'

'I made it this far,' she said quietly. 'And believe me when I say that no man will force me to marry the Ard-Righ. I will go to the west and live out the remainder of my days in peace.'

'I was leaving the abbey to return to my men,' he said gruffly. 'I'll take you with me.'

But although she ought to be grateful for his offer, she sensed that he had his own motives.

'Eat,' he repeated, holding out the bundle.

She glanced at the food he offered and noticed that he'd roasted a rabbit. So that was where he'd gone—to hunt for meat, as he'd promised before. Her stomach growled, and she couldn't stop herself from reaching for the hot food. It was as if she could never get enough to eat, after all the years of suffering.

'You need not bring me very far,' she said quietly. 'Laochre is hardly more than a day's journey. If you bring me there, the MacEgans will see to my care after that.'

It was a reasonable solution and one that would not trouble him any more than was necessary. She waited for him to agree, but those green eyes narrowed upon her. Instead, he seemed disinterested in her suggestion.

'Or I could escort you to the west, if that is what you want.' He spoke with no emotion, his gaze not meeting her eyes.

Now that, she didn't believe for a moment. Raine de Garenne had admitted that he was occupied with the king's orders. He would have to return to his soldiers and commander. Nothing had changed, so far as she could tell.

'Where are your men?'

He shrugged. 'They are camped east of here. But I could delay my return to them.'

Her senses went on alert, and she didn't at all believe he would journey with her, out of the goodness of his heart. 'You want something from me, don't you?'

He leaned forward and broke off a piece of the meat, his hand brushing against hers. She jolted at the contact, and his expression fixed upon her. 'Perhaps I do.'

Her mind flashed back to the kiss, though she knew that was not the reason. Her cheeks reddened, and she asked, 'What reason would bring you from your duties to act as my escort?'

Raine picked up another piece of meat and guided it to her lips. The simple gesture undid her good sense, crumbling away her thoughts.

His thumb edged her mouth, reminding her of the shared embrace.

She chewed and swallowed, feeling a mild panic rising. Was he trying to seduce her? Had she inadvertently suggested that she wanted more than a kiss?

'Not that,' she insisted, returning his stare. He didn't smile in teasing, nor did he react. 'If you're wanting a reward, silver pieces are all I can give to you.'

'You have knowledge of the kings of Éire-ann, have you not?'

The pieces fell into place then. He could gain permission from his commander to escort her west if she gave him political information. He wanted her to share what she knew, so he could use the information against his enemies. But she was not a traitor.

'I can tell you nothing,' she argued. 'All I know is what I have heard from my father. My knowledge would be of no use to you.' And even if she did know something, she would never betray her countrymen to the Norman army.

Raine leaned in closer on the bed, balancing his weight upon both hands. At his nearness, she wanted to back away, but she forced herself not to be intimidated by him.

'Your father made certain you were taught the Norman tongue, didn't he? Because he wanted you to be able to negotiate between the Normans and the Irish. A useful skill for the Queen of Éireann.'

'And for speaking to you,' she countered. Her posture stiffened. 'There is nothing I can tell you. And if that is what you want, then I must go to Laochre alone.' She had no desire to reveal information that was never meant for a Norman's ears.

'You haven't the strength for that journey,' he argued.

Although he was right, she saw no alternative. 'I will do what I must.'

'Your father's men will find you,' he predicted. 'And they will force you to return to the High King for your marriage.'

Perhaps they would try, but she wasn't about to surrender. 'I will never wed a man like the Ard-Righ.' She ate more of the rabbit, sating her hunger. 'Or any man, for that matter.'

'Your father won't give up until you're found.'

'He can try to find me,' was her reply, though she knew it was true. Her father would not stop searching for her, no matter how long it took. Brian was a stubborn, proud man who delighted in having his own way—but he did love her. He wanted her to be Queen of Éireann, for it reflected well upon him.

Raine sat back, sharing the meat with her. It seemed that the more she ate, the hungrier she became. It had been so long since eating had not caused her stomach to seize with cramping. She savoured the food, and then he unfolded the bundle again, revealing dried apples.

'Where did you get these?' she asked, startled to see the fruit.

'I found them stored within the kitchen.' He gave them to her, and she was grateful for the fruit, almost greedy at the taste of it. But as she devoured the apples, she was reminded that the monks who had once lived here were now gone. It felt even more like they were trespassing like scavengers.

'What happened to the priests who lived here?' she asked him.

'They died in the fire.' He offered nothing else, but the dark tone suggested that he felt responsible for the deaths. She stopped eating, studying his expression in the hopes of glimpsing the truth. He claimed that he was a Norman warrior, and she suspected he was a man accustomed to killing.

And yet, there was an empty bleakness in his eyes, like a haunted man. As if he didn't enjoy killing, the way a warrior might. She didn't know what to think of that.

Why had he returned to this place? What interest would a Norman soldier have in an abandoned abbey? She couldn't understand it.

'Do you want more to eat?' he asked her.

She shook her head, recognising his desire to avoid speaking of the priests. So be it. Likely it was better if she didn't know what had happened here.

'I intend to leave tomorrow at dawn,' she told him. And as far as she was concerned, she didn't need his help—especially if he was looking for information she could not give.

'It would be better to travel at nightfall,' he countered. 'It's too easy for them to track you. They won't be far away, and we would be unable to avoid them.'

We? So he was still thinking of accompanying her. She regarded him with a frown, for she hadn't agreed to that. 'They are travelling towards Tara, and *I* am moving in the opposite direction.' She wanted it clear that she didn't need him to escort her. He could return to his men, if needed.

Raine evaded her searching gaze and answered, 'The High King's men have split up to search for you. If we do not wait and let them travel farther, then they *will* find us.'

Carice didn't know why he was insisting on helping her, but it was time to be clear with him. 'I would be grateful if you would take me to Laochre,' she said, 'but I cannot give you information about the kings of Éireann. I know nothing, and even if I did, I would not betray them.' She eyed him sharply and added, 'I can grant you a reward of silver for your assistance, but nothing more. And if you choose not to escort me there, I'll go alone.'

Raine studied her, but his expression held a silent challenge. She didn't know what to think of that, but she would not lower her eyes in surrender. Instead, she faced him down with her own strong will.

There was a faint hint of respect in his expression. 'You won't go alone.' Though he didn't acknowledge her offer of a reward, she suspected that he might still try to press her for knowledge.

'Thank you.' Yet despite his compromise, she sensed that the battle of wills was not over.

Raine gave a slight nod and commanded, 'Rest now.'

She leaned back and huddled beneath the coverlet while he finished eating. Beneath the woollen blanket, her feet and hands were freezing. She tried to rub her hands to warm them, but they were numb from the time she'd spent in hiding.

There was no chance she would fall asleep in such discomfort. She managed to sit up, and swung her legs to the side of the bed, intending to go stand by the fire. But Raine stopped her. 'What is it?'

'I'm freezing.' She hoped he might find her another blanket while she warmed herself at the hearth. Before she could get out of bed, Raine pressed her back down.

He reached for her hands and rubbed them between his palms. The heat of his skin felt so good, she closed her eyes, wishing for more. Then he bent down to her feet and did the same, massaging the frigid skin. She tried to stop herself from shivering but could not repress the instinct.

'Do you want me to lie beside you for

warmth?' His offer meant no harm, but she questioned the wisdom of accepting his body against hers.

'I don't know.' She met his gaze, uncertain of what he intended. This man unnerved her, and she worried about sleeping at his side.

Raine didn't seem to care about her wariness. Instead, he stretched out beside her, pulling her body against his. He pulled his cloak over both of them and did the same with the blanket. His gesture was only meant to help her get warm, but against her nape, she could feel his breath. A sudden rush of awareness slid over her, bringing goosebumps to her skin.

He is not to be trusted, her mind warned. She knew that, even as she nestled closer to him. His presence was so dangerous to her good sense. Never before had she lain this close to a man. And especially not one who wanted her to act as a traitor.

She was fascinated by the contrast between them. He was muscular, a large man with a great deal of strength, whereas she was weak and softer. The hard planes of his body offered a shelter she welcomed. Even wrapped within the coverlet, she could feel the warmth of his arms around her. For a moment, she imagined that this was what it was like to lie with a husband.

A fragile twinge of regret caught her. At one time, she had dreamed of a life where she would be Lady of Carrickmeath with a husband and children. When her father had betrothed her to Rory Ó Connor, she'd been filled with terror and loathing. Brian had believed he was giving her a dream, not a nightmare.

But she felt no loathing beside Raine de Garenne. Instead, his embrace was welcoming, granting a solace that made her grateful. She had needed the warmth of his body, and he had offered it to her. Though she should feel guilty about resting beside him, she didn't. Raine was a stranger to her, a man who might escort her to Laochre Castle, and then it was doubtful she would see him again.

She tried to close her eyes and find sleep, but the longer she remained in his arms, the more she grew aware of the heavy chain mail he wore. He could not possibly rest, wearing such armour.

'You could…remove your armour if you want to sleep. It's difficult in chain mail.' She couldn't imagine trying to sleep with the weight of the metal links pressing down.

Raine didn't answer at first, but then he sat up, pushing back the coverlet before he walked towards the fire.

She never took her gaze from him as he turned to face her. Though he remained silent, she felt the censure in his stare. Out of courtesy, she closed her eyes. 'I won't look, I promise.'

'Carice,' he said quietly. 'Would you prefer it if I left you to sleep alone?' His stare held an intensity that made her uncertain of what he truly wanted. But it did seem that he was trying to determine whether his presence had made her uncomfortable. And that wasn't it at all.

'No,' she answered. It made her feel safe to have him near. 'I would rather have you stay. Unless…you do not wish to be near me.'

'I will stay.' His green eyes held her spellbound as he removed the leather corselet. 'But trust that I will not harm you. If you want me to leave you alone, I will.'

He set aside the corselet and reached for the chain mail hauberk. Though she knew she shouldn't watch, she couldn't tear her gaze from him. His blond hair gleamed against the firelight, and he fixed his attention upon her as he removed the armour. Only a linen undertunic remained, but it was unlike those she had seen before. This one was worn, but made of a finer weave of cloth, like one a nobleman might wear. It hung open at his neck, and she spied angry, reddened flesh.

'Are you hurt?' She hadn't realised it before. 'Your skin looks as if it's still healing.'

His expression tightened, and he paused a moment before lifting away the undertunic. His torso was rigid, resembling the honed body of an ancient god. There were scars of battle, but the reddish markings near his throat spread over one shoulder. He turned his back to her, and she saw that the skin was red and mottled, as if he had suffered from burns.

It hurt to look at the healed flesh, knowing how badly he must have suffered. 'What happened to you?'

'I was caught in the fire when this abbey burned. I nearly died.' He still remained facing the hearth, not looking at her. 'I saw the flames when my men were camped nearby,' he said. 'I alerted my commander, but he didn't want to intervene. "It's not our battle," he told me.' Raine rested his hands upon the stone wall, and the muscles in his back flexed. 'I went there anyway, but I was too late to stop the raiders.'

Carice was glad to hear that he hadn't been

responsible for the men's deaths. But she sympathised with him, imagining what he must have endured. 'And you were trapped in the fire?'

He turned back and nodded. 'One of the monks helped me escape. Then he died from the smoke. He couldn't breathe.' Raine's voice was cool, as if it didn't matter. But beneath his expression, she sensed guilt and regret.

'Why did you return?'

'After my wounds healed, I received permission to bury them. I do not think the bishop was notified, for the bodies were rotting when I arrived. But soon, they will come to rebuild this place.'

She couldn't suppress a shudder, but she now understood why he'd come back. It was the right thing to do. His actions made her wonder more about this man and who he truly was. He was keeping so many secrets, it was difficult to understand him. 'And now? After you take me to the MacEgans, where will you go?'

He lifted up the linen undertunic and donned it once more, setting the chain mail aside upon a chair. 'I will return to the king's men and my commander.' He didn't offer anything further but went to sit upon the foot of the bed.

'What of your family?'

There was a trace of unrest that passed over his face. 'Go to sleep, *chérie*. I have no wish to speak of them now.' He stretched out beside her, on top of the coverlet. She remained facing the fire, acutely conscious of his presence.

But she found it impossible to sleep with him so near.

Chapter Three

Being so close to this woman was slowly killing him. Carice's scent allured him, tempting him to hold her close as he had earlier. She wasn't speaking, and he knew she was only feigning sleep.

And yet, the raw need to touch her was pushing away his good sense. He might claim that he was only intending to warm her, but the truth was, he longed to hold this woman. She was innocent, utterly fragile, like a newly-opened blossom.

He flipped back the coverlet and slid beneath it, well aware that he should not be sharing a bed with her. Though they were alone, with no one to cast blame, he understood how dangerous this was. Already he had tasted her lips, and he knew how soft and yielding they were.

He wanted to kiss her again, but it would only heighten the temptation.

She moved back to him, snuggling her backside against him, drawing his arms around her body. The moment she did, he gritted out, '*Dieu*, you're cold.' She was slender and hardly seemed to have any body warmth at all.

'I am sorry,' she whispered. 'But it's impossible to sleep when I'm so freezing.'

He pulled her body against his, bringing his leg over hers, to keep her even closer. She sighed and murmured, 'That's so much better. Thank you.'

It wasn't at all better for him. Her presence aroused him, and he could not prevent the instinctive response. He had a beautiful woman in his arms, and despite her cool skin, his mind was envisioning other ways to warm her.

Her brown hair was silk against his cheek, and her limbs were tangled with his, seeking comfort. His conscience warred with his body's needs, and he couldn't stop thinking of the way she had reached for him earlier. Despite her boldness, he didn't at all believe she had any intention of seduction.

In time, her breathing slowed, and her skin was not so frigid. He lay awake, staring at the fire, wondering if this was what it would be like to have a wife. He had never married, not after all that had happened after his parents had died.

But a part of him hungered for a life such as this. To lie with a woman at night, to take comfort in her softness. War was a part of his blood, and he lived in a world where killing was expected of him. There was no peace, no sense of contentment.

Whether or not she knew it, Carice Faoilin was bringing him towards a greater temptation. And each day he spent with her made him more aware of the loneliness surrounding him.

With reluctance, he rose from the bed and went to stand by the fire. He'd revealed his burns to her, expecting her to be repulsed by them. Instead, she'd sympathised and had lain close to him.

He should take her to Laochre as she wanted. She needed to remain in a safe place where she could be surrounded by friends—not with a man like him. He walked over to stand by the bed, reaching for one of her long curls. He traced it between his fingertips before releasing it.

There was a restless energy within him, the sense that all was not right. He put on shoes and his cloak, taking his weapons before closing the door behind him.

The air was frigid, and his breath formed clouds in the air. He decided to go and check the grounds, to ensure that there were no intruders. Once he was convinced it was safe, he might be able to sleep.

The scent of Lady Carice haunted him, tempting him to taste those lips once again. He strode down the stairs, needing the cold night air to temper the fire rising within him.

Raine seized a torch from the wall and walked outside. It was snowing lightly, the ground covered in a dusting of white. As he walked the perimeter of the ruined abbey, he thought of King Henry's orders. The man had no intention of allowing Rory Ó Connor to reign over the lands he wanted for his own. Henry was ambitious and ruthless, a man who would stop at nothing to get what he wanted. The High King's death would ensure his success.

Raine stopped beside the graves of the monks, the burden of their deaths troubling him.

He pressed his hand against the skeletal remains of the building, remembering the vicious pain of the burns. His men had taken him away, and over the course of several weeks, he'd gradually healed. But he'd needed to return, to silence the ghosts that dwelled within him.

Dieu, what was he still doing here? He'd been granted two days, no more. He had to return to the soldiers, to face his commander and obey the orders given to him. Time was slipping away from him, and he had to uphold his duties.

But the woman waiting in bed for him could not survive on her own. He had to either use her to get close to the Ard-Righ—or he had to bring her to Laochre and wash his hands of her. Leaving her behind was not an option.

Reluctantly, he returned to his quarters, stomping the snow from his feet before he ascended the stairs once more. The moment he opened the door to his chamber, he saw the dim glow of the fire illuminating Carice's face. Her features were softened in slumber, and she had the face of an angel. From deep within him came the desire to guard her, to protect this woman from all harm.

She reminded him of a life he could have had, if tragedy had not befallen his family. For a moment, he allowed himself to dream of being a husband…or even a father. Guilt slashed through the vision, reminding him of his purpose. His family had died, while he'd been too stricken to move. He could not set aside the blame, and a life of solitude was what he'd earned.

Raine removed his boots and strode towards the bed. It was better if he left Carice alone to sleep before they departed. But he remembered the softness of her body pressed against his, the womanly allure that held him captive. And most of all, her kiss.

He cursed himself, even as he slid beneath the covers. When he reached towards her, he felt the coolness of her skin. She still wasn't nearly warm enough. The moment he moved closer, she rolled to face him, snuggling as near as she dared.

Her touch was like a slow flame, consuming him. She was a physical torment, tempting him in a way he couldn't resist.

Raine shut his eyes, forcing himself to remain utterly still. Though Carice was pressed up against him, he didn't touch her, nor did he let himself imagine anything more. It was nearly an hour before he managed to calm the urges of his body, and even longer before sleep came.

But when it did, the nightmares returned.

* * *

He heard the sound of screaming. Raine bolted awake in his chamber, not knowing what was happening. He dressed quickly, not even bothering with armour, and seized his sword. His heart thundered with worry for his family or worse, their liege. King Henry was visiting Peventon Castle, along with fifty of his soldiers and servants. The scream was a woman's, but whose?

Raine hurried down the stone stairs, his weapon drawn. He froze at the sight before him, unable to believe what he was witnessing. His father's face was purple with rage, and he clenched a dagger in his fist. King Henry held his own blade and stared back at Neil de Garenne with arrogance.

'You dare to draw your weapon before me?' Henry said, his voice icy.

A sinking feeling caught in Raine's stomach, a rise of mingled fear and nausea. To threaten the king was a death sentence. His father knew that, so why would he do such a thing?

'You dared to touch my wife,' Neil shot back. 'I care not that royal blood runs through your veins. If you have harmed her, I will spill every damned drop.'

Only then, did Raine notice his mother weeping in the corner. Estelle sat on the floor, holding her knees, her clothes torn and in disarray.

God help them all.

Raine started to move towards her, but a soldier caught him by the arm. 'Stay out of this.'

He ignored the man and wrenched his way free, moving towards his mother. Tears streamed down her face, and her expression was filled with terror.

'She knows better than to deny her king. Sheathe your weapon, de Garenne, and apologise.'

But his father lunged at Henry, a war cry roaring from him. One of the king's soldiers came from behind and stabbed Neil.

Raine froze in place. His limbs felt as if they were iron, bolted to the floor. He stood in shock as his father's blood spilled over the stones. Estelle rushed forward, reaching for her husband.

And though he knew he had to move, had to help them, he could do nothing.

Too fast. It had all happened too fast for him to respond.

Then, Raine watched in horror as his mother seized her husband's knife and stabbed herself.

* * *

Raine gasped for air, jerking awake.

Carice startled at his motion, and realised that he was sweating, his breathing uneven. 'What is it?'

When he didn't answer her whisper, it seemed that he was still under the spell of a bad dream. 'It's all right,' she murmured, touching his shoulder. 'I am here.'

The top of his tunic had come unlaced, and her palm brushed his bare skin. He jolted as if she'd burned him, but his eyes flew open. Even then, he did not appear aware of who she was. 'It was only a dream,' she whispered, reaching out to stroke his cheek.

He gripped her wrist roughly and shoved it against the coverlet. 'Do not touch me.'

His abrupt transformation frightened her. In his eyes, she saw a wildness of a man who was gripped with visions that were all too real. She pulled back, bunching the covers around her. This time, he got out of bed and donned his chain mail once more, adding the leather corselet atop it.

'What were you dreaming of?' she asked.

But he would say nothing about the nightmare. Instead, he ordered, 'We should leave now. It's nearly dawn.'

She wanted to argue with him, but the look in his eyes was shielded, as if he were holding back terrible memories. Instead, she rose from the bed, reaching for her shoes. She found that she was hungry again, and she took some of the food he had brought last night. Though her weakness lingered, at least the vicious stomachaches had abated.

Carice drew her cloak over her gown, tying it closed. Raine eyed her appearance, his expression stoic. 'You won't be warm enough in that cloak. It snowed last night.' He gave her his own outer garment, before he dragged one of the blankets off the bed and draped it around her shoulders. Carice gathered it up like a *brat* and added the extra layer.

'You should take back your own cloak,' she insisted. 'You're only wearing chain mail armour.' She couldn't imagine that he could stay warm in that, despite the leather corselet.

'The cold won't bother me.'

Of course not, she thought drily. Men didn't get cold. Or if they did, they'd never admit it.

Raine opened the door and waited for her to follow him. In the narrow corridor, he reached for a torch from one of the sconces. It cast shadows upon the wall while she descended the stairs. As he had predicted, she felt the cold chill of the night air slipping beneath the layers of wool.

Once they stepped outside, she paused a moment to watch the fat snowflakes drifting from the sky. There was beauty in them, and she held out her palm, trying to catch one. A bemused smile crossed her face, and she reached down to form a snowball.

'Do not consider it,' Raine warned.

But Carice smiled. 'I was just thinking of my brother, Killian. He used to throw snowballs at my face when we were children.'

'You never spoke of a brother.' The hint of censure in his voice made her stop a moment.

'He's not really my brother. At least, not by blood.' She struggled to explain it to him. 'We had different parents, but Killian lived at Carrickmeath, and we grew up together.' A pang caught her, for she did miss him. 'He's the brother of my heart, I suppose you could say.'

'If he was like a brother, then why didn't he escort you to safety?' Raine led her towards the horses, and she dropped the snowball. She didn't miss the implication that Killian had failed in his duties.

'It's…complicated. Killian is the High King's bastard son.'

'Then does he want you to wed Rory? To bring himself back into favour with his father?'

She shook her head. 'It's the last thing he wants. In fact, he wanted to help me escape, but I had the chance to play matchmaker instead.'

The confused expression on Raine's face made her hide a smile. 'I have no regrets. Lady Taryn of Ossoria needed an escort to Tara. Killian needs to make peace with his father. And the fact that Taryn and Killian cannot keep their eyes off one another made it even better. I made him stay behind with her when she was in trouble.' She folded her arms over his chest and saw the look of exasperation on his face. 'Don't tell me. If you were my older brother, you would never let me go on my own.'

He sent her a sidelong look. 'I am *not* your brother, *chérie.* Nor would I want to be.' The sudden edge in his tone made her remember sleeping beside him, their limbs tangled together. She sobered instantly at the thought.

'If it makes you feel any better, Killian will

join me at Laochre before I go west,' Carice said. 'Our separation is only temporary.'

'Why did you leave before Trahern could arrive?'

She lifted her shoulders in a shrug. 'I grew nervous when he didn't come. I saw a chance to escape the High King's men, and I took it.'

Raine took her by the hand and guided her towards the stables. 'What you did was dangerous.'

'I didn't think so at the time. But yes, it was.' She squeezed his hand, feeling embarrassed at her weakness. 'I am glad I met you. And I am grateful for your help.'

He met her gaze for a moment before saying, 'We should go now.'

Although she didn't understand why he was in such a hurry, she supposed his nightmare had set him on edge. He was right that there was indeed a risk that she would be caught or found.

The snow dotted Raine's dark blond hair, and he led her inside the stables. Although she was still weary, it would be dawn within hours. With luck and good speed, she would reach Laochre tonight and possibly find Killian and Lady Taryn waiting for her there.

Raine prepared his horse, and Carice waited

until he led the animal by the reins. He lifted her onto the horse and swung up behind her. Though it was still dark, there was a dim haze of morning on the horizon. Against her spine, she felt Raine's strong presence. She had grown accustomed to the hard lines of his body, but there was no peace within him.

It shouldn't matter. By nightfall, she would reach Laochre, and their paths would diverge. She steeled herself, knowing it was meant to be this way. Even so, she felt traces of regret. Raine was the first man she had ever kissed, and he had given her a glimpse of a different life. With him, she almost felt like an ordinary woman—one who had a life ahead of her instead of numbered days.

You're going to die, the voice of reality intruded. *No man will ever fall in love with you.*

She had no right to hope for more time with him—not when she was dying. It was better to let him go and relinquish the idle dreams. What man would want to be with a woman who could never give him companionship or children? Moreover, he had to return to his Norman commander.

When they reached the gates, Raine paused a moment and turned to look back. The ruins of the abbey were scarred by fire, but the stones remained. On the far side, she saw the graves he'd dug, and though he said nothing, she understood that he felt responsible for the destruction. Perhaps those were the dreams that burdened him.

Snow lay upon the ground, crisp and white. As they rode, it continued to fall. She loved watching the swirl of flakes upon the wind, and when they reached the open meadow, she leaned back to watch. Raine stiffened, and she glimpsed a frown upon his face. 'Do you not like snow?'

'I don't enjoy sleeping in it.'

Her smile faded, for as a soldier, he had likely slept out of doors during many battles. 'I suppose you're right. I've always enjoyed watching it fall from the sky, though. It's beautiful. Except when my brother shoved it in my face.'

'And did you seek revenge upon Killian?'

She glanced behind. 'I didn't hit him with a snowball, no. But I did cry until he brought me a kitten.' Nothing had bothered her brother more than tears, and she'd been ruthless in using them to get her way. But even though her cat, Harold, had comforted her over the years, the animal still doted upon Killian.

'You manipulated him, then.' Raine tightened his arms around her as he quickened their pace. 'It doesn't surprise me.'

'I used the weapons I had. It could be called strategy, really.' She could feel Raine's chain mail armour against her back, and they were a tangible reminder that he was here to guard her. The metal links were a boundary between them, allowing no warmth at all.

But she remembered well, what it was to sleep beside him. His scent, of warm male and a hint of leather, was comforting.

After they rode together for many miles, she said, 'Thank you for escorting me to Laochre. I hope your duties bring you prosperity and that you see your family once again.'

He gave no answer, but slowed the pace of their horse. 'I doubt I will ever see my family again. And especially not if I disobey orders.' This time, he drew the horse to a stop, his hand resting upon his sword hilt.

'Is something wrong?' she asked. They were not nearly close enough to Laochre. He cut off her words with his hand, guiding the horse west, towards a small circle of trees. Her heartbeat quickened, though she could not see the invisible threat.

Against her ear, he whispered, 'Someone is following us.'

She didn't see how that was possible, given that it was not yet dawn, and she had heard nothing at all. But there was no reason to doubt him.

'I'm going to dismount, and I want you to ride to those trees. Stay there until I come for you.'

Carice wasn't certain it was a good idea to be alone, but she gave no argument. He got off the horse, and before he could leave, she caught his hand. 'What if there is a threat within the trees? Do you have a weapon I could borrow to defend myself?'

Raine unsheathed a small dagger at his waist. 'Take this. But do not use it unless you have to.'

She took the blade and secured it within her girdle. He was about to move away, but she reached out to his cheek. 'Be careful, Raine.'

He covered her palm with his own and squeezed it, before he retraced their tracks. Carice watched him for a short time before retreating towards the trees on horseback. When she reached the grove, she moved through the woods to the opposite side.

The horse's hooves crunched through the

snow, and she turned one last time to look back at Raine, hoping he was safe.

Then men closed in on her so fast, she had no time to react. Strong arms dragged her off the horse, and a scream tore from her throat.

Raine cursed when he heard Carice cry out. Damn it all, but he should have checked the woods before sending her there. A few paces back, he'd spied a single man following on his own horse. The man was a giant, taller than any man he'd ever seen. It had to be Trahern MacEgan, the man who had been meant to guide Carice back to Laochre. Raine had seen the man in battle, years ago, and never had he met any man taller.

He sheathed his sword and charged towards the woods, even knowing it was futile to fight against several men. But he hoped the rider would assist him. 'MacEgan!'

The rider turned his head and rode up alongside him. 'Was that Lady Carice?'

Raine nodded. In the Irish language, he added, 'She needs help!' Without waiting for a reply, he continued running towards the woods. Another scream escaped Carice, and the sound of her panic intensified the need to reach her.

He'd sworn to keep her safe, and he would keep that vow.

With his sword drawn, he entered the woods and seized a fallen branch to use as a makeshift shield. Carice was being held by two men, and she gripped his dagger in one hand. It didn't seem that they intended to harm her, but he recognised one as the soldier he'd released. Half a dozen more men were armed and standing nearby.

'Don't let them take me,' she pleaded with Raine, struggling against the guards. But she lacked the physical strength to fight them, and within moments, one twisted her wrist so the dagger dropped to the snow.

At her gasp of pain, Raine threw himself at the soldiers. His sudden attack caught them off balance, and he jerked Carice free. 'Go! Trahern is close by.'

She didn't argue, but scrambled backwards. Raine had no time to see her there safely, but he struck out at the first soldier with his fists, knocking the man down. He seized the dagger from the snow and buried it in the throat of the next man.

The haze of killing came upon him then, and he moved with swiftness, his sword cutting through bone and flesh. Dimly, he was aware of Carice urging Trahern to help him. He was relieved to know that he'd been right about the man's identity.

The MacEgan fighter unsheathed his own sword, and his brute strength offered a welcome assistance.

'Take her to Laochre,' Raine commanded.

'There are too many of them,' Trahern argued. 'You can't hold them off alone.'

'Get her out. Now, before more of them come.' He seized a fallen branch to block a soldier's sword, lunging hard with his own blade. MacEgan hesitated, but Raine insisted, 'You have no choice. Take her to safety. Leave me behind.'

Trahern sent another man sprawling from a punch, and Raine blocked a third soldier who had come up behind the Irishman.

'Take my horse, then,' the Irishman ordered. 'I'll take her mount.' Trahern sent him a wary look and added, 'Meet us at Laochre if you can.' He shoved another soldier, and there were four men remaining.

Raine stole one last look at Carice. Her long brown hair fell across her shoulders, dampened with snow. Her pale skin was flushed, and fear filled her eyes.

He drank in the sight of her, not knowing if he would live or die. And if Carice's was the last face he saw before dying, he would hold no regrets.

Carice leaned heavily upon Trahern Mac-Egan when they reached the *donjon*. They had spent all afternoon and evening riding towards Laochre, and she could barely keep her eyes open.

Trahern was so tall she had to lean back to look at him. He was also a bard, and he'd entertained her with stories during the journey. It had been a welcome distraction, but she could not stop worrying about Raine.

Was he alive? Had he managed to defeat the soldiers? They were mostly the High King's men, mingled with a few of her father's, but she had not seen any sign of Brian Faoilin.

'Will you be all right?' Trahern asked her, slowing down their mount as they entered the gates. 'Can you walk the rest of the way?' His eyes grew concerned, and she knew he was well aware of her weakness.

She paused a moment. 'I can, yes. But I keep

thinking about the soldiers. We shouldn't have left Raine behind. It wasn't right.' After all that he had done to protect her and care for her, it felt as if they had turned their backs on him.

'He's alive, Carice.'

'There were four of them,' she insisted. 'Four men against one.' Her throat tightened at the thought of him being surrounded. Surely no man could survive such a battle. And though he had sacrificed himself for her sake, the guilt weighed down on her.

'He's a trained Norman soldier,' Trahern argued. 'Believe me when I say that he lives. He did not want you to see him slaughter those men.'

She knew she ought to feel pity for the soldiers. They had died obeying orders, attempting to bring her back. But it had always been against her will. They had been part of the chains binding her to a marriage she had never wanted. A numbness settled over her, the regrets so hard to bear.

'I need to know what happened to him,' she murmured. Had Raine escaped, as Trahern had predicted? Or had he died, his body bleeding out in the snow? She pushed away the thoughts, afraid of the answer.

God help her, she could not forget the memory of his kiss. He hadn't wanted to be with her at first, but the moment his lips had captured hers, she was unable to breathe or think clearly.

'I will find out, if you wish,' Trahern said. He guided her inside, his palm against her back. 'But for now, you are safe.'

The lighted torches were bright within the room, and heads turned at the sight of them. She took a deep breath, and relief flooded through her at the sight of her brother, Killian. The worry on his face dissipated the moment he saw her, and from his roughened looks, it appeared that he'd been fighting. There were signs of swelling upon his face, and a hint of blood on his lip.

'Both of us are in need of food,' Trahern called out as he escorted her inside.

Carice pasted a smile upon her face, but she wasn't feeling at all overjoyed. The worry over Raine distracted her from all else. She knew not if she would ever see him again. It felt as if they'd abandoned him, and she couldn't bear to think of it.

Killian rushed to her side, and she gripped her brother hard as he embraced her. 'Thank God.' Despite all her worries, being in his arms made her feel safe once more. Of all the men here, Killian understood the Ard-Righ's cruelty and he would ensure that she had an escort to continue her journey west.

'Were you pursued by your father's men?' he asked.

She nodded. 'And the High King's men. I had to take shelter at the abbey.' For a moment, she considered telling him about Raine, but then thought the better of it. Killian had the protective instincts of an older brother, and he would only be more worried about her if she spoke of being alone with a Norman soldier.

Trahern might tell him, but when she glanced back at the Irish giant, he held her gaze. It seemed he would not intervene, allowing her to say what she would. She suspected the bard was quite good at keeping secrets. Trahern approached his older brother, King Patrick, who sat upon a dais at the far end of the Great Chamber. While the king appeared amiable, there was also a veiled strength within him. Carice suspected that few men dared to cross him.

Her brother was staring at her with a sense of uneasiness, as if he expected her to fall over at any moment. To break the tension, she ruffled Killian's hair and smiled. Then she leaned against him, and they walked together towards the dais to pay their respects. She wasn't certain if she was expected to dine with the King of Laochre, but she would follow the necessary courtesies. As they drew closer, she saw Lady Taryn. The woman met her gaze with a warm welcome in her eyes, but there was a sudden tension in Killian.

Interesting. Because if she was not mistaken, he had fought on behalf of Lady Taryn. When Carice studied his bruises and swollen knuckles closer, she became more certain of it.

She leaned upon her brother and beckoned for the young woman to join them. Taryn wore an overdress of cream, trimmed in silver threads. Golden balls hung within her hair, against her cheeks, but Carice knew the real reason for the elaborate styling. It was to hide the scars on Taryn's cheeks. Though she didn't know how the young woman had become disfigured, she understood how it felt to have everyone staring.

Though some would think it an unlikely match, Carice believed that Killian deserved a woman who recognised the good man he was. And Killian didn't seem to mind Taryn's scars at all.

She leaned in to her brother and murmured, 'You like her, don't you?'

'Stay out of this, Carice.' Her brother gave her a very clear *Stop meddling* look.

'But you do. You fought for her, didn't you? That's why you're bruised and have swollen knuckles.'

He squeezed her palm in a silent threat: *Leave it alone.*

She sent him an answering smile. *Make me.*

Their silent argument was interrupted when Killian led her to the table directly below the dais where they were invited to dine. He helped her to sit down, and Lady Taryn joined Carice on the opposite side. The woman smiled at her and said, 'I am glad you arrived safely.'

'So am I. It was not easy to escape my father.' Carice turned back to Killian, and the expression on his face had darkened. He knew, as she did, that Brian would never give up. He wanted his only daughter to be queen of all Éireann— no matter what the cost might be.

Never, she swore to herself. She would rather be dead than allow the High King to claim her. Not only because Rory Ó Connor was a brutal man, but because she did not want to spend her last months wedded to a monster.

Although she ought to feel safer at Laochre, she could not relinquish the fear that her freedom would soon be at an end. Even surrounded by so many MacEgans, her father and the king's men might find her and force her to return with them. She needed to leave quickly—and she desperately wished that Raine were here to escort her.

It was a foolish thought. He had no interest in protecting her—only in serving his king. Even if he did come to Laochre, she doubted if he could travel west with her.

Taryn passed over a trencher of roasted meats and cheeses, and Carice chose some food for herself. She was exhausted from the journey, hardly able to eat at all, but she needed to keep up what little strength she had left.

Her mind blurred as she conversed with her brother and Lady Taryn about the High King. Though Killian had promised not to do anything dangerous, she had her doubts. He was watching over Taryn as if he intended to fight for her—and the young woman seemed uneasy about it.

Seeing them together reminded her of Raine. He had looked at her that way on the night he had slept beside her. Although they were hardly more than strangers, she had felt the tangible attraction to him. She was warm and safe in his bed, and despite all the reasons it was wrong, she had enjoyed sleeping with his hard body against hers.

The wistful thought caught at her heart. *I want to see him again.*

Never in her life had any man awakened her to such feelings. And if she only had a few months remaining, she wanted to seize every last moment she could.

Her head spun with dizziness, and she gripped the table to keep from fainting, taking slow, deep breaths. Although she no longer had the stomach cramps she'd experienced before, the weakness had not diminished.

The moments she'd spent with Raine had taunted her with unfulfilled hopes. She had no right to let herself imagine a future with any man, much less a Norman soldier. By next winter, she would likely be dead. It was a reality she didn't want to face, but it was inevitable. It was better that they had parted ways, for it avoided heartache.

There was no future for her—but there could be for her brother and Lady Taryn.

Was it not better to spend her last few months

bringing joy to others? Carice saw an opportunity to bring her brother happiness. He needed a woman to love him for the man he was. And she had no qualms about pushing Lady Taryn and him together.

When Taryn was about to leave, Carice took her by the hand. 'Don't go yet. I would like to stay and talk with you a while.' She turned to Killian. 'Give us a few moments alone, won't you?'

If all went to plan, her brother would spend the next few days alone with Taryn. A little scheming wasn't a bad thing, so long as it brought happiness to others. With any luck, after she was gone, they would have each other.

Chapter Four

Raine wasn't about to let Carice Faoilin go. Not like this.

Her face haunted him in a way he'd never anticipated. All he could think of was her riding off with Trahern MacEgan, her eyes filled with fear. Though she'd trusted him to bring her to Laochre, Raine didn't know the man.

His instincts sharpened with the need to follow her and ensure that she was safe. And though he knew it was impossible—for he was already late reporting to his commander—he couldn't deny the urge. Never had any woman lain beside him at night, seeking comfort. She had soothed his troubled spirits, pushing back the loneliness.

Now, it had returned threefold.

He had finished burying the bodies of the

remaining guards he'd killed. The fight had ended quickly, after Carice and Trahern had gone. Most men would have been afraid of the odds, but Raine hardly cared if he lived or died. It gave his fighting an advantage, for he struck out with no fear. And he'd won.

A few scattered flakes of snow drifted against his face. His arm was aching from a shallow cut. It was an annoyance, nothing more, but he wanted to wrap it to keep from dripping blood everywhere.

He trudged through the snow, back to where Trahern's horse was tethered. Then he rode towards the abbey, trying to settle his mood. *You can't go after her,* he reminded himself. *She's gone, and it's better that way.*

He knew that—and yet, his thoughts lingered upon her beauty, her soft hair and the taste of her mouth. A dream was all she would ever be. It was best to let her go.

The moment he walked through the abbey grounds, he saw the horses and armed men waiting for him. The sight of the soldiers was enough to remind him of the duties he'd neglected.

His commander, Sir Darren de Carleigh, stood just past the graves. He still wore his conical helm, and he crossed his arms with a knowing stare. Although Sir Darren was not a tall man, he was heavily muscled from training. 'You're late, de Garenne. You were supposed to return two days ago.'

'I was unable to return.' He pushed back his chain mail coif and held up his wounded arm as evidence.

The knight's eyes narrowed at the sight of Raine's wound. 'What happened?'

'Just a small fight.' He thought quickly of what to say next, knowing he could not claim that he'd been attacked while hunting.

'And who were you fighting?' Sir Darren's voice was quiet, but it held a deadly edge. 'Did someone follow you here?'

Raine thought a moment before speaking. He didn't want to tell them about Carice, and yet, he saw no alternative. The Norman soldiers would learn the truth, whether or not it came from him. He had to choose his answers carefully. He shrugged and remarked, 'A few of the High King's men were travelling through the woods. I questioned them.'

It wasn't exactly true, but it gave him the means of redirecting Sir Darren's curiosity. 'What did you learn?'

Again, he held back, unsure of what to reveal. Some of the Irish soldiers had retreated, returning to Carice's father. If the Normans continued east, Sir Darren might encounter the men and demand more answers.

The truth was the only way to protect Carice. And there *was* a way he could see her again, even if it meant using her to achieve his purpose.

'They were in search of the High King's bride,' he said at last. 'Lady Carice, of the Faoilin tribe, went missing a few days ago. She was trying to avoid her marriage.'

Just as he'd suspected, the knight smiled at the information. 'This could be useful to us.'

Useful perhaps—but Raine didn't want the Norman soldiers anywhere near Carice. They would frighten her or even threaten her. He couldn't let that happen.

Instead, he offered, 'I know she was travelling towards Laochre Castle. Let me track her down. I can try to convince her that I'll protect her and bring her to safety.'

'And why would she believe you?'

Raine paused and then admitted, 'Because she was here. I gave her shelter for the night before Trahern MacEgan escorted her to Laochre. She trusts me, because I kept my word.'

A slow smile curved over his commander's face. 'So you'll let her believe that you're helping her to escape her marriage…but you'll bring her back to the High King instead,' Sir Darren finished. 'Good. That will give you a means of infiltrating Tara.'

Raine felt the trap closing in around him. Although he tried to tell himself that he would guard Carice, he wasn't so certain he could keep that vow once they reached Tara. He had to carry out his orders to kill the High King. The task was dangerous beyond anything he'd ever attempted. He was a pawn in a game played by two kings—and no one would care if he died.

Carice Faoilin shouldn't mean anything to him…and yet, he didn't want to betray her like this. All she wanted was to die in peace, with her freedom.

He could understand that. But freedom was not a gift given to him. He had surrendered his life into the guise of a king's soldier, in order to save his sisters' lives. And the only means of regaining their freedom was to sacrifice hers.

Sir Darren began walking towards the kitchens, beckoning for Raine to join him. 'We will dine with you, and you will tell me everything you know.'

He inclined his head and led the men into the kitchens. There was a little meat left, and he divided it among the soldiers, letting them feast upon it. While they ate, he cleaned the cut upon his upper arm and bound a length of linen around it. The cold air had slowed the blood flow, and he kept the binding tight.

'Take your men and go on to Tara without me,' Raine suggested. 'I will find Lady Carice and bring her to you. It will be easier to protect her if I go alone. She will not willingly go with all of us.'

'She may not agree at all.'

He doubted it, for Carice had already asked him to accompany her west. He simply had to convince her that he'd changed his mind. 'I will not fail in this.'

Sir Darren nodded, wiping his hands and reaching for a cup of ale. 'Remember that your greater task is to kill the High King.' The knight sent him a measured look. 'You would not wish King Henry to be displeased by your actions.'

Raine caught the man's insinuation. He masked the anger churning inside him and regarded the Norman knight. *Oui,* he knew the power the king held over him. The man had already seized their family's lands. But worst of all was the fate of Raine's sisters.

'After I kill the Ard-Righ, I want Nicole and Elise released.'

That was not negotiable. The fate of his sisters was the only power the king held over him now. Raine cared nothing for his own life or fate, for he had already lost everything. The only reason he'd agreed to the orders was to win their freedom.

Sir Darren said, 'You will be rewarded, if you succeed in the assassination.'

'I want them freed, not a reward.'

His commander met his gaze and acceded, 'If it is possible, I will intervene for their sake.' Darren turned sympathetic, and in that sudden moment, the boundaries shifted. The knight admitted, 'I have sisters, as well. I understand your concern for them.'

'They are innocent in this.' God only knew what had happened to Nicole and Elise in the past few years. He'd hated having to leave them, remaining so far away. But that was the cost of their lives, and he'd paid it. His orders were clear—become a Norman soldier and obey the king in all things.

Yet, if he succeeded in the assassination, there was the risk that King Henry would not release them. It was a dangerous game Raine played, one he doubted he could win.

He exhaled slowly and said, 'What of my lands? Will they ever be returned to me?'

Darren shook his head. 'That, I cannot say. After your father's betrayal, I do not think Henry will give them back.'

'I have never given him reason to question my loyalty.'

'Then give him a reason to reward you,' Darren countered. 'Rory Ó Connor's death will encourage Henry to intervene. You will disappear after it is done and never set foot in Ireland again. It is very likely your sisters will be released as well.'

But if he was unsuccessful, Henry would lay the blame at his feet and order his death. That much was certain. 'What will happen to my sisters if I fail?'

Darren said nothing, and his silence was the answer Raine had expected. He had no choice but to obey.

'So be it.' He stood back against the wall while the soldiers finished eating. The grim finality of his life hung over him with the knowledge that there was no escape from this. Invisible chains bound him to a fate he didn't want.

'Find the High King's bride and bring her to us,' Sir Darren said to him. 'She will give you the means to get close.'

He inclined his head but added, 'Do not follow me. I will bring her to Tara, but only if you stay away from us.'

His commander didn't respond, and Raine understood the unspoken words. They didn't trust him to uphold his promise.

'Nicole and Elise's lives depend on my obeying orders,' he insisted. 'I would never put them at risk. I will bring Lady Carice to the High King—be assured of it.'

And he could only hope that Carice would forgive him for this.

Carice sat in the solar with Queen Isabel and Lady Genevieve, Bevan MacEgan's wife. Despite being in the company of the two women, she felt restless. Her brother, Killian, had left only yesterday with Lady Taryn on a journey to plead with the High King. Lady Taryn's father was being held captive at Tara, and Killian had agreed to escort her there.

It felt as if her brother were walking into the lion's den. And yet, she knew the reward that awaited him if he succeeded in saving Lady Taryn's father. It would give him another life, one where he was no longer treated like a *fuidir* or a bastard son. She wanted that for him, and she prayed for his safety.

Although the MacEgans had offered her the chance to stay longer at Laochre, her own protection was fragile, at best. It was only a matter of time before her father found her here. The sooner she left, the safer she would be.

She knew that the MacEgans would help her, but she couldn't stop thinking of Raine. Trahern had offered to find out what had happened to him, but it would take time. It might be better to travel towards the abbey on their way west. Then she could see for herself if he was still there. The thought reassured her.

'Liam, come back here,' the queen demanded. When her young son only giggled, staggering in his attempts to walk, Isabel put aside her sewing and scooped him away from the fireplace hearth. 'I vow, this child terrifies me. Every moment I turn my head, he finds a new danger. Yesterday, I caught him trying to touch Patrick's sword.' She snuggled him close, and Carice smiled at the baby's antics.

'At least my Duncan cannot walk yet,' Genevieve countered. Her own son was sitting up, chewing upon a piece of fur, while the young mother was seated at her harp. She had played music for them the night before, and the soothing sounds filled the room.

It helped keep Carice's mind off her churning stomach, for the illness had returned again this morn. She'd tried to eat a little bread to calm the aching, but the pain had only worsened.

Carice let out a slow breath and lowered her gaze to her sewing, pretending as if nothing was the matter. If she didn't eat at noontide, it might help.

As a distraction, she asked Genevieve, 'May I hold your son?'

The young woman smiled, still plucking at the harp strings. 'Of course.'

When Carice took the babe in her arms, Duncan seized handfuls of her hair, offering a gummy smile. She spoke nonsense words to him, but the moment was bittersweet, reminding her of the children she would never bear. Her heart grieved at the truth of it.

She braved a smile at the babe, trying to

imagine what it would be like to live her days without pain. Or what it would be to have a child of her own.

Resentment gathered in her stomach, for she knew it would not happen. The sense of unfairness heightened, for what had she done to deserve this illness? Why should she have to die when other women could live and leave a part of themselves in their offspring? It made her wish that her sickness was a tangible enemy, one who could be struck down by a blade. She wanted a different life than this one, and she wished to God there was a way to have it.

A knock sounded at the door, and when the queen called out for the person to enter, an adolescent boy peered inside. He sent a brilliant smile towards Carice and said, 'Queen Isabel, there is a man at the gates.'

The queen sent the boy a wry smile. 'Ewan, that's not very useful information. Who is there?'

His smile widened, and he entered the solar. He gave a dramatic bow before Carice and added, 'It's a Norman soldier. And he's asked to see the lady.' Then he knelt and offered, 'Would you like me to slay him for you?'

Carice straightened, startled by the lad's declaration. The only Norman soldier who knew she was here was Raine. Her emotions threatened to spill over, and she fought to hold them back. Raine was alive, and he'd come back for her. The rush of anticipation made her pulse quicken, though she knew her thoughts were running away with her. She was no longer a silly adolescent girl, and she needed to calm herself.

Queen Isabel groaned. 'Save us your chivalry, Ewan. He's only a Norman soldier, not a dragon.' To Carice, she added, 'Ewan is my husband's youngest brother. He believes he will be the greatest warrior of the MacEgans.'

'And so I will be.' He flexed skinny muscles and shot her another wide smile. 'When I'm stronger.'

His good spirits made it impossible not to be amused. Carice returned his grin and said, 'I believe I know who the soldier is.'

Before she could elaborate, the queen intervened. 'Who is he? And why is he here?'

'He is here for me,' Carice answered. 'He saved Trahern and me when we were pursued by King Rory's men.'

'Where are the rest of his men?' Isabel demanded. 'Norman soldiers don't travel alone.'

Ewan shrugged. 'This one did.'

The queen's suspicions dimmed her elation, for it almost seemed that Isabel would not allow Raine to enter.

Carice fumbled for an answer. 'He was supposed to return to them. They were travelling back to Tara, I think.'

Isabel glanced over at Lady Genevieve. 'Why would Norman soldiers go to Tara? It doesn't sound right.' Her expression turned troubled. 'Our countries are at peace now. There is no reason to bring any soldiers there.' To Ewan, she added, 'Allow him to enter, but I will expect you to find out everything you can about this man. Ask him to wait in the Great Chamber. If he is truly alone, he may be no threat to us, but Connor and Bevan should be there.' The lad nodded and quickly departed their chamber.

'Do you think King Henry is planning another visit to Éireann?' Genevieve suggested. When the baby began fussing, Carice handed Duncan back to her. The young mother took him and adjusted her *léine,* allowing the baby to nurse.

'Perhaps.' Isabel appeared unconvinced. 'But Patrick should know of this. He may want to warn the *Ard-Rígh.*'

'Raine did not come here to fight,' Carice insisted. 'I am certain of that. Ask Trahern, and he will tell you.'

It was likely that Raine had come to ensure that she had made it safely to Laochre. She stood up, intending to go downstairs, but her knees swayed, and she had to sit down once more.

The queen's expression transformed into sympathy. 'You aren't feeling well, are you?'

'It's nothing.' Carice steadied herself, but her stomach felt as if knives were carving it into pieces. She struggled to push away the illness, desperate to see Raine again. The idea of retreating to her bed was not at all what she wanted. She closed her eyes, tightening her mouth as she fought to remain standing.

'Our healer should come and see you,' Isabel suggested. 'She may be able to find out what ails you.'

'After I see Raine,' she insisted. And no matter how much her stomach was bothering her, she would push back the pain.

Genevieve exchanged a look with Isabel, and it was obvious that neither of them believed she was capable of walking across the room, much less going to see Raine.

She took several deep breaths and stood up again, grimacing against the stomach pains. Isabel picked up Liam and balanced him on her hip while she stood beside Carice.

'You may see the soldier if you wish,' Isabel said slowly. 'But take slow steps. And promise me you'll let our healer look at you afterwards.'

She braved a smile at the queen, who seemed to understand her reasons. 'Thank you.'

'I suppose if it were me, I would not let anything stop me from seeing Patrick.' Isabel walked beside her, keeping the pace slow. Liam squirmed in her arms, but she bent to him and kissed his cheeks. 'You did not mention this man before. And I don't think Killian knew of him either, did he?'

Because her brother would have been over-protective and angry with her for taking such a risk. It was better if he knew nothing.

'No, I didn't tell him about Raine.' She didn't miss Isabel's curious look, but she saw no reason to elaborate. 'If it weren't for him granting me shelter, I wouldn't have survived my escape.'

Carice leaned against the wall as she made her way towards the hall. Isabel was leading the way, but Genevieve had stayed behind to finish nursing Duncan. Dizziness washed over Carice when she reached the stairs, but she forced herself to continue.

When she made it to the bottom of the stairs, she paused a moment to catch her breath. Isabel guided her into the Great Chamber, but there was no sign of Raine anywhere. The din of conversation within the space was a roar within her ears. Carice chose a seat on one of the low chairs near the wall, trying to remain out of the way while she mustered her remaining strength. Most of the trestle tables had been pushed aside, but many people had gathered within the space. Soon enough, several MacEgan guards emerged, and behind them, she saw Raine.

When he removed his iron helm, his dark blond hair was dampened with snow. He wore the same chain mail armour and tunic she had seen earlier. He kept his posture rigid as he entered the chamber, and a broadsword hung at his side. From the linen bandage on his forearm, she realised that he'd suffered a minor wound, but it was the only injury she could see. And for now, she was so relieved to see him alive.

She wished she could run towards him, to embrace him and thank him for all that he'd done. But if she dared to leave this seat, she would drop to the floor in a faint. A slight smile played at her lips at the thought of collapsing before him. It wasn't exactly the way she wanted to welcome the man.

Two of the MacEgan men shadowed Raine as he strode towards the dais. Queen Isabel had joined her husband, and although she was Norman herself, her expression held wariness. Carice didn't understand the tension between Isabel and the king. Why would Raine's presence bother the queen? He had not come with an army, intending an attack—he'd come for *her*.

She stood, and a tunnelling rush of air made her dizzy. *Don't faint,* she warned herself. Slowly, she pushed her way through the crowd of people who had gathered. Trahern had joined his brother at the dais, and at the sight of him, she breathed a little easier. He could attest that Raine had saved their lives.

'Who are you and why have you come to Laochre?' the king asked. He spoke in the Irish tongue, and when Raine didn't answer at first, the queen translated for him in the Norman language.

'I am Raine de Garenne.' He sent a direct look towards Trahern. 'And your brother knows why I am here.'

The Irish warrior took a step forward, but there was wariness in his expression. 'I found him with the Lady Carice. We were attacked by the High King's men, and he stayed behind so that I could bring the lady to Laochre. I invited him to join us, and I presume he wanted to see if the lady was safe. Unless he came for another reason?' He raised an eyebrow in silent question.

A rushing sound filled Carice's ears, and she took a shaky breath, moving closer to Raine. Then he saw her, and his green eyes turned possessive. He looked upon her as if she belonged to no one but him. 'I have come at the Lady Carice's request.' His eyes held warmth, reminding her of the days they'd spent together.

She wanted to speak to Raine, to tell him how glad she was to see him once more. But his voice seemed to come from far away, the words echoing within her ringing ears. Her knees were weak, hardly supporting her steps at all. And suddenly, her sight grew fuzzy and the room tipped. Though she fought to remain conscious, darkness closed over her.

And then, there was nothing.

Raine rushed towards Carice, but two men held him back. *Dieu,* she'd been so pale. He didn't know why she'd fainted, but it was clear her illness hadn't abated. Instead, she seemed to be getting worse.

'Let go of me,' he demanded. The primal need to protect her overrode all else. He elbowed his way free of one guard, and then smashed the face of another. He heard the crunch of bone and raised his arm to ward off a blow. Two of the MacEgan brothers seized him, but he wrenched his way free. Before he could reach Carice, Trahern hauled him back.

'Leave her be.' The Irishman spoke in the Norman tongue and tightened his grip on Raine's forearm. 'Our healer will look after her.'

Though he knew they were right, fury roared through him with the possessive need to guard Carice. He knew it was irrational, but he didn't like seeing her in such a state.

The king intervened, stepping forward as he spoke the Norman tongue. 'Lady Carice will be well enough in the care of our healer. But I have questions for you about your involvement with King Rory.' The sharp tone within the man's voice held suspicion and a silent threat.

Raine fell silent, his attention fixed upon Carice as the healer took her away. He wasn't surprised that the MacEgans didn't trust him. They had good reasons not to.

A moment later, they switched into Irish, speaking quietly in front of him. He understood most of what they were saying, but decided to keep that knowledge to himself. Though he could speak a few Irish words, his listening skills were far stronger.

Patrick turned to his brother Trahern and asked, 'Why do you think the Normans are gathering at Tara? Henry is not visiting, and there is no reason for an army.'

Raine was careful to keep his expression fixed, making it seem as if he didn't understand a single word. But their suspicions were raised by his very presence.

'He knows something,' Trahern remarked. Raine could feel the man's searching gaze upon him. 'But he'll never tell us.' To the younger blond warrior, he asked, 'What do you want to do, Connor?'

The young man's face grew serious. 'Question him further.'

The king seemed to agree. 'We cannot allow the Normans to attack Tara. We've fought too hard for this peace.' He exchanged a look with his wife, who came forward and took his hand.

Raine continued to behave as if he understood none of their words. But he knew that more questioning could lead to imprisonment or worse, torture. The MacEgans had allies among both the Irish and the Normans, and they would do whatever was necessary to keep the High King alive.

Which put them at cross purposes. Rory Ó Connor could not remain alive if Raine intended to gain his sisters' freedom.

'Come,' Trahern spoke in the Norman language once more, leading him towards the back of the Hall. 'My brothers and I want to speak with you in private.'

Raine said nothing, knowing that if he dared to protest, it might reveal that he understood their language. 'I came to see Lady Carice.'

'And so you will, when she is feeling better.'

All of his instincts flared up, for he knew not where they would bring him. If he broke free now, they would never let him near Carice. But if he agreed to go with them in private, the 'questioning' might take a darker turn.

They had already taken her above stairs, and it was killing him not to follow her. Not only because he needed to take her with him to Tara, but also because she was unwell. He vowed to himself that after he had answered their questions, nothing would stop him from finding Carice.

The men led him to a smaller chamber in the very back of the *donjon*. King Patrick faced him, while his brothers, Trahern and Connor, stood on either side of him. 'My wife was a Norman before she married me. I have kept my peace with them, but only for her sake. My loyalty lies with my kinsmen and with the kings who battle for the good of Éireann.'

Raine straightened and faced the king openly. 'Why am I here?'

Patrick took a step forward, meeting him eye to eye. 'Because you slaughtered the High King's men instead of giving Lady Carice back into their care.'

'She did not want to wed the High King. I defended her from becoming their captive.'

'A woman you've only known two days?' The king's mouth tightened. 'I believe you had another purpose in mind.'

Before Raine could counter the man's prediction, Patrick continued. 'According to Lady Carice, you intended to return to your army at Tara. I want to know why. Why are the Normans gathering around the High King?'

'I am a soldier, and I obey orders,' Raine answered. 'I know not why they are travelling there.' He kept his voice quiet, as if he cared nothing about the Norman army.

'A lie,' Trahern said. 'If you were obedient, you would have been with your commander instead of alone.'

'I was granted a short leave to bury the holy men who died in a fire,' he said.

Trahern exchanged a glance with his brothers. Connor seemed to read his distrust and came to stand behind Raine. It was a not so subtle reminder that he was surrounded by men who could easily kill him where he stood.

'Instead of returning to the Normans, you came back for the lady,' Trahern said. 'Those are not the actions of a loyal soldier.'

Raine gave no response at all, knowing that silence was the best answer.

'You were planning to use her, weren't you? Because then you would be close to the High King.' Trahern moved even closer, using his height as intimidation. 'For what purpose?'

Raine pretended as if he'd heard nothing. Over and over, they questioned him, but he let their words fall upon deaf ears. Instead, he envisioned Carice's beautiful face and the long brown hair that hung below her shoulders to her breasts. He remembered her smile and the light blue eyes that held worry for him.

When they realised that he would answer no further questions, Patrick switched into the Irish language. 'Do you think he's dangerous?'

Trahern gave a slight nod. 'To King Rory, yes. Not to us or to Lady Carice.'

The king thought a moment. 'We cannot let him stay within the castle. He might try to take the lady during the night.'

Which was exactly what Raine had planned. It took an effort not to reveal that he understood every word of their conversation. But these men were far too astute about his intentions.

'What do you want to do?' Connor asked.

The king only pointed towards the door. 'Take him.' His brothers seemed to understand Patrick's orders, and they guided Raine back through the Great Chamber and outside. Connor kept his weapon unsheathed, and it was clear that they were treating him as a prisoner instead of a guest.

As they approached a smaller tower, Raine studied the number of MacEgan soldiers in the courtyard. There were at least two dozen men, half of them patrolling the inner bailey, and others stood at intervals at their posts along the top of the outer wall.

He could try to escape—and might even succeed if he moved quickly—but they would only believe him guilty. At the moment, he had simply refused to answer questions. Even if they imprisoned him, there was no cause for punishment.

At least, not yet.

They had guessed his intent to bring Carice to Tara, but they knew nothing about his role in killing the High King. If they did, they would slit his throat where he stood.

'Where are you taking me?' he demanded, as they guided him across the inner bailey. Their silence was an answer he should have anticipated, as a subtle retribution for his own refusal to speak.

When they reached the stone outbuilding, he didn't miss the solid wooden door leading inside the guard tower. Raine halted his steps and stared at the men. 'Is this how you treat all strangers who visit Laochre?'

'It's how we treat Norman strangers,' Trahern countered. 'At least, those who keep the truth from us.' He narrowed his gaze at Raine and said, 'Unless you have answers you'd prefer to give now?'

'I have done nothing to threaten you,' he reminded them.

'No. But your army threatens the Ard-Righ.'

Raine stood before them and said, 'We have only a small group of soldiers. And there is no threat in men travelling to Tara. What their reasons are, I know not.' He kept every trace of untruth from his expression, masking all emotion.

'If you answer our questions openly, there is no need to remain here for long.' Trahern nodded to his brother. 'Connor, show him inside.'

The man pushed open a wooden door, but it was so dark, Raine could see nothing within the space. There were no windows, no torches to light the interior. Before his eyes could adjust, they guided him to stand at the back wall. Iron manacles were shackled to his wrists, and Raine struggled against their grip as the pins were hammered into place. Damn them all. He hadn't expected it to come to this. 'There is no need to imprison me,' he accused. 'I have done nothing wrong.'

A moment later, a torch flared, and they closed the door. Although he saw no weapons of torture, he didn't delude himself into believing he was safe.

'Tell us the reason why the Norman army is gathered at Tara, and we will free you now,' Trahern offered.

'I have told you. I don't know their purpose.' Which was a lie, and all knew it. Raine realised he never should have come within the gates as a guest. It would have been far better to slip inside and steal Carice away before anyone knew what had happened. The MacEgan men were far too shrewd, for they were the best-trained warriors in Ireland.

'What do you want to do?' Patrick asked in the Irish tongue.

'Leave him here overnight,' Trahern answered. 'He may speak more, once he's spent a few hours here.'

'And what if he is telling the truth?' The king crossed his arms. 'What if he means no harm?'

Connor glanced back at his brother. 'If the Norman army is planning to attack Tara, the men we sent with Lady Taryn will be in danger. We need to know why they are gathering.'

The men stepped back, still discussing his fate. Then Patrick switched back into the Norman tongue. 'Have you anything else to say? What are your orders at Tara?'

Raine gave them no reply at all, for anything he said would condemn him. Instead, he leaned back against the wall, steeling himself for an uncomfortable night. Although the enclosure was sheltered, it wasn't warm.

'Leave him here,' Patrick commanded. 'He may give us answers on the morrow.'

Raine held his silence as they left him in darkness. There was nothing he could tell them, and he wasn't certain how he would gain his freedom.

The utter absence of light was unsettling, but he was able to sit down on the dirt floor.

The stone walls did nothing to keep out the chill. He would survive the night, but it was unlikely he would find any sleep—not locked away in this place.

Raine ignored the physical discomfort, for he supposed it was a just punishment for the killing he had done. But as he waited, he could not stop thinking of Carice. Had the healer been able to ease her pain? Or was she still suffering?

As the hours crept onward, his only solace lay in his thoughts of her.

* * *

Carice awakened in the middle of the night, unaware of what had happened. Her mouth tasted like it had been stuffed with wool. She realised that the healer had given her a tea to help her sleep. Slowly, she sat up and tried to gather her thoughts.

Raine. She remembered that Raine had been here yesterday. Where was he now?

When she tried to recall the memories of the last evening, she could not seem to make sense of them. It was a blur of visions, mingled with the desire to sleep longer.

She slid her feet over to the side of the bed and reached for a cloak. Her stomach had calmed, and she put on her shoes, returning to the Great Chamber. The MacEgans might have given Raine a place to sleep among their guards, and she wanted to speak with him.

She rested her hand against the stone wall as she walked down the spiral stairs. The Great Chamber was quiet, and men were sprawled on the floor, sleeping among the dogs. But there was no sign of Raine. The MacEgans had retired to their own chambers, and she had no idea where to look for him.

She spied the king's youngest brother sleeping against the wall. Ewan—that was his name. Carice leaned down to the young man, shaking his shoulder. The boy swatted her away, but she persisted in waking him up. When Ewan opened sleepy eyes at last, she whispered, 'Where did they take Raine? I know you must have seen it.'

Ewan yawned. 'They took him to the guard's tower.' Then he closed his eyes and rolled over to go back to sleep. A moment later, he was snoring.

The guard's tower? Now why would he be there? Carice frowned at the thought. When she reached the outer doors, a servant slid back the heavy bolt upon the doors. She walked outside and down the stairs, pulling her cloak tighter. The sky was black, but torches lined the walls at even intervals.

The guards noticed her presence immediately, and one came forward. 'Is aught amiss, my lady?'

'I want to speak with Raine de Garenne,' she explained. 'Can you bring me to him?'

The man's expression tightened. 'He is being held in the tower over there.'

'As a captive?' Carice was incredulous at the idea. 'But why? What has he done?'

'He refused to answer our king's questions.' The guard started to escort her back inside, but Carice would have none of it.

'I must speak with him.' She began walking towards the tower, and the guard shadowed her. When she reached the door, she found it locked. To the man, she commanded, 'Open this now.'

He shook his head. 'You would not be safe with him.'

'He protected me for several days,' she protested. 'Don't be foolish. Open the door, and you can stand here to guard me.'

The man shook his head. 'No, my lady. I am sorry.'

She eyed him and then sat down in front of the door, gathering her cloak around her for warmth. 'I suppose I'll wait, then.'

He strode away from her, obviously believing she would never stay outside in the cold. Snow flurries drifted downward from the sky, and she rested her cheek against the wood. 'Are you there, Raine?'

'*Oui.* I am here.' His voice sounded weary, and she was terrified of what had happened to him.

'What did they do to you?' She got on her

knees, speaking through the locked door. 'And why are you a prisoner?'

'They chained me in the dark because I could not tell them of my commander's orders.'

She couldn't understand why the MacEgans would do such a thing. It made no sense at all, for Raine had done nothing wrong.

'Why *did* you come to Laochre?' she asked. 'Did something happen?' There was a shifting sound, and she heard the metallic jangle of his chains as if he was moving closer to the door.

'Why do you think I came, *chérie?*' His voice was low, but there was a trace of warmth within it. Carice pressed her hand to the door, and it was almost as if she could sense his hand on the opposite side. This man had become a friend to her, and seeing him imprisoned was wrong.

She wanted to imagine that he'd come to escort her to the west, but it was unlikely. He did have orders to obey. Queen Isabel's warnings held truth in them—a Norman soldier could not do as he wanted. His life was sworn to the king's service. 'I think you came back to see that I arrived here safely.'

He didn't answer, but she suspected that he could not admit such a thing, even if it was true.

Raine de Garenne was a Norman soldier, not a man who held any feelings towards her. Even so, she wanted it to be true, for he had fought to keep her protected.

'I wish you were here to help me travel away from this place.' Her voice held her wistful imaginings, and she lowered her palm from the door. 'My offer stands, if you're willing.'

'Whether I am willing is not the question,' he said. And in the answer, she realised that his duties imprisoned him as surely as these chains did.

Carice shivered against a gust of wind, and saw that the soldier had turned back to watch her. When she didn't move, he crossed the inner bailey to stand before her.

'You should go back to your chamber, my lady. It is far too cold for you to remain here.'

'I will be glad to obey, if you will grant me a few moments inside with Raine.' She needed to know what could be done to get him out of this place. And while she suspected that the Norman army intended to invade Tara, none of that mattered to her, for she would be nowhere near the High King. And neither would Raine, if she could convince him to come with her.

He didn't behave like a soldier, she realised.

More like a commander or even a Norman lord. There was a sense about him as if he would never yield or break.

The soldier eyed her. 'If I grant you a little time, you must vow to return to your chamber.'

She offered him a blinding smile. 'I so vow it. And I thank you for whatever time I may have.'

'If you break that promise, I will carry you back against your will.' With that, the guard unlocked the door.

Carice pushed it open and saw that it was impossibly dark within the space. 'Raine, I am here.' She didn't want to startle him, particularly if he couldn't see her. To the guard, she asked, 'May I have a torch?'

He left to get one, and Carice took off her cloak, bringing it to Raine. In the dark, she knelt down and spread it over him. His skin was icy, his muscles rigid from the cold.

'I'm so sorry that this happened,' she began. 'Why did they lock you in here? I still don't understand.'

Before Raine could answer, the guard returned with the torch. Carice took it from him, setting it within a sconce on the wall. He eyed her and said, 'You may remain only for a short while, my lady.'

The moment her eyes adjusted to the dim light, her mood turned grim. Raine's wrists were bound in iron chains, and he had nothing to protect him from the cold night air. She moved to sit beside him and took his hand in hers. His fingers were freezing and she tried to warm them. 'What can I do to get you out of here?'

'I will get myself out,' he said. The dark timbre of his voice made her wonder exactly how he planned to do it. And she didn't want more death.

'I will talk with King Patrick and see what can be done.' She rubbed his hands, trying to bring warmth into them. 'I am sorry you were treated like this. Especially after all you did for me.'

He gripped her hand. 'Do you still want me to take you away from here?'

His question startled her, for she didn't know if it was possible, given his position within the Norman forces. 'Would your commander allow this? I thought you had to return to them.'

He regarded her, and the intensity of his gaze made her look away. 'No. He would not allow it. But if they believe I was held prisoner and could not return…'

She understood what he was implying. If he claimed that the MacEgans had held him captive here, the Normans would know the truth of it. 'It will not take long,' she said. 'If we ride swiftly, we can be there within a few days.'

The thought of journeying with Raine brought about a rush of eagerness. Yet she felt a slight worry about his reasons. Although he had offered once before, she hadn't wanted to accept his help, after learning what he wanted.

'Why do you want to travel with me?' she asked. 'Is it because you want information? I have told you already, there is nothing I can tell you.'

'That isn't the reason why.' His thumb slid over the pulse point upon her wrist. The simple touch undid her senses, and she pushed back the rush of longing.

'Then is it gold or silver that you want?' Her uncle, who dwelled on the Dingle Peninsula, would give a reward for her sake, she was certain. It would not be much, but enough for his trouble.

'No.' The chains rattled slightly as his hands moved to her waist. 'That's not what I want.'

Her heart thundered within her chest, and she

didn't know if she was imagining the interest in his voice. 'Then what is it?'

He paused a moment before his hands fell away. 'There were…people I wanted to protect once. I failed in that. But I can protect you.'

She started to protest, 'It's dangerous. And I don't think—'

'Does there have to be a reason?' he prompted. When she said nothing, he added, 'We both know the MacEgans will not want to cause trouble between your clan and their tribe. It is easier if you allow me to be your escort.'

He was right, but she still wasn't certain about the answer he had given. There was something missing, something he wasn't telling her. She took a step backwards and was startled when the world seemed to tip. Raine caught her before she fell.

'You look pale. Are you still unwell?'

She took a moment to steady herself. There truly wasn't a good way to answer his question, for she was always unwell. Instead, she responded, 'There are good moments and bad. I've learned to live what's left of my life from hour to hour.'

He didn't appear pleased to hear that. 'You should go back to your chamber and rest.'

Aye, he was right. 'I will. Give me a few hours, and I will try to arrange your release.' If that was even possible. She didn't know how King Patrick would agree to free him. 'But what shall I say to the king? He wants answers from you.'

'Tell him I will break my silence.'

Carice moved in and removed her cloak, placing it around his shoulders. 'Try to stay warm until then.' She tucked the wool against him, and he caught her wrists with his chained hands. In the freezing darkness, a sudden heat rose up within her skin. She was conscious of every breath between them, and her breasts tightened against her gown.

It was a foolish response, but one she could not suppress. Raine took the edges of the cloak and drew them around her, cocooning both of them in the wool. Her heartbeat stuttered within her chest, while her body yearned to move even closer. On impulse, she hugged him, hiding her burning cheeks against his chest.

God help her, she was wanting far too much. Her feelings were shifting past the brink of friendship into something more. And it was dangerous to both her wayward heart and her mind.

Don't, she warned herself. *He is going to leave.*

She knew that, but she also knew that every fragile moment of life was to be treasured. In a matter of hours, she could be curled up in a ball once more, her stomach raging with pain. Moments like these were rare, and she wanted to savour the feeling.

An aching caught inside her, while her emotions weakened beneath the weight of yearning. She knew there was no future with this man or any other. If she dared to let herself dream, it would only break her heart when he left her. And he *would* leave. He had to return to his duties, and she was fleeing a marriage from the most powerful man in Éireann.

Not to mention, she was dying.

Raine's palms moved up her spine, and her fingers tightened around him in response. She had no right to reach out to this man.

But when he caught her mouth in a kiss, all her resistance melted. The heat beneath her skin transformed into a shocking fire that burned within her. She felt her body melting against him, like candle wax beneath a flame. She wanted to be closer, and when his tongue slid inside her mouth, she felt the echo within her womb.

He spoke against her lips. 'The guard is watching us.'

'Is he?' She kissed him back, welcoming the invasion of his tongue. He threaded his hands into her hair, claiming her mouth with a raw power that consumed her. Never in her life had she ever been kissed like this.

And she wanted more.

Chapter Five

Raine held the cloak through the rest of the night, the scent reminding him of Carice. The guard had forced her to go, but the warmth of her body lingered. He didn't understand why she got under his skin, but he couldn't resist the urge to kiss her. And he knew, all too well, what might happen if they travelled alone together.

He reminded himself that no harm would come to her when he brought her to Rory Ó Connor. She would be protected, as the High King's bride. And Rory would never have the chance to lay a hand upon her—Raine would make certain of that.

Morning light filtered through the bottom of the wooden door, and he heard footsteps approaching. The door swung open, and the sudden light was blinding. Two men came inside the tower, but he had not seen these guards before.

'King Patrick wishes to speak to you again,' the taller man said. 'Come with us.' They bound his hands with rope before unfastening the manacles and chains. Raine bent down to pick up the fallen cloak, and before they could protest, he said, 'This belongs to Lady Carice. She will need it.'

One of them took the cloak, and they led him back to the *donjon*. The ground was blanketed with snow, and it coated the top of the walls. He walked up the stone stairs leading inside, hiding his annoyance at his hands being bound.

Once he entered the Great Chamber, the scent of food nearly brought him to his knees. What he wouldn't give for a piece of roasted meat or warm bread. His mouth watered, but he held back his hunger when he was brought to the king. Patrick sat upon a carved wooden chair with his wife Isabel beside him. This time, Lady Carice was seated at the queen's side.

When Carice caught sight of him, she smiled. Though her face was wan from lack of sleep, there was a brightness in her blue eyes. Despite all that she'd suffered, her beauty tightened the breath within him. It was a dangerous game he was about to offer, one formed of lies and betrayal. If she agreed, she would despise him when it was over.

He was a cold-hearted bastard who didn't deserve to walk upon the same dirt. The kiss he'd taken had been born of the desire he'd struggled to hold back. This woman was a trusting innocent, and he, a man whose life was clouded by a ruined past.

And yet, Carice's smile took apart all his plans to stay away from her.

'I understand Lady Carice went to speak with you during the night,' King Patrick began, using the Norman language. 'Why?'

'She asked me to escort her to the west, away from the High King's men.' He knew not what she had said to Patrick, so it was best to keep to the truth.

'One of our men can bring her there,' the king responded. 'She would be safer with Trahern or Connor.'

'It is her choice to make.' Raine knew the man had every right to be suspicious. *Oui,* Lady Carice would be far safer with the MacEgans. But he faced the king and let the man draw what conclusions he would.

'You never answered my questions last eve.

Are you prepared to speak now?' The king leaned in, resting his forearms upon the table.

Raine thought a moment, trying to decide how to begin. He turned to Queen Isabel and addressed her first. 'I understand that your family is Norman, my lady.'

She glanced at her husband and nodded. 'I was, yes. But my loyalties lie with my husband.' Her voice held a warning, as if he should tread carefully.

Raine acknowledged her with a nod. 'Then you understand what a Norman soldier must do. And what happens to him if orders are disobeyed.' He kept his posture stiff, never taking his eyes from hers. 'Or what happens to his family.'

The king and queen sobered as they understood his meaning. Carice's smile faded, and she asked, 'What happened to your family, Raine?'

He met her gaze but merely shook his head. This was not the place to speak of such matters. Instead, he directed his attention to the queen. 'I have no choice but to obey my orders. And if I betray my commander by revealing them, it is not only my life at risk.' He kept all emotions from his voice, revealing nothing. 'As I told you before, I was granted a few days to bury the holy men who saved my life from the fire.'

The king seemed uninterested by that and pressed again, 'The Normans are gathering at Tara. I want to know why.' His voice was edged with steel, making it clear he expected answers.

Raine hesitated, choosing his words carefully. 'It is no secret that King Henry wants command of Erin. But he does not wish to use force to seize it. An attack upon Rory's men is not his intent.' Those were the only truths he could give.

'I sent several of my men to accompany Killian MacDubh and Lady Taryn of Ossoria on their journey to speak with the High King,' Patrick said. 'Are they in danger?'

'Not from the Normans,' he admitted. And this was true. Sir Darren's interest lay in the death of the High King and nothing else.

'Why did you refuse to speak to us last eve?' the king queried. 'You could have avoided an uncomfortable night.'

'Because I needed time to make my own decisions. My orders are to return to the soldiers. If I do not, the penalty is death. And my family will suffer for it.' He eyed Carice. 'But I am willing to take a greater risk.'

'And what is that?'

This time, he looked at Carice and offered, 'I have agreed to grant Lady Carice's request to escort her to the west before I return to my duties.'

'It is not necessary,' the king began to argue, but Carice raised a hand and intervened.

'Forgive me, Your Grace, but I would prefer to go with Raine. It means that none of your men would be held responsible for my disappearance.'

The queen's look grew discerning, her lips tight with worry, though she said nothing.

'If I take her alone, it is easier to remain hidden,' Raine said. 'But in return, I would ask that you let others believe that I am still your captive.'

'Then your commander would not hold you responsible for your absence.' Patrick exchanged a glance at Isabel, but the queen's attention was upon Carice.

'Is this what you want, Lady Carice?' The woman's face had grown serious, almost as if she wanted the answer to be no.

'I trust Raine,' Carice said, braving a slight smile. 'He will not harm me.'

At her words, the burden of lies grew heavier.

He intended to use Carice, delivering her into the hands of her greatest enemy. She would never forgive him for this.

But perhaps when the Ard-Righ was dead, he could bring her to the sanctuary she wanted, as a means of atonement.

She will never trust you again, his conscience asserted. *She would rather die than travel at the side of a murderer.*

He vaguely heard the voices of the king and queen mingled with Carice's, as they spoke of the journey. But when he looked upon her beautiful face, he remembered the stricken faces of his sisters.

'Raine, don't let them take us,' Elise had *begged. Her eyes were shining with tears as the soldiers had seized her and Nicole. 'Please.'*

He'd lowered his weapon, staring into the eyes of the Norman commander. It was Sir Darren de Carleigh, and there was no sympathy in his expression.

Raine had forced himself to step over his parents' bodies. 'My sisters are innocent of this,' he told Sir Darren. 'Let them go.'

'Your father was a traitor, and the king has given his orders for all of you to be taken and questioned.'

King Henry had already left, only moments ago. Undoubtedly, he would expect to see them all executed, innocent or not. A chill washed over Raine at the thought of his sisters being violated and killed.

'They are women,' he said slowly. 'Elise is only four and ten. What harm could they do to anyone?'

'My orders are—'

'Your orders be damned.' Raine moved forward, using his height to intimidate the commander. 'Take me in their place.'

'All of you will be prisoners of the king,' Darren repeated. But a flicker of distaste came over him. He lifted a hand. 'But there is something you can do to protect them.'

The words were a salvation he'd never expected. 'Name it.'

'You are a man of strength, a better fighter than I've ever seen. Become one of our soldiers, under my command. So long as you fight for us and give us your loyalty, your sisters will live. And no one will touch them.'

He hadn't understood, at the time, why Sir Darren had wanted a traitor's son to join Henry's forces. Now, he knew that they had wanted a man they could manipulate, someone to fulfil the tasks they could not—a murderer.

From the moment he'd set foot on Ireland's shores near Wexford, over two years ago, he had obeyed Sir Darren's orders blindly. He'd fought with the Norman forces, attacking the Irish throughout Leinster and proving that he would follow their commands without question.

He sobered at the memory, for it was the first time he had encountered the MacEgans. King Patrick did not remember him, for Raine had been only one of many soldiers fighting that day. He'd watched Patrick and his brother Bevan kill men Raine had fought alongside, their swords striking down their enemy. He knew the strength and courage of the MacEgans.

And he'd witnessed their fury and anguish when their eldest brother Liam had died that day.

The Irish had long memories and would not forget what was done. Despite the fragile peace, the death of the Ard-Righ would upset the balance. And Raine would be responsible for it.

They were interrupted by two guards approaching the dais. One raised a knee in deference to King Patrick and said, 'Forgive me, my king, but Brian Faoilin has arrived. He wishes to know if you have located his daughter.'

The king raised a hand. 'Do not let him in yet. Keep the gates closed for the moment.' To Carice, he turned and remarked, 'I cannot refuse him the hospitality of Laochre. What do you want to do?'

Raine was startled when she stood from her place and went to stand beside him. 'We will leave now and travel while my father and his men are inside. You may tell him the truth— that you gave me a place to stay before I left.' She unsheathed a blade from her waist. 'Raine has told you everything. Now I ask that you let us go.'

The king's expression grew serious as he turned back to Raine. 'You would not have spent the night as our prisoner, had you spoken the truth.'

He believed that, but he hadn't known what answers to give. Then, too, he didn't deserve to spend the night in comfort, after all that he had done—and for what he was about to do.

'Now you may tell anyone honestly that I was held in chains.' He held out his wrists while Carice cut the ropes. 'And when I return to the

Normans, you have my word that no harm will come to any of the MacEgan men.'

At that, the king's tension relaxed. 'Lady Carice, what say you? Do you want to leave Laochre now or await your father?'

'I want to travel with Raine,' Carice insisted, 'until I reach my mother's family in the west.'

She went to stand at his side, and when she placed her hand upon his arm, he forced himself to think of his sisters instead of her. No one had shown mercy to Elise or Nicole. Despite Sir Darren's promise that they were safe, he was uncertain about it. And whether or not they had been abused, he could not say.

If he killed the High King, they would be free. And although he didn't relish the idea of murder, for his sisters he would pay any price.

Raine tried to ignore the warmth of Carice's palm and the soft scent of her skin. He didn't want to think of how hurt she would be when she learned that the man she trusted had betrayed her. He shut it all out, turning his thoughts to stone.

Queen Isabel reached out for her husband's hand and regarded them. 'We will grant you the time you need to escape. But you must go now.'

Patrick lifted a hand in dismissal. 'So be it.'

One of the soldiers returned Carice's cloak to her, and she leaned against Raine as she fastened it. He realised that, although she had masked her illness well enough, she was still weak.

To the king, she asked, 'May we take one of your horses?' The king agreed and ordered a servant to guide them out to the stables. But Raine had his doubts about leaving during the daylight. 'If we leave now, the soldiers will see you. Even if we wait until they've entered the gates, we will still be visible from the castle walls.'

Carice's expression grew drawn. 'You're right.' She thought a moment and her gaze centred upon one of the soldiers. 'I am too easily recognised if I am dressed like this. Perhaps instead, I should disguise myself in the armour of one of your guards. I could keep my hair hidden inside the cowl and then we could ride out past them.'

'They still might recognise you, if there are only two of us,' Raine said. But her idea had merit. Brian Faolin's kinsmen were unlikely to find her if she wore armour.

'King Patrick, could several of your guards

travel with us?' Carice pleaded. 'Only for an hour or two?'

'She's right,' Isabel agreed. 'It would be safer. And they can accompany both of you far enough that no one will notice if two soldiers do not return.'

Raine gave a nod, but inwardly, he wondered if Carice had the strength to wear chain mail armour. Before he could voice the thought, she turned to him with a slight smile, 'Will you help me find the smallest soldier here?'

The chain mail was heavier than she'd ever imagined. It was like having stones crushing her shoulders and torso. Carice was barely able to sit upright on the horse, but she forced herself to endure the weight. About a dozen men rode with her, and Raine remained at her side in the middle of the entourage. She kept her gaze averted while they departed and her father's men entered the gates of Laochre. Though she knew there was no reason to fear, uncertainties closed over her. Only a few hours of daylight remained, and she knew not where they would find shelter this night. The king and queen had given them supplies, including a tent, blankets, and food. Yet, her fears did not diminish.

Thus far, no one seemed interested in the soldiers, and they continued to ride as a group towards the north. Raine had suggested it, and since her family lived near the Dingle Peninsula, they would have to travel in that direction regardless.

For many miles, they rode in silence. Her shoulders sank down, and she struggled to keep her seat on the horse. It was like trying to keep a stone pillar upon her shoulders, and she gripped the reins so hard, her knuckles whitened.

'Are you all right?' Raine asked.

She managed a nod. 'How much farther will we ride?'

'Just to the edge of those trees.' He pointed towards the horizon, and she wanted to weep. He seemed to sense her dismay, and he brought his horse alongside hers. 'When we reach the forest, you can remove the armour. I'll send the soldiers away.'

'Where will we stop to sleep for the night?' She suspected they might have to make camp in the forest, but the idea made her worry. It was so difficult to stay warm, she dreaded the thought of sleeping within a tent.

'It depends on how swiftly we travel,' he answered. 'We might reach the village of Casheldrum if we ride in haste. Possibly by later tonight.'

The idea of riding all day made her ache just to think of it. She didn't know how she would manage it in the armour. Carice tried to tell herself that a few hours wouldn't matter. But she knew how weak her body was, and she didn't want Raine to hear her complain.

There was no question that he was right—her father *was* close by, and Brian Faoilin might catch up to them if they didn't continue riding. There was no choice but to keep on the journey.

'You're tired, aren't you?' His voice was cool, but beneath it, she sensed that he was aware of her fragility.

'I am. But I will do what I must.' She squared her shoulders, fighting back the pain of the chain mail. 'I should probably warn you—I'm going to fall off this horse soon.'

'Then fall towards me.' He reached out for her glove hand. 'I'll catch you, *chérie.*'

He would, she knew. And the knowledge warmed her. She had come to depend on this man, and though she worried about the consequences of him escorting her, she was glad of his presence.

Carice squeezed his fingers, meeting his gaze.

'Thank you, Raine. I am so grateful that you changed your mind about travelling with me.'

He acknowledged her thanks with a slight nod, but there was an unreadable expression on his face. They continued riding with the Mac-Egan soldiers until Laochre lay far beyond the horizon.

The harsh landscape was mottled with white snow and darker mud. To take her mind off the journey, Carice tried to think of the west coast. She had visited her family there only once, but she had never forgotten the stark beauty. The water had been sapphire, while green fields embraced the rocky hills. The sky was so vast, the clouds seemed to drift down to the water's edge in feathered wisps.

It was a good place for anyone to live out their remaining days. Weariness slid over her, and she leaned against her horse, resting her head against the animal's mane. She rode for the last mile, imagining a life where she could sit and simply watch the world go by.

'Carice,' came Raine's voice. She opened her eyes and saw that they were near the forest. 'We're here.'

She nodded in relief, and he spoke quietly to the MacEgan soldiers before dismissing them to return to Laochre. When they were alone, he helped her dismount and led her into the shadowed trees.

Frost coated the fallen leaves upon the ground, leaving tips of silver. She leaned against Raine as he led her deep into the forest. When they were surrounded by trees, he turned his back. 'I'll stand guard while you remove the armour and put your *léine* on once more.'

She fell silent for a moment, wondering if she could manage this by herself. Though she could remove the helm and coif, letting her hair fall to her shoulders, the rest of the armour was heavier than she'd ever thought it could be. It was impossible to lift her arms above her head. And while most women would simply struggle their way through it, she knew her limitations.

'Would you help me?' she asked quietly.

He stiffened at her request, though he must know how difficult this was. The illness had taken too great a toll upon her body, and she needed his assistance. Slowly, he turned around and regarded her. She tried to hold out her arms, needing him to lift the chain mail hauberk from her torso. 'Lift your arms,' he bade her.

At that, her mouth twisted into a smile. 'If I could do that, I wouldn't need your help.'

The sudden flare in his eyes made her self-conscious. She was well aware of how this must seem to him. Already they were alone, and now she had asked him to undress her. But what did it matter? She was incapable of removing the armour.

Raine reached for the heavy sleeves and held each one while she pulled out her arms, one at a time. Then he rested his hands at her waist.

He could have lifted the hauberk away. But instead, his green eyes caught hers in invitation. Carice was fully aware of his hands tracing her silhouette, gently skimming her flesh as he moved higher.

Her attention grew fixated upon his mouth. She wanted him to kiss her again, the way he had only yesterday. Desire flowed through her, and she craved more from this man. She leaned closer to him, reaching out to touch his forearms. His skin was hot, his muscles tight as he drew the armour over her head.

She was relieved to be rid of the heavy weight, but the shift she wore was too thin to offer any protection from the cold. She shivered, crossing her arms over her breasts. But inwardly, her thoughts were in turmoil. She wanted this man in a way she'd never anticipated. And though it was an immoral, terrifying thought, she wanted his touch upon her skin. Something about this Norman soldier transformed her from quiet and sickly into a woman who craved a different life. With each day she spent at his side, she felt stronger, more whole.

He was still going to leave her behind—she had to remember that.

Raine moved to her horse and reached inside the leather pouch to find her *léine* and overdress. She watched him, wondering if he was having the same thoughts.

He tossed the garments to her and turned his back once more. 'Clothe yourself, Lady Carice.'

Apparently she was wrong. Her cheeks flushed with embarrassment as she dressed quickly, struggling to remove the trews. When she had finished, she told him, 'You can turn around now.'

Raine took the armour and folded it, placing it inside another saddle bag. Then he found a flask of water and drank for a moment, passing it to her. She sipped the water, wondering if she had imagined the desire between them. He had kissed her the morning he'd been in chains and had agreed to come with her on this journey.

But now, it seemed that he was trying to keep her at a distance. Did he feel any attraction at all towards her?

'You need to eat,' he said, returning to the saddle bag. Her cheeks warmed, and she was all too conscious of her thin frame. Her illness was as unpredictable as the rain, and she could never tell if it would be a good day or a bad one.

Raine brought out a cloth-wrapped bundle of food. Inside was half a wheel of cheese, slices of beef, and dried cherries. She stood near him, and he tore off a piece of meat, passing it to her. The food tasted delicious, and she savoured every bite. The ground was too cold and wet to sit down, so they both remained standing. Raine held out the cloth bundle between them.

'You seem to be feeling better,' he said. 'From earlier, I mean.'

'I am still tired,' she admitted, 'but my stomach doesn't hurt so much.'

He ate some of the cheese and passed it to her. 'Has it always been this way? Do you not eat because it hurts?'

She shrugged, reaching for more of the beef. 'When I was younger, it wasn't this bad. It was only during the last year when it hurt every day to eat.' She had grown to loathe mealtimes, for they only brought pain and suffering. Whenever her father hosted a feast, she tried to avoid them, for every time she ate, she grew ill.

'Could someone have been poisoning you?' he prompted. 'Someone who wanted you to die?'

She shook her head. 'Others ate the food that I could not bear to touch. The healer tried everything to help me. He bled me, he tried teas. Nothing worked.' Just remembering those days made her stomach ache. But despite her certainty that it wasn't poison, she couldn't help but wonder why some of her symptoms had lessened after she'd left Carrickmeath. Was it simply that she'd felt suffocated at home, surrounded by healers and her father's overprotective ways? Was it this taste of freedom that had made her want to embrace whatever time remained? She didn't know. But the longer she spent time with Raine, the more she felt as if a burden had been lifted from her shoulders. She would not have to endure a marriage to the High King and a wedding night. Here, with Raine, she was free.

Between them, they finished the rest of the food, and Raine took her hand. 'Come. We'll ride towards the village and find a place to sleep for a few hours.'

He helped her to mount her horse, and they rode through the forest for a time. The food and rest had made her feel better, as well as being free of the chain mail armour. 'I don't know how soldiers endure that armour, day after day,' she remarked. 'It's impossibly heavy.'

'We grow accustomed to it. Sometimes I hardly notice the weight.'

She lowered her gaze, thinking of his muscular form. As strong as Raine was, undoubtedly the armour weight was hardly more than a cloak to him. She recalled the silhouette of his hardened skin and the reddened scars upon his back. Despite all that he'd suffered, she'd been fascinated by his bare skin.

A secret smile passed over her face, for they were naught but idle daydreams. She knew better than to imagine Raine would ever be attracted to a dying woman. He believed she was too thin, and her illness made him uncomfortable. So be it. But she intended to savour every moment of life that remained, seizing what joy she could.

Raine continued leading the horse northward, and when they reached the edge of the woods, she spied a narrow frozen stream. It reminded her of a time when she was younger and had loved to play upon the ice. Her brother Killian had taught her to glide on skates made of deer antlers, and they had raced one another upon the pond. Although he had won every race, she'd loved the feeling of gliding across the hard surface of the frozen ice.

'How close are we to the village?' she asked, wondering if there was time to stop.

'A few miles more. We'll be there by nightfall.'

Raine kept his pace swift, seemingly intent upon reaching shelter quickly. He certainly would have no interest in stopping—especially for a reason as foolish as a moment of fun.

But with her time slipping away, Carice no longer wanted to live her life doing what was expected. The food had given her a new energy, and while she was feeling good, she wanted a chance to enjoy it, even for a few reckless moments. Certainly Raine de Garenne would believe she had lost her senses, but she didn't care.

'I want to stop for a moment,' she told him, bringing her horse to a halt. Then she swung down and stepped towards the ice.

* * *

Raine stopped immediately, wondering if Carice was about to be sick. He drew his horse to a halt and dismounted, releasing the reins. 'What is it?'

She turned back and sent him a secret smile. 'Only an impulse.'

He didn't know what she meant by that, but it didn't seem that she was feeling unwell. He watched her for a moment before he dismounted.

Snow blanketed the stream banks, and Carice trudged through it, moving towards the frozen stream. The water was hardly a stream at all, only twice the length of his arm. He doubted if it came up to his knees when it wasn't frozen solid.

She approached the stream and touched the ice gingerly with one foot. He couldn't, for the life of him, figure out what she was doing. Was she thirsty?

'What is it?' he asked.

This time, she stepped on the ice and turned back to look at him. 'Killian and I used to race upon the ice when we were young.'

He continued staring at her, not understanding at all. Was she suggesting that they stop their travels to…run upon ice?

She beckoned to him. 'Come here, Raine.'

He shook his head. 'You're going to fall and get hurt.' What she was suggesting was not only a waste of time, it was also dangerous.

'It's only ice. It doesn't hurt that badly. Or I may fall into the snowbank.' She crooked her finger to him. 'I'll wager that you can't beat me in a race.'

Why on earth would she want to race? She hardly had the strength to walk, much less run. He dismissed the idea immediately. 'We don't have time for this. Your father—'

'My father would have to ride for hours to catch up to us. And it will only be for a little while. Unless you think I'm going to win? Or perhaps you're too frightened of the ice?'

It was a bold dare, and the teasing look she shot him was bewildering. He hadn't seen this mischievous side to her before. When he reached the frozen stream, he stepped carefully onto the ice, amazed that it didn't shatter or break beneath their weight.

'What is your wager?' he asked.

'Whoever reaches that bank first can choose the reward.'

He sent her a sidelong glance, wondering what she meant by that. There was nothing he could give her, and he couldn't see any point to this.

'I do not need anything from you.' He started to step back towards the snowbank, but she caught his hand and pulled back.

'You're assuming you're going to win.'

Of course he would. 'You've been ill,' he reminded her. 'We've been riding for hours, and you need to preserve your strength.'

She looked back at him, and in her eyes, he saw the look of a woman whose days were numbered. 'I want to enjoy the time I have left, Raine. Before it's gone forever.'

The thought of her dying was a reminder he hadn't wanted to face. He might not know Carice very well, but he knew how hard she'd fought to live. He'd watched her suffer, and he'd seen her smile. He knew the taste of her lips and the softness of her body in sleep.

'Only for a moment,' he acceded. 'But you're going to lose.'

She ignored his prediction and said, 'Killian and I used to play in return for power.'

He frowned at that. 'What do you mean?'

'If I won, I gave him commands for an hour.

If he won, he told me what to do, and I had to obey.'

Though he knew she was speaking of children ordering each other around, her suggestion made his wayward thoughts grow stronger. The idea was wicked, and he ought to tell her no.

'Are you ready?' she murmured.

'We're both going to break our necks,' he predicted. But when she gave the signal, he began sliding his feet across the ice, struggling to run. His feet went flying out from under him, and he hit the ice hard while she continued sliding one foot, then the other, in a steady pace.

'Are you all right?' she asked, grinning at him. Her brown hair had fallen loose from its plait, and it tousled around her face. There was a brightness in her light blue eyes, and she continued moving forward.

Raine got back to his feet and took longer strides, attempting to catch up to her. When he reached her side, she tried to push him down, but he maintained his balance.

'No cheating,' he warned. But as he spoke the words, he pushed back against her, moving ahead. Almost there…

At the last moment, she leaped from the ice back into the snowbank. She raced ahead of him, running through the drifts until she reached the end of the ice. 'I won.'

He was incredulous at her declaration. 'No, you didn't. You left the ice.'

'I never said we had to stay on the ice,' she countered. 'You made that assumption.'

Her brazen cheating made him determined to claim the victory. 'You cannot win by breaking the rules.'

'Do you mean to say you won't follow my orders?' She reached out for his hand, leading him off the ice. From the tone of her voice, his suspicions sharpened. He tightened his palm around hers and lifted her back onto the horse. Her face was flushed from the exertion, and in that moment, she looked like a woman who had just awakened from sleep.

'What orders?' he asked, mounting his own horse.

She sent him a secretive smile and answered, 'I'll tell you later.'

Chapter Six

They arrived at Casheldrum by nightfall. Carice had never been to the settlement before, especially one so remote. The small crannog had a wooden walkway across a half-frozen lake that led to a gate and a ringfort at the centre of the island. Several wattle and daub roundhouses were gathered in a semicircle. Though it was isolated, it would provide a good shelter for the night.

She was in good spirits after winning the race. It had felt so good to run and feel the wind against her cheeks. Seeing the expression on Raine's face after she'd won had made it even more enjoyable. Although he was a stoic man, she'd detected a softening within him. This day, she was feeling stronger than usual, and she was confident that her health would continue to improve.

Before they dismounted, Raine removed his helm and hid it among their travelling supplies to ensure that he appeared like an ordinary visitor instead of a soldier. The guards allowed them to enter, and Carice spoke to the chief, since Raine's grasp of the Irish language wasn't strong.

'Have you travelled for long?' the chief asked her. He was a man similar in age to her father, and she wondered if he knew Brian Faoilin. She hoped not, for she didn't want him to alert her father's men.

'We visited with the MacEgans last night,' she answered. 'We are on our way home again.' She reached into a pouch on her horse and withdrew a handful of silver, offering it to the chief. 'I hope we may compensate you for your hospitality.'

The chief waved it away. 'No. We do not take silver from our guests. Stay with us awhile, since my son and his wife are away. You may use their home for the night. And if we ever visit your lands, then return the same hospitality to us.'

He seemed friendly enough, and he bade one

of his men to help Raine move hot stones into the space to heat the interior of the hut. Carice was glad that they would have their privacy, and she did not dissuade them of the assumption that she and Raine were husband and wife.

They joined the rest of the clan for an evening meal out of doors. Carice sat upon a log near the fire and accepted a bowl of venison stew. The hot broth and meat were soothing after a long day of riding, and she enjoyed the flavours of the stew. Raine sat beside her, and she took comfort in his presence. His arm rested behind her, almost in a half-embrace. Though she knew it was only to maintain the pretence of marriage, her skin warmed beneath his hand.

After she finished her meal, she leaned her head against his shoulder, fighting against the weariness that passed through her. As she watched the other women with their husbands, Carice envied them. She wanted so badly to live like a normal woman, to enjoy her days without pain.

Was it possible? She wanted to believe it, though her body was now growing tired from all the travelling. With each day, she grew stronger. And whether her body was simply healing or whether she was finding happiness in her last moments, she clung to hope.

Raine had kept silent throughout most of the meal and had only given a few minimal responses to the chief's questions. 'You look weary,' he said, lowering his mouth to her ear. 'Do you want to sleep now?'

'I would, yes.' She thanked the chief once more for letting them stay the night. Raine led her back to the hut, and inside, the space was now warm. He ducked inside and closed the door behind him. A few clay lamps were lit, illuminating the dark interior. There was a bed of furs in the corner, and it was so inviting, Carice longed to do nothing but collapse on top of the pallet.

But first, she wanted a moment alone with Raine. There were only a few days left with him, and she wanted to know him better. She still didn't understand why he had agreed to set aside his duties and travel with her.

Carice turned back to him. 'I never gave you my command, after I won our contest.'

'You didn't win. You cheated,' he reminded her. But she sensed he wasn't angry at all, from the softness in his tone.

'I won,' she insisted. 'And now I wish to collect my reward.'

His expression turned wary. 'And what was it you wanted?' He moved closer and stood before her. In the faint light, she studied his harsh features. His dark blond hair was damp from the snow flurries, his face rough with bristle. She found herself staring at his mouth, wondering if she dared voice her true desire.

Kiss me, she wanted to say, but didn't. Not because she was afraid he would refuse…but because she was afraid she wouldn't want to stop.

'Well?' he prompted. 'Name your reward.'

She tried to think of something and at last blurted out, 'Never have I seen you smile. I would like to see that.'

Silence descended between them, and he remained stoic. It was a simple request, one he would have no difficulty obeying. But instead, he answered, 'I have no reason to smile, Carice.'

His words troubled her, and she longed to understand what had happened to his family. But she would not press for secrets. 'You endured a difficult life, I know,' she acceded, 'but surely you have smiled before.'

He released her hands and folded his arms

across his chest. From the dark expression on his face, it was clear that he had no desire to indulge her—almost as if he believed he had no right to be happy about anything. 'Go and rest now. We've more travelling to do, and you'll need your sleep.'

She ignored his excuses and reached up to touch his cheeks. With her thumbs, she lifted the edges of his mouth, hoping to coax a smile. Instead, his face hardened, and he caught her wrists. 'Don't mock me.'

'I—I wasn't.' That had never been her intention at all. It was merely idle teasing, nothing more than that.

'My father was killed by King Henry's men and his lands were seized. My mother killed herself after he died. We lost our home, and my sisters were taken by the king's men.' He softened his grip on her wrists and drew his hands down her sides to rest at her waist.

She was shocked by his words, unable to form a single word. Her heart ached for his suffering. 'I didn't know.'

But he wasn't finished. 'Do you think I don't know what's happened to my sisters? How many men have hurt them during the years I've been gone? But I obey the king's orders to keep them alive. One day, I may be able to save them.' His hands remained at her waist, and his green eyes stared into hers. 'I have no reason to smile any more. Not even for you.'

The grief and helplessness behind his words broke her feelings into pieces. Carice stood on tiptoe, drawing his mouth down to hers. She kissed him in the need to offer sympathy and comfort, for words would do nothing to allay his pain. 'I'm sorry,' she murmured against his mouth.

He took her offering, kissing her back. She wasn't afraid of the kiss, even though it over-powered her senses. Instead, she welcomed the intrusion of his tongue, feeling the aching echo between her legs.

Now she understood his reluctance at helping her. By disobeying his orders as a soldier, he was risking the lives of his sisters. Guilt cloaked her emotions, even as she slid her arms around Raine. He was strong in a way that went beyond physical prowess. He was the sort of man who would never stop fighting for those he loved. Undoubtedly, he would go back to find his sis-ters—she was certain of it.

Her own feelings were weakening, for with each kiss, she was more drawn to him. She didn't want him to return to the life of a soldier...she wanted him to stay with her, impossible as that might be.

He continued kissing her, his hands sliding within her hair. He caressed the length of it, and she pressed her body against him, feeling the heated length of his arousal.

Need and desire poured over her, and she found it difficult to breathe. Right now, she wanted more, and he seemed to be fighting against his own urges. She shuddered when his mouth went to the line of her jaw, and she ran her hands over his hair, down to his broad shoulders. He was still wearing the chain mail, and she wanted it gone.

'Take off your armour,' she commanded. 'Since you will not smile for me.'

He stepped back, and his eyes burned into hers. Though he said nothing at all, he obeyed, lifting the tunic away and then the chain mail hauberk and undertunic. His torso was bared, and she saw the hard ridges of muscles and the scars of battle. The need to touch him was undeniable.

Carice rested her fingers upon his chest, staring back at him. 'If you had won our race, what boon would you have demanded of me?'

For a moment, he said nothing, and she wondered if his thoughts were as tangled as hers. 'I have no commands for you, *chérie*. Sleep now, if that is your wish.'

It wasn't. And so she eyed him once again. 'May I touch you?' The boldness that swept over her was born out of her realisation that every moment might be her last. She could not say what would happen between now and her last days. But she had this time with him.

'It would not be wise.'

She knew that, but she wanted to. 'I find myself not caring about wisdom any more. And we've only a few more days together.' For a breathless moment, she studied him, wondering if he desired her at all.

'Why would you want to? I am a Norman soldier.' The tone of his voice held the edge of a tortured man, as if he believed himself unworthy. Though it was true that his back held the scars of the fire, she did not find him unattractive.

'You are the man who saved my life,' she said, meeting his stare.

He was looking at her with an expression of stone. For a moment, he said nothing, but merely took her hands in his. His eyes darkened, and he gave a single nod. 'Do as you will.'

She explored his bare skin with her hands, tracing the muscles of his chest. He had the body of a soldier, and she admired the toned flesh. On impulse, she pressed her mouth to his heart, kissing his skin. He let out a ragged breath, revealing that he liked her touch.

She brought her lips to another part of his chest, marvelling at the feeling of him. But when her hands moved to his spine, she felt the scars from the fire. She walked around him and touched his shoulders, tracing the edges of the reddened flesh. She knew he had suffered in the flames, and that one of the monks had pulled him out. His scars had healed, but the flesh was mottled and red. Carice pressed her lips to his scars, as if she could heal him with a kiss.

And that was his breaking point. Raine spun and lifted her up, kissing her hard as he carried her to the pile of furs. She delighted in the flood of desire that rolled over her in a wave of pleasure. He pressed her down and lay atop her, his erection nestled against her stomach. The sensation of his body upon hers awakened a craving that could not be satiated. She felt the need to arch her hips, to welcome him within her.

Though she was a virgin, instinctive needs rushed over her skin. Between her legs, she was wet, and with every kiss, her desire heightened. Raine was thrusting against her skirts, his eyes closed as he fought for control.

This was what a wedding night was meant to be—a desperate urge to be joined with the husband she desired.

She closed her own eyes, afraid that she might indeed be falling in love with this man. Never in her life had she wanted anything as much as she wanted him.

He rested his weight upon her, his expression tight as he slowed down. '*Dieu*, Carice, you're killing me.'

She reached up to his hips. 'I trust you, Raine. I know that you would never, ever do anything to hurt me.' The words were meant to reassure him, but instead, they seemed to have the opposite effect.

He stopped immediately and rolled to the side. His expression grew shielded, allowing no emotions. 'I should not have let it go this far.'

'We only kissed,' she started to say, but he touched a finger to her lips.

'We did more than that, and you know this. It was wrong, Carice.'

'I wanted to touch you,' she confessed. 'Why was it wrong?'

'Because you are not mine to take.' He stood up and donned his armour and tunic once more. 'You don't belong to me and never will.'

His words cut through the desire, leaving her cold. She didn't know what to say, but it felt as if he'd tossed her aside. She should have been prepared for his response, but instead, her feelings were bruised by his rejection. Everything about his demeanour had shifted into cool indifference. She swallowed back the hurt. 'Are you leaving?'

He nodded. 'I'm going for a walk. Stay here and sleep. I'll return soon.'

And when he closed the door behind him, an unexpected wave of anger passed over her. All of this was unfair…the illness, her body's weakness. Why did this have to happen? What had she done to deserve this pain and suffering? Nothing at all.

Like as not, Raine had left because he thought her too fragile. He did not want to touch her because he found her thin body unattractive. Or perhaps he saw her as a duty, nothing more.

Clearly, he had no interest in exploring the rising feelings, and his refusal had humiliated her.

Carice clenched her fingers in a fist and punched the furs. For the first time in years, she had reached for something she wanted, daring to let herself have feelings for a man. She'd wanted to believe that he had travelled with her because he cared, because he'd felt something too.

And it wounded her to realise that she was wrong.

Raine cursed himself with every step he took. *I know that you would never, ever do anything to hurt me*, she'd said.

Damn it all, but he loathed himself for betraying her like this. He had no right to her affections, no right to touch her. She wasn't his, and he was a bastard for delivering her into the hands of her enemy. He didn't deserve to touch her soft skin or taste the pleasures of her flesh.

Even if he wasn't about to betray her, he couldn't do it. How could he take comfort in her arms when he'd been helpless to save his mother and sisters? He had been trained to fight, and he should have done something…anything. Instead, his hesitation had resulted in death and suffering.

He lived with that guilt every day, and he was unworthy of happiness. Not with Carice, not with anyone. She thought he had honour, when that was the furthest thing from the truth. His life was cloaked in deceit and cowardice. All he could do was continue forward on this path he'd forged, with the hope that he could some day save his sisters.

Raine told the guards at the crannog that he would be back soon, and he trudged across the wooden walkway that crossed the lake. The punishing night air was what he needed right now—something to cool the fires of lust that she'd kindled within him.

He walked through the forest leaves, his feet crunching against the ice. The moon was low in the sky, for it was early yet. They had come north, but now it was time to turn eastward. If they travelled by night, and slept during the early part of the day, Carice might not notice the direction of the sun. She would protest, but with any luck, this part of Ireland would be unfamiliar to her, since they had gone towards the north.

Raine paused when he reached the deepest

part of the trees, resting his palms upon two narrow trees. God help him, he should have known better than to kiss her. Carice Faoilin was entirely too desirable. Her touch had been an ember, slowly burning through his common sense. He couldn't grasp clear thoughts around her.

It was best to make a strong break, to keep himself apart. If he didn't, he would never be able to go through with his plans. She was a means to an end, a way of getting close to the Ard-Righ.

A soft sound caught his attention, and he unsheathed his sword, turning sharply.

'You found the High King's bride, I see.' Sir Darren lifted his palms to show he meant no harm, and Raine returned his weapon to its scabbard. His commander wore armour and a cloak lined with wolf's fur. The man's face held a slight smile, but there was an unspoken warning in his expression.

Raine had asked them to travel ahead to Tara, but it was clear that Sir Darren was unwilling to remain at a distance. 'You cannot follow us this closely,' he warned the man. 'Lady Carice will see our men and grow suspicious.'

'Then she came willingly with you?' The

knight's interest was kindled, and he gestured for them to walk farther through the woods.

Though Raine obeyed the silent command, he didn't want to reveal too much. Sir Darren might try to interfere, and he couldn't allow that. 'Lady Carice believes I am taking her to her relatives along the western coast, far away from Tara.'

A slow smile curved over the knight's face. 'Good. I am well pleased that you have succeeded in capturing her. Without her knowledge, of course.' He slowed his pace when they neared the crannog. 'My men are camped half a mile back from here. I will give them orders to keep their distance. But should you have need of us, we won't be far.'

Raine had no need at all for soldiers, but he gave a nod. 'I am leaving with her after midnight.' Before Sir Darren could speak, he continued. 'Do not follow until dawn. She cannot see you, or all of this is for naught.'

The commander nodded. 'So be it.' He eyed Raine a moment and said, 'I hope you succeed in bringing down the Ard-Righ. King Henry will undoubtedly grant you whatever reward you seek.'

All he wanted was his sisters' freedom.

Raine said nothing at all, but kept his face impassive. 'Hold your distance, Sir Darren.'

'So long as you keep to our plans, I see no reason to interfere.' But the subtle threat in his commander's voice was unmistakable. *Falter in this, and your family will suffer.* Sir Darren would have no choice but to tell Henry if the outcome resulted in failure.

As the knight retreated, remaining in the shadow of the woods, Raine kept himself hidden. With any luck, Carice would be sleeping upon his return.

Carice knew exactly why Raine had fled. And while she understood that he was acting out of honour, she wasn't at all interested in sleeping. Aye, she was tired, but more than weariness, she was tired of waiting to begin her life.

As an adolescent girl, she had waited to be betrothed. She had journeyed to Tara at her father's command, and it was then that she had caught the eye of the High King. Rory was nearly as old as Brian, and she had been appalled to realise that her father's ambitions had led him to sacrifice his firstborn at the altar of matrimony, in order to raise his own status.

The idea of consummating a marriage with

the High King made her stomach turn. But it would never happen. Not if she escaped with Raine.

Carice suspected he was already regretting his decision to escort her west. She had allowed her heart and body to steal all common sense from her. He was right to push her away before it went too far. Her body was too weak and unattractive anyway. He wouldn't want to lie with her, simply because she wanted to be in his arms.

The brittle hurt encircled her with a truth she didn't want to face. No man wanted a dying woman. She pushed back the rise of tears, and lay back against the furs, studying the herbs that hung in neat bundles from the ceiling.

Raine returned at last, but she didn't look at him. Instead she behaved as if nothing at all had happened between them. 'Did you have a nice walk?'

He didn't respond to the question but said, 'I thought you would be asleep by now.'

'No.' She couldn't sleep at all, both from her body's physical frustration and her own regrets. 'I was waiting for you to come back.'

Raine didn't acknowledge the remark and said, 'I'll awaken you before dawn, and we'll continue our journey. Your father's men will be sleeping by then, and we can stay far away from them. We should be able to see our way if we follow the river.'

He didn't wait for an answer but moved to the opposite wall, making it quite clear that he had no intention of sleeping anywhere near her. Stubborn man. Carice tried not to let her feelings be hurt as she snuggled beneath the furs. But she didn't want him so far away.

'I wonder about the people who live here,' she mused aloud, studying the interior of the hut. 'They haven't been married long, I'd wager.'

In answer, Raine closed his eyes, remaining silent. Carice didn't let that deter her. She knew he was trying to avoid her, and she was feeling restless. She wanted to be with him, to feel the warmth of his body against hers while she slept. Even if it was only in friendship.

'I don't think they have children,' she continued. 'At least, not yet.' The dwelling was small, with only one sleeping place. An emptiness slid over her with the knowledge that she would likely never bear a child. She would never know the sensation of movement within her or what it was to bring life into the world.

The dream was one she yearned for, but it would never be.

'You don't have to avoid me, Raine,' she told him. 'There is room for both of us here.' To lighten the mood, she added, 'Besides that, my feet are cold.'

'I intend to sleep right now,' he countered. 'Just as you should.' The tone of his voice brooked no argument, putting up an invisible barrier between them. He had made it clear that he wanted no part of her.

Her heart trembled, but Carice forced herself to ask, 'Did I make you angry when I kissed you? I only did it because I felt badly for what happened to your family.'

He hesitated a moment but then said, 'I wasn't angry.'

For a long moment, his pause hung between them. She said nothing, uncertain of what she should have done.

'But I cannot sleep near you, Lady Carice.'

She closed her eyes, feeling her face warm with embarrassment. 'It's all right. I only meant that we could keep each other warm.'

'It's not safe,' he warned. 'I don't trust myself not to touch you.'

The words were an invisible caress, and she

imagined his hands upon her skin. Or better, his warm mouth. Her breasts tightened into hard nubs against her gown. She buried her face in the fur, not understanding the heat coursing within her. This man breathed life into her in a way she'd never anticipated. He made her crave everything, though she understood his desire to remain distant. She simply had never known how much it would hurt to be spurned.

The silence filled up the space between them. She wanted to speak to him, to bring back the friendship that had been there when they had raced upon the ice. And so she broached the subject that troubled her. 'Sometimes I wonder how much time is left for me before I die.'

'None of us knows when we will take our last breath,' he said quietly. 'I could be killed in battle at any moment.'

She knew it was true, and yet, the thought brought a sense of fear within her. Raine did live a dangerous life, more so than her own. He rolled over to his side, facing away from her, and the silent message was unmistakable.

Despite his rejection of her offer, Carice didn't like the idea of him sleeping with no protection from the cold ground. She stood and picked up her fallen cloak, spreading it on the ground beside him. 'You can sleep upon this. To stay warm.'

He opened his eyes and gave a grudging nod, rolling himself inside the cloak.

Though he tried to sleep, she sensed that he was not truly resting. 'I am sorry about your sisters, Raine. I hope you believe that.'

But when he gave no reply, she started to think about his decision to help her. Something wasn't right. A man who had sworn to protect his sisters, who had agreed to do the king's bidding, would never escort her to the west without a reason of his own. His defiance could cause the women to be harmed even more— especially if the Normans learned that he had been released from captivity so soon.

An icy chill caught her, though she knew it was foolish. Surely her suspicions were unfounded. Raine was helping her because he wanted to—because beneath his grim exterior lay a man of honour, one who remained true to what was right instead of what was expected. Her suspicions had no merit, and she had to believe in him.

Besides, it would only be a few days before they reached the Dingle Peninsula. Somehow, she would find a way to reward him for all that he'd done.

But as she closed her eyes and sought to find sleep, she couldn't quite let go of the feeling that something wasn't right.

True to his promise, Raine awakened Carice in the middle of the night. He hadn't slept at all, and he didn't care. His body was aching for her, and being surrounded by her scent within the cloak hadn't helped.

'Do we have to leave now?' she whispered, her voice heavy with sleep.

'*Oui,*' he answered. 'We must. Else we risk being discovered.' He helped her to rise and tore a loaf of bread in half, giving her food to sustain her before the journey. Then he fastened the cloak around her. Carice's long brown hair hung beneath her breasts, and her blue eyes stared into his. She didn't understand the temptation she was, and he would not take advantage of her body, no matter how badly he wanted her.

The only reason they were leaving now was so she would not see the morning sunrise and realise that they were travelling eastward. If she slept until midday, he might manage to hide their whereabouts.

She's going to find out what you've done, his mind warned. He knew that, for Carice was an intelligent woman. It was a matter of time. He only hoped they would get close enough to Tara before she discovered his ruse...and that one day she would come to forgive him.

Outside, the snow crunched beneath their horses' hooves, and the moonlight guided their path. Raine began leading the horses east, following the river as he'd promised. He altered their path through another forest, hiding their trail. Though he told her it was to avoid her father's men, the truth was, it was meant to confuse her.

Carice was half-asleep as she rode, and she leaned heavily upon the mare as the hours passed. She looked so fragile, the guilt sank into his conscience. The deception would cause her to hate him, but he could see no other means of gaining his sisters' release. It was one of many reasons why he'd refused to seduce her. She would despise him even more if he dared to take her innocence, when he'd intended to betray her all along.

He found a small sheltered space at the side of a hill, with a dolmen built upon the mound of earth. The table-shaped rock formation would protect them from the elements, and he guided her towards it. 'We should be far enough away from your father's men,' he told her. 'You can rest a little longer if you wish.'

The truth was, the light was changing and the faintest touch of rose creased the eastern horizon before them. If he gave her time to rest, it was unlikely that she would notice their path.

He helped her dismount and then brought out a fur that the chief had given them. 'Go and sleep,' he bade her. 'You can wrap yourself in this to keep warm.'

She nodded drowsily, stumbling forward until he helped her inside the small space. He used a heavy blanket of wool to cover the opening. But he knew she would need more warmth than that. They could not risk a fire—even the presence of the horses might alert strangers, if anyone came upon them. He would have no choice but to share the space with her, to keep her from freezing.

Carice huddled underneath the dolmen, her body trembling from the cold. He wanted to go and warm her now, but he had to care for the horses first.

He led them to drink and ensured that they had all they needed and were protected from the elements before he returned to the dolmen. He pushed aside the wool and crouched low, sitting beneath the stone shelter. Carice was curled up in the fur, and she was shivering hard.

'I c-can't seem to get warm,' she said.

Without a word, he reached out to her waist and pulled her body against his, adjusting the fur coverlet so it warmed both of them. The moment he felt her curved backside against him, he grew hard. But he forced his idle thoughts away, rubbing Carice's arms to bring warmth to them. She took his hands in hers, crossing them beneath her breasts. 'Thank you. This is so much better.'

But it wasn't. She was revealing all the temptation he wanted but couldn't have. He gritted his teeth, wishing to God that he didn't crave her like this. She was killing him.

'Don't move,' he commanded. 'Sleep.' Because if she moved against him again, he was going to lose control.

She let out a soft sigh. 'You're the one who needs to sleep, Raine. I know you're tired.'

He was. But there was no way to gain any sort of relaxation with her so near. She had strung him so tight, he could hardly breathe from the arousal.

But then he realised she wasn't truly trying to sleep. Instead, Carice had her hands gripped together, her body tensed, as if in pain.

'You're hurting, aren't you?' He drew back to give her space.

Her mouth tightened at his prediction. 'I'll be all right. It's just that my stomach is hurting again.' Her breathing was irregular, almost rough. 'I thought I was getting better. I suppose I was wrong.'

He didn't like this at all. Last night, she had seemed well enough, but now, the illness had renewed its attack upon her. 'What can I do to help you?'

'Just—leave me alone for a while. It will pass.'

It went against every instinct he had, but he moved out of the dolmen. She might want some water from the cold stream if he broke through the ice. Food would likely make matters worse.

Dieu, he wished he had some knowledge of medicine. But she was holding her knees, doubled over in pain. Seconds later, she bolted from the space and ran into the woods.

'Carice!' he called out, hurrying to follow.

'Stay back,' she pleaded. 'I need a moment.'

Raine wasn't going to listen until he realised

that she was going to be sick. There was a reason why she didn't want him to witness her illness. He let her go, and when she returned a little while later, her face was the colour of frost. Her pace was slow, and she moved as if every step pained her.

'What is it?'

She dropped to her knees, her eyes shut tightly. 'Sometimes I wish I could just die. I hate this. I really do.'

He lifted her into his arms and led her back towards their shelter. 'Do you want to sleep?'

She buried her face in his shoulder, and he could feel the dampness of her tears. Never in his life had he felt so helpless, and he wanted to find a way to ease her.

'I wanted to get better,' she wept. 'For a while, when we were travelling together, I thought—' She stopped speaking, as if the right words wouldn't come. But he knew what she wanted to say. She'd thought things were changing.

It bothered him to see her like this, so upset over a body she couldn't command. He knelt down and laid her inside the shelter, sitting beside her. She leaned back against him, and admitted, 'If I had the choice of two final days of life without pain or two years of this suffering, I would take the two days.'

Raine lay beside her, and she rested her cheek against his chest. He brushed away the tears, unable to do anything except hold her. Though he'd known she was suffering, he'd never seen her this sick. It suddenly made him aware that he was bringing her towards a greater danger. He'd reasoned that there would be no harm for she was never going to wed the Ard-Righ. Now he realised that she might not survive the journey across Ireland. She believed he was bringing her to spend her final days with her mother's family.

Her eyes remained closed, her mouth tight with pain. 'Only a few weeks ago, I thought of taking a potion to end my life. I suppose that makes me damned in the eyes of Heaven, doesn't it?'

He tightened his arms around her. 'Don't ever do such a thing, Carice.'

Her face held weariness. 'If I had been brought to the High King, I would have done anything to escape him.'

The guilt threaded through him even tighter, binding him towards self-loathing. 'You will never wed him. I promise you that.' At least this was one vow he could keep. 'Would you like me to bring you water?'

'No.' Her voice came out in a whisper, and she leaned her head against the earth. 'Just lie with me a little while. And maybe I won't feel so alone.'

Raine pulled her into his arms, stroking back her hair. It had been too easy to forget her illness over the past few days. He despised himself for endangering her in this way.

'Promise me something,' she ventured softly.

'What is it?'

'If I ask it of you, will you leave me behind?'

He started to refuse, but she rolled over to face him. 'Raine, I don't want you to watch me die. I want you to remember me in another way. Mayhap the way we were yesterday, when you let me race you on the ice.' Her blue eyes stared into his with regret, and she reached up to touch his cheek. 'Be my friend and allow me that mercy.'

'No.' He would never leave her behind to die. 'That, I will not do.'

'Stubborn man,' she whispered. 'Why not?'

'Because I had to leave my sisters, and it was not my choice. They were helpless, and are now prisoners of the king. I won't turn my back on a woman again.' His voice came out sharper than he'd intended, but he would never abandon her.

It struck him hard to realise that he would miss her, too. This fragile woman had somehow entwined herself within him.

'Then…if I do not survive the rest of this journey, promise me that you'll stay until I breathe my last breath.'

He didn't even want to imagine it. 'You won't die alone,' was all he could manage.

She smiled then and kept her hand upon his cheek. 'I will always be grateful that you saved me from a marriage to Rory Ó Connor.'

Her palm was a brand upon his blackened soul. 'I am sorry,' he said. Sorry for what he had done and for what he still had to do. But she misunderstood him, believing he was apologising because of her illness.

'Don't be.' She let her fingers trail down his arm. 'I have enjoyed these days with you. I am glad you changed your mind about escorting me to the west. I only hope I can finish the journey.'

Her words humbled him, yet the idea of this woman dying was a blow he didn't want to face. Her smile, her passion—she captivated him in a way no woman ever had. If she died, he would mourn the loss of her.

Instead, he held her tightly and tried not to think of it.

Chapter Seven

Carice awakened, feeling warm and beloved. She was lying in Raine's arms, and it gave her a sense of peace. *I don't want him to go,* she thought. But, of course, that wasn't realistic. He had to return to his commander, and after that, she wouldn't see him again. The emptiness at that knowledge struck her hard. She had grown accustomed to having him at her side, and it had driven back her loneliness.

Her stomach ached from hunger, but the pains from earlier had abated. Though she was still weak, she thought she might be able to eat a little. Perhaps dried fruit or meat.

She turned to study Raine in sleep. The bristle of his beard lined his cheeks, and the worry upon his face had softened. For once, he appeared contented, and she found herself longing to kiss him.

Truthfully, she wanted more than that. She wanted to run her hands over his hardened chest, to bring his mouth to her own skin. She wanted to know what it was to love this man and to have him love her in return.

Dear God, her time remaining was slipping away so fast. She had thought she'd accepted it, only to realise that Raine gave her a reason to fight harder. He gave her a reason to live.

And whether or not it was right, she wanted him.

Softly, she touched his hair, smoothing it back from his brow. His green eyes opened, and the worried expression returned to his gaze.

'How do you feel?' he asked.

Carice gave a nod that she was all right, but instead, she ran her hand to the back of his neck. She needed to touch him, needed to feel his strength. 'I am better today. But I am feeling a little hungry.' She almost hated to voice it to him, knowing he would have to leave to fetch her food.

'I'll bring you something to eat.' Gently, he moved away from her, tucking the furs around her before he left the shelter of the dolmen.

The moment he left, she forced herself to straighten and come out of the shelter. The fire Raine had built hours ago had burned down to low embers, so she found a few dry branches to coax it back to life. Carice stretched her stiff limbs, and when the cold wind struck her, she reached for her cloak. A new layer of snow had fallen, and she smiled at the frosted branches within the woods.

Raine brought her some dried venison from their supplies, and she ate, struggling to chew the hardened meat. But the nourishment eased her, and he gave her even more when she had finished.

It was noon, and the sun was directly over them. She was grateful for it, but it only reminded her that they needed to travel farther. This landscape was unfamiliar to her, but she sensed that they were not terribly far from the sea. Which was strange, since they had a greater distance to ride. Had they travelled farther than she'd remembered?

'We should go,' she told Raine. Aye, she was weary, but she knew the necessity of moving forward.

'I don't know if we should,' he hedged. 'You

were very ill last night, and it might be better if we wait until nightfall.'

'My stomach doesn't hurt quite as much right now,' she admitted. 'I'd rather travel while I'm feeling better.'

He didn't appear convinced but helped her onto the mare before mounting his own horse. Carice gripped the reins and felt lightheaded for a moment before she steadied herself. Raine drew his horse alongside hers. 'You must let me know if you're feeling unwell and need to stop.'

She gave a nod. 'I will.' His concern lifted her spirits, and as they rode, she wondered what he thought of her now. She had reached a low point during her illness, not only because of the pain, but because she had never wanted him to see her in that way. She'd grown to care for this man, and for him, she wanted to be well and whole.

Raine kept their path steady through the hills, and as they continued on, the snow revealed damp patches of grass and mud. They were silent for a while, and at last, she brought her horse alongside his. 'I am sorry for what happened earlier.'

He didn't answer at first, as if he were choosing his words. 'It is not your fault, *chérie.*'

'I know. But this was not what you were anticipating when you agreed to escort me to the west.'

'I knew you would have difficulty on this journey.'

Although his voice was matter-of-fact, she hated the thought of being a burden upon him. 'Even so, I am sorry for what I said to you about dying. Sometimes when I am in a great deal of pain, the future frightens me.'

He pulled the reins of his horse, and Carice halted her mare as well. 'No one welcomes death. But we cannot be a prisoners of a fate that hasn't happened yet.'

He was right. She'd been so consumed by pain and suffering, she couldn't look past it. Although the stomach pains had diminished somewhat, they were always with her. But perhaps it was better to go on living, one hour at a time, as best she could.

She tried to muster a smile, but he didn't answer it. Raine spurred his horse forward and kept glancing behind them from time to time, as if he suspected they were being followed.

'What is it?' she asked. She hadn't noticed anyone nearby in the past few miles.

'Just a bad feeling.'

She followed the direction of his gaze but could see nothing. And yet…there were tracks ahead of them. Many horses had come through this way during the night. Although there was no reason to feel uneasy, she asked, 'Who do you think rode through here?'

'I can only hope it isn't the High King's men with your father.'

She let out a slow breath. 'He hasn't given up searching for me.'

'Nor will he.' Raine guided her towards the trees again. His expression remained guarded and he asked, 'Is there another reason you fled his men? Did any of the soldiers ever harm you?'

She shook her head. 'My father is ambitious, not cruel. But he would never listen to me when I said I didn't want to be the High Queen of Éireann. Sometimes I felt like a pawn in a political game instead of his daughter.' But even so, she did know that her father loved her. After her mother had died, he'd spent a great deal of time with her. 'Brian never wanted to admit I was sick. He couldn't face the truth, and he believed that I would get better and marry the High King.'

'Will you regret never seeing him again?'

Though Raine's voice held no hint of reproach, she understood his caution. Before she went to the west coast to die, she might wish to see her father one last time.

'Perhaps,' she admitted. 'I would see him again to say farewell if he would only let me go afterwards. But he won't.' She glanced around them at the frosted branches. 'I am surprised that he would search this far west. He was at Laochre the last time we saw him. I wonder if the MacEgans told him where we went.' She glanced all around her, but it was impossible to tell where they were now with the trees surrounding them.

Before she could ask Raine for their whereabouts, the sound of a woman screaming pierced the silence. Carice didn't hesitate, but spurred her horse towards the noise. Raine joined her, but he held up a hand. 'Be careful. We don't know what's happening.'

She fell back a few paces while he unsheathed his sword and rode forward. Over the rise of the hill, she saw half a dozen soldiers surrounding a woman who was immensely pregnant. The men wore Norman armour, and fury washed over Carice at the sight of them.

Why would they attack a pregnant woman? It was unforgiveable.

'We have to help her.' She kept her voice low but knew that he heard her. Raine was studying the men, his face grim. Carice guessed what he was thinking—six men were too many to fight by himself. And if she tried to help him, she might fall into their hands. But neither could they leave a pregnant woman in danger.

Raine raised a hand towards the men, and in that second, the Normans spied him. They stopped encircling the woman and began to ride towards them.

She brought her horse near his. 'What do you want to do?'

He kept his gaze fixed upon the approaching men. 'You cannot remain here. Go towards the woman and help her towards the woods while I speak with them.'

It was a grave risk to split up, but she didn't want to abandon the woman. With a wry smile, she offered, 'I should have worn my chain mail armour.'

'I don't believe falling on top of the soldiers would be the best idea,' he admitted. There was a hint of humor in his eyes, before it vanished.

'They are coming to speak with me, and there is no need to fight—yet. But you must leave now.'

He kept his hand upon the sword hilt. 'I will distract them enough for both of you to get away. You can help bring her to the trees and hide until I return for you.'

'There are too many soldiers,' she protested. 'What if you are hurt?'

'I won't be.'

His confidence should have made her feel better, yet she feared the men might attack him. 'But—'

'Go now,' he insisted. 'I will try to negotiate.'

The men had almost reached them, and she worried that they might know Raine's commander. 'What if they demand that you return with them?'

She didn't understand the searching look in his eyes. Raine studied her as if he were holding something back. 'I will not go with them. You have my word.'

'And if they give you no choice?'

He held her gaze for a moment. 'Then keep to the woods until they have gone. There is another ringfort not far from here.'

She reached out to touch his forearm. 'Be safe.'

In answer, he leaned down and kissed her swiftly. 'I will come for you.'

The gesture startled her, and colour flooded her cheeks with confusion. Carice raised the hood of her cloak and rode away, just as the men arrived. Raine moved his horse to face them, putting himself in the path of the soldiers.

She didn't look back as she rode, uncertain of whether this would work. Raine was facing the worst sort of danger, with so many Norman soldiers. But to her surprise, they didn't seem to be attacking him. Instead, he gathered them near and spoke to their commander. She could not hear what was said, but it didn't matter. The distraction was enough.

Carice dismounted from her horse and approached the pregnant woman. 'Did they hurt you?'

The woman was weeping, holding her swollen stomach as if to protect her unborn child. She wore a long cloak and her reddish-brown hair held loose braids, barely covered by a veil. From the fine weave of her gown, Carice suspected she was an Irish noblewoman. 'N-no,' the woman stammered. 'You came before they could harm me.'

Thank goodness. 'Can you ride, if I help you onto my horse?' Carice asked.

The woman shook her head. 'I can hardly move right now. I tried to run from them, but I couldn't get away.'

Given the woman's advanced pregnancy, Carice wasn't surprised. 'Can you reach the safety of the trees? We can hide from the soldiers until Raine returns.'

'I'll try.' But the woman was struggling with every step. Carice put an arm around her and helped her as best she could. Glancing behind, she saw that Raine was still talking with the men.

'What is your name?' she asked the woman. 'And are you alone?'

'I am Aoife,' she answered. She did not offer her tribe's name, which only made Carice more convinced that this was a lady of importance who did not wish to reveal too much. 'I was travelling home when I was taken from my escorts. I tried to run, but with the baby, I cannot get very far.'

Carice could understand that. Although the woman was hurrying as fast as she was able, her girth made it impossible to move quickly. Even now, each step was an effort. She wondered if they would reach the grove of trees. Although Raine had managed to keep the soldiers away, it would be all too easy for them to catch up.

'Where do you live?' she asked the woman. 'Perhaps Raine and I can take you home.'

There was a sudden uneasiness that passed over the woman's face, as if she had no wish to reveal her destination. 'If you help me get back to my husband's men, they will escort me home.'

'We will try,' Carice promised. 'Is your husband with them?'

Aoife shook her head. 'He is in Leinster.'

Then the woman had a long journey ahead of her. Carice wasn't at all certain that Aoife could make it that far east, particularly if she could not ride. It made her wonder how she had been separated from her escorts and why the Normans had attacked. Surely her men had to be nearby.

She continued guiding the woman towards the woods, though her own strength was beginning to diminish. The moment they reached the trees, she searched for a place to hide. The slender trees offered no means of concealing them, but there was a large stone monolith near the clearing. It was an obvious place, but their only choice.

Carice helped the woman continue through the trees, and when they reached the monolith, she bade Aoife to sit down. 'Are you all right?' she asked.

Aoife was out of breath, but she managed to nod. 'I need to rest.' She closed her eyes, pressing her hands against her swollen belly.

'How long before your child is born?' Carice asked. She worried that the woman might have already begun her labour.

'A few weeks, perhaps.' Aoife shrugged. 'It's difficult to tell.' She sat upon another stone and leaned back against the monolith. For several moments, she calmed herself, and then she added, 'I was taken from my escorts about a mile east of here. If you could help me return to them, then that will be enough.'

'Shouldn't they be searching for you?'

The woman closed her eyes and shrugged. 'I was travelling with eight of my father's men. Some of them provoked a fight with the Normans. Four were killed.'

It wasn't surprising. Although a year had passed since the invasion at Port Láirge, many of the Irish despised the Normans—especially if their loved ones had died in battle.

'The other four men might still come for you,' Carice offered. 'But we will try to reach them.' Inwardly, she wasn't certain how this woman could possibly travel a mile—not unless Raine returned and helped her mount one of their horses.

What was happening with the Norman soldiers? She had heard no sounds of fighting, nothing at all to suggest that Raine was in danger. He must know the men, she reasoned. Else they would have continued their attack.

But her sense that all was not right only heightened. She kept her attention on Aoife, hoping the woman could continue walking. And in the meantime, she prayed that Raine would return to them.

Raine faced his commander and regarded him. 'You were supposed to remain behind us. Lady Carice doesn't know where we are travelling, but she saw your men.'

'It won't matter in another day,' Sir Darren countered.

No, but if Carice realised how far to the east they had travelled, she would refuse to go any farther. 'I have kept my word to bring her with me. Wait for us at Tara, and we will join you there.'

His commander didn't seem to trust him at all. 'We will continue to follow you, but I will order my men to wait—for now. You should know that we encountered her father's men. I made an agreement with Brian Faoilin to help him search for her.'

Raine kept his face neutral, though he suspected that Sir Darren's patience was waning. But neither did he want Carice to learn the truth until it was necessary. 'I will not abandon my duty. But Lady Carice is unwell. She needs another day or two to rest before we can leave.'

Sir Darren shook his head. 'I have more men already gathered at Tara. We cannot delay for too long, for I have someone on the inside who may be of use to us.'

A traitor, he meant. Raine's mouth tightened, and he gave a nod. Sir Darren would not hesitate to use any advantage he held.

The knight's gaze sharpened upon Raine. 'I saw the way you kissed her. You've grown too close to her. What will you do when you have to leave her with Rory Ó Connor?'

He would slit the High King's throat before

he'd allow the old man to touch Carice. But his commander was right—Raine had to let her go. He'd slept hard with her fragile body against his own. It had felt right to hold her in his arms. And when she had spoken of ending her own life, the idea had filled him with dread.

He understood suffering. There were moments when he'd been recovering from the burn wounds when he'd longed for a respite from the endless pain. But he'd fought back to regain his strength. He would never consider seeking his own death, for his sisters were relying upon him.

After his mother had taken her life, the priests would not allow her to be buried upon consecrated ground. Her body had been placed near the woods, far away from the family graves, and all of her possessions had been seized by King Henry's men. Raine had been left to grieve for a woman who had loved her husband more than her children. He had not been able to forgive her for making that choice, and he would never let Carice even consider the idea of suicide.

He changed the subject, wanting to divert Sir Darren's attention away from Carice. 'Why did your men attack that woman? Were they so desperate to harm a woman expecting a child?'

Sir Darren shrugged. 'Her men attacked ours, and we retaliated. She has wealth, so we thought of ransoming her. My men raided their wagons and found gold. She was merely a distraction.'

'I thought you had more control over your men than that, Darren,' he said softly. 'They're turning into common thieves.'

His commander stared at him, his expression stony. 'They are away from their homes and families. So long as they obey my orders, I care not if they seize an opportunity where they find it.'

The man's blatant disregard for the law irritated him, but there was nothing Raine could do. 'Let the woman go. I am taking her back to her escorts.'

Sir Darren's gaze narrowed. 'So long as you bring Lady Carice to Tara, it matters not what you do with the other woman.' He wheeled his horse beside Raine. 'But if you do not join us at our camp by evening on the morrow, we will come and take her from you.'

It took an effort to hold his tongue, but Raine knew arguing would accomplish naught. They were outnumbered, and if he did not follow orders, they might hurt Carice. 'We will be there.' As he left, he sent his commander a warning look. 'But if any of your men threaten her, I will tear them apart.'

Carice breathed a sigh of relief when she saw Raine approaching. He drew his horse to a halt and said, 'Tell the woman the soldiers won't bother her any more. I've sent them away.'

She translated for him, but Aoife appeared uncertain of whether or not Raine was telling the truth. She clenched her hands together, looking exhausted and afraid.

Carice wanted to ask questions, but the look in his eyes warned her to say nothing. She guessed that he knew the Normans and had used that influence.

'This is Aoife,' she said to him, introducing Raine in turn. 'Her escorts are about a mile from here, maybe less.'

'You are one of the Normans,' Aoife accused. To Carice, she demanded, 'Why would you trust this man?'

'He is a Norman, yes. But he has earned my trust, and I swear to you, he will only protect us. I hired him to escort me to the west.'

The woman rested her hands upon her swollen belly, and she looked uneasy. 'I need to return to my men. They were taking me home to my husband.'

Carice translated for Raine, and he spoke in Irish, 'We will take you to them.' Although he'd spoken clearly, his discomfort with the language was obvious. She questioned how much Raine had understood of what Aoife had said.

'Can you ride?' he asked the woman gently. He spoke in the Irish language, but his Norman accent was strong.

She nodded. 'I think so.'

He dismounted from his horse and easily lifted Aoife atop his mount. Though it was awkward, the woman managed to hold on to the reins. Carice worried about Aoife keeping her balance. 'I don't want her to fall.'

'She won't.' Raine helped her to mount her own horse and then swung up behind her. Carice leaned back against him while he drew their horse alongside the young pregnant woman.

As they made their way through the woods, Carice translated Raine's questions. They learned that the woman lived in the north and was travelling home from her father's dwelling. A sadness crossed her face, and she admitted, 'He died last year, and I went to visit the home of my childhood. It lies a few miles east of here.'

'Would you rather return there?' Carice suggested. To her surprise, Aoife refused.

'No. There is no reason to go back, and my husband is expecting me to join him.'

Though she questioned whether the young woman could reach Leinster, given her pregnancy, it was not her place to interfere. Carice questioned her on Raine's behalf. 'Have you enough supplies?'

Aoife lifted her shoulders in a shrug. 'They took gold, but I don't think they stole our food. We can manage until we are home again.'

'I spoke with their commander,' Raine said, speaking slowly to give Carice time to translate. 'They will not trouble you again. I promise you that.'

And Carice believed that he would keep that vow. Raine had behaved honourably towards her, and he'd given her no reason to distrust him. He had the physical strength she lacked, and with this man, she felt protected.

As they rode east, she leaned back against him, enjoying the feeling of his arms around her. His male scent allured her, and she grew distracted with thoughts of him kissing and touching her. God forgive her, but she wanted this man. She wanted to forget about her body's weakness and lose herself in his embrace. She was aware of every hardened line of his body, his powerful thighs surrounding her, and the chain mail armour he wore.

When they found Aoife's escorts, there were two men present, one of whom was badly wounded. Their leader appeared visibly relieved. 'My lady, I am so glad to see you unharmed. The other two men are still searching for you.'

Aoife's face hardened. 'They did a poor job of it. But thankfully, I was found by Lady Carice and this Norman soldier.' She motioned for her guard to help her down. Then she turned back to them, returning the horse to Raine. 'I owe you my thanks for bringing me back. My husband will see to it that you're rewarded for this.'

Carice translated for Raine, as well as his reply, 'There is no need for that.' He dismounted from their horse and took back the other mount. 'I am only sorry that the soldiers took what was yours.'

Aoife leaned down from her horse and twisted off a ring. 'You will need shelter for the night. If you ride towards the east, you may stay at my father's house. Take this, and one of my soldiers will accompany you, to ensure that you are treated as a guest.'

If they journeyed towards the east, it meant they would be backtracking. Carice told Raine of Aoife's offer, but started to argue that it wasn't needed.

Raine ignored her protest and spoke slowly, 'That would be…kind. We accept your offer.' He took the ring and slid it onto his smallest finger.

What was he doing? 'We're travelling west, Raine. I don't think—'

'You need to regain your strength,' he argued back. 'I don't want you sleeping out of doors another night. Not when you've been so ill.'

Though she knew it was only concern, her greater worry was being found by her father. And travelling east made that a true danger. 'I'll be fine. I can manage.'

He ignored her and directed his attention back to Aoife. To Carice, he ordered, 'Translate for me.'

She didn't want to, but obeyed, repeating his words. 'If one of your men would guide us to your father's house, we would appreciate it.'

Aoife offered a smile. 'I am thankful for your kindness. And please tell my father's steward that I am in need of more escorts.' She gave instructions to one of her men to lead the way while the others began burying the fallen soldiers.

The guard chosen to accompany them said, 'We must travel south and then east.'

Raine didn't argue with the man, but Carice thought this was a terrible idea. Not only would it bring them towards her father's men, but there was no need for it. She drew her horse alongside his and said, 'Why would you have us go the wrong direction, Raine? I am not so weak that I cannot sleep outside.'

He stiffened in the saddle, but eyed her. 'You could barely move only a little while ago. If I push you too hard, you'll collapse.'

'I can manage the journey,' she insisted. 'Really, there's no need for this.'

He eyed her, and in his gaze, she saw the gravity of his concern. 'What does one more day matter, Carice?'

'What about the soldiers you spoke with? Won't they recognise you and tell your commander what you've done? I don't want you to be punished on my behalf.'

There was a hint of unrest in his eyes. 'They care not what I do during these next few days, so long as I return to my duties within a sennight.'

He was lying; she was certain of that. She started to argue again, but then understanding dawned within her. 'You bribed them, didn't you? And if it seems that you are travelling east, they will think you are obeying.'

He neither agreed with nor denied her prediction. It did make sense, however. She supposed another day wouldn't matter too much, if it meant protecting him from the ire of his Norman commander.

But as they travelled, it bothered her to realise that they were not retracing their path. It made her wonder exactly where Raine had taken them. In fact, it seemed that they were moving forward instead of backwards. The uneasy suspicions were hard to silence, but she told herself that she had never been to this part of Éireann before. One meadow looked the same as the next.

But she was beginning to wonder if there was a reason for her misgivings.

They arrived at the settlement in the late afternoon. Raine hardly spoke to Carice at all, for fear that he would reveal too much. They were only two days' journey from Tara, and his misgivings heightened. He didn't want to see Carice's eyes fill up with hatred towards him—not after he had fought so hard to take care of her.

You've grown too close.

His commander's words were true enough. Raine had intended to distance himself, to be her escort and nothing else. But when she'd raced him on the ice, when she'd slept in his arms, some of the emptiness had abated. Being with Carice had softened the rage he'd held within him during the past few years. She brought a sense of peace that took away the loneliness. With each moment, he found himself wanting to remain at her side.

You will never have a woman like her. Not after what you've done.

The knowledge filled him with regret. He followed the guard inside the gates, trying to shut out the voices of guilt. His sisters were depending on him. Their lives rested upon the decisions he was about to make. He had no right to put one woman's needs before his family's.

'I feel as if I know this place,' Carice said. 'It seems familiar somehow.' Her expression grew discerning, almost thoughtful as she studied their surroundings. Then a moment later, she seemed to dismiss the idea.

He only shrugged. 'I have not been here before.' Although it was a smaller property, it boasted a large stone *donjon* and several out-buildings. Thatched roundhouses encircled the space, and he guessed that the outer walls were twelve feet tall and two feet thick.

The guard introduced them to the steward, and they showed the man Aoife's ring. Carice explained what had happened, and her words were verified by the guard who had accompa-nied them. All the while, Raine grew aware of how pale she appeared, as if each step was an effort. Although Carice was putting on a brave front, she needed to rest.

While the guards arranged for more escorts to return to Lady Aoife, the steward ushered Carice and Raine inside. 'We are so very grate-ful that you protected our lady.' He led them into the tower where they were given the fin-est room. A large bed stood at one end, while a warm fire crackled within the hearth. 'Our household would be glad to prepare a feast for both of you.'

Raine glanced at Carice, and addressed the

steward in Irish. 'We would prefer to eat within this chamber. My lady is unwell.'

She sent him a sharp look, but didn't argue. Her face was troubled, as if she didn't want to admit the pain she was suffering.

'Would you like our healer to examine your wife?' the steward offered, and Raine nodded, not correcting the man's assumption. He wasn't about to leave Carice alone for any length of time. Besides that, he did want someone with healing skill to see her.

Seeing her so frail and weak the other night had heightened his worry. Not only because of her sickness, but because she had spoken of death so freely.

'I will get food for you,' he promised Carice, after the steward had left them alone. 'Let the healer look at you, and she may have medicines that will help.'

'I know I have become a burden to you,' she said softly. Then she went to stand by the window. 'You never wanted this journey with me. Especially when your sisters were in danger.'

The sadness in her voice held more than regret. He didn't know what had prompted her melancholy, but he didn't want her to speak of it now. Their time together was running out, and he didn't want it to be shadowed by regret.

He crossed the room to stand behind her. She rested her hands upon the wall on either side of the window, and he wrapped his arms around her waist. 'You were never a burden.'

She turned to him, and her blue eyes were filled with such pain. 'I think I wanted to believe that there could be something between us. I always thought you were a handsome man, even if you were stern.'

He drew his hand over the curve of her cheek, uncertain of what to say. 'If our lives were different, perhaps there would be something more.'

'But they aren't, are they? You must return to the Normans…and I must live out the remainder of my days alone.'

He cupped her face, wishing to God he didn't have to betray her. 'I must obey my duties. But that doesn't mean I regret the moments with you.'

'Don't say it,' she whispered. 'I've been foolish to imagine that you might stay with me.'

Mon Dieu, how he wanted that. But he had no right to her. 'You know I cannot.'

She lowered her gaze, and he pulled her into

his embrace. 'These days were a gift to me, and I do not regret them.'

She clung to him a moment before she lifted her mouth to his. The gentle brush of her lips sent a bolt of heat raging through him. Although she might be physically weaker, Carice had invisible weapons of her own.

God help him.

An hour later, Carice relaxed in a small wooden tub filled with steaming water. Her hair was bound up in a knot at the top of her head, and she sighed with relief. The hot bath was sprinkled with herbs that the healer had recommended for her, and the old woman had given her hot tea made with crushed mint. The drink had soothed her stomach, and with each hour, she felt better. She was grateful for the chance to be warm, though her heart had gone cold.

Raine had gone below stairs to fetch food, and while he was gone, it had given her a chance to think. Her mood was heavy, her mind torn apart with anger and grief. Though he had not recognised this place, she knew it was the home of Diarmuid MacMurrough, the Irish King of Leinster. Lady Aoife was his daughter who had been given in marriage to Richard de Clare,

the Norman leader also known as Strongbow.
King Diarmuid's lands were only a short journey southwest of Tara.

Carice drew up her knees in the small tub,
so torn about what to do. It was clear now that
Raine had brought her to the east instead of the
west. His desire to travel at night was a means
of deceiving her, and she suspected he had been
obeying orders all along. More than likely he
had intended to deliver her into the hands of
the High King.

The thought made her want to scream, to
pummel her fists against his chest and release
a cry of rage. He had taken advantage of her
illness, knowing that she could not stop him.
She had been so stupid to believe that he would
help her.

Hot tears welled up in her eyes, for she ought
to confront him. She should demand that Raine
leave her here, though she knew he wouldn't.
Instead, he might take her away and give her
over to the High King. Or perhaps to the Norman soldiers they had encountered a few hours
ago. She was certain now that they were his
men, and undoubtedly, they had followed him
from the beginning.

Hurt balled up inside her that she had let

herself believe he cared. When he had touched her, she had come undone, her emotions crumbling beneath his caress. Beneath his lies, she'd also sensed the traces of guilt and regret. Perhaps he *did* care about her, though he might not admit it. He could have insisted that they continue travelling; instead, he had stopped here in the afternoon.

Why? Was it because he worried for her health? Or was it because he was wavering in his decision? He had not yet given her into the hands of her enemies.

A grain of an idea took hold within her. Was it possible to change his mind? Aye, Raine was a soldier, a man bound to the king's will who could not put his own desires first. But what if he decided not to go through with his plans? What if she could convince him to let her go?

Confusion clouded Carice's thoughts, for she knew not what Raine thought of her. He had protected her, time and again…but was it only out of duty? Had he kissed her, wanting only to deceive her?

She leaned her head back and closed her eyes. Whatever time they had remaining was sliding through her fingers like droplets of water. She didn't know if there was a way to turn him back from this course. Was it possible?

The door opened quietly, and she shielded herself, only to realise it was him. Raine had a tray of food in his hands, but he turned away immediately. After he set down the tray, he lowered the latch to bolt the door. 'Forgive me. I didn't realise you were—I mean, I should not have entered without knocking.'

'It's all right.' But even so, she felt the blush all over her skin. Had he seen her naked body?

Did you want him to? The voice of her conscience was chiding, and she closed her eyes, stammering. 'The—the healer thought if I bathed in these herbs, it might help.'

He kept his distance, standing on the far side of the room, his gaze averted. 'And did it?'

'Yes. It felt good to be warm.' She studied him closely, wondering what thoughts were going through his mind. A hundred questions passed through her, but she kept silent. If she pretended that she didn't know what was happening, he might reveal more of his intentions.

Raine's shoulders were lowered, and he said, 'I'll leave the food here and return later. Shall I send for a maid to help you?'

'Don't go,' she murmured. 'Stay and talk with me a while.'

He kept his back turned. For a while, he remained silent, as if he knew not what to say. 'What do you want from me, Carice?'

I want to know why you've brought me here. And if you intend to go through with this betrayal.

She bit her lip, wondering what answers he would give. 'How much longer will we travel?'

'A day and a half. Perhaps two at the most.' He stood with his palm against the wall, and at least this was an honest answer.

'I suppose you'll be glad to be rid of me,' she whispered. 'After all the trouble I've given you.'

And because it will bring you into the High King's favour.

But what purpose would that serve? He didn't need King Rory's favour—he needed the favour of his own ruler, King Henry. Was that why he had been sent? To deliver her into their hands as a show of good faith? The Normans and Irish had a deceptive peace, one that hovered on the brink of war.

'No, I won't be glad to leave you,' he said. His voice was husky, and she didn't know whether it was desire or regret she heard within the tone. Her foolish heart wanted to believe that there could be more.

'Come here,' she bade him. She wanted to look into his eyes, to read the thoughts he would not speak.

'I must leave you alone to clothe yourself,' he said. 'But I will return.'

He started to go, but she called out to him, 'Bring me the drying cloth first.'

Raine hesitated before he reached for the cloth. 'I am trying to be honourable with you.' There was a strain within his voice, of a man who was battling his own urges.

Good. She wanted him to be frustrated, to feel the crushing weight of guilt. But more than that, she wanted him to abandon that path, to walk with her in whatever days remained. To find the fragmented pieces of honour that would convince him that surrendering her would not bring his sisters back.

As he approached, he kept his gaze downcast. But she watched his tall form, she let her gaze settle upon his muscled body and the blond hair that gleamed against the fire. She had touched his warm skin, feeling the beating of his heart against her palm.

He held the drying cloth out to her, but there

was a slight tremor in his hands, as if he were hovering on the brink of his control.

Carice was beginning to understand that she was in a position of advantage. And if she could coerce him into changing his mind, this she would do. She would never wed Rory Ó Connor, for she was done with obedience. The illness had stolen away the life she'd wanted to have, the children she'd wanted to bear.

And she would go down fighting before she would let Raine de Garenne hand her to an enemy.

'Will you help me from the tub?' she asked.

The drying cloth fell from his hand. 'You don't know what you are asking.'

He was wrong in that. She knew exactly what she was doing—using every possible means of changing his mind.

'I may fall if I try to get out of this tub without your assistance.' She kept her tone light, but he didn't smile. He held the drying cloth, but when he stared at her, she felt a sudden wave of shyness.

She was asking him to come closer, this man who had lied to her and brought her closer to her enemies. He might have conspired with her father, for all she knew. And yet, when she looked into his green eyes, she saw a man haunted by the past. The lines of his face revealed untold suffering.

'You ask too much of me. If I lift you from that tub, I'll not be able to stop myself from touching you.'

She kept herself hidden within the water and regarded him. 'Is that what you want?'

His green eyes burned into hers. 'What I want and what is right are two different things.'

At that, she stood up from the tub, revealing herself to him. Water trickled down her naked body, down the slight curves of her breasts and her body that was too thin. Inwardly, she was trembling from fear. She was taking the greatest risk, hoping that he would somehow turn away from duty. 'I understand.'

This was seduction, an offering she should not give. She knew that these were the actions of a woman of loose virtue. But there was far more beneath the surface of her offering. There was fear, a trace of shame, and worry that he would remain fixed upon his decision. Her heart was pounding, and at his silence, she wondered if she had made a mistake.

'Look at me,' she commanded, 'and answer

me with truth. In two days, will you be relieved that you will not see me again?'

He bent down and retrieved the drying cloth, his knuckles clenching against the linen. Slowly he lifted it around her shoulders, the cloth shielding her body.

He lifted her from the tub and brought her to stand before him. 'You know not the man I am. Or the things I have done.'

Oh yes, she did know. But what she wanted to know was whether she could change his course. Carice reached up to take his face in her palms. 'Is that the man you want to be? Or would you forsake your duties to stay with me?'

He closed his eyes, and she saw the rigid tension within him. 'Do you want these hands upon you? These hands that have slain countless men?' He dropped his voice even lower. 'Why do you offer yourself to me, when we both know I will leave?'

'Because I believe that you don't want to go.'

He captured her hands upon his face, and the expression in his eyes was of a man drowning in need. 'I don't deserve a woman like you. Not after what I've done.'

His words took on a deeper meaning, for she

was well aware of it. 'Then change it. Be a different man.'

He brushed his thumb over her lips, sliding his hand down the curve of her throat. 'Would that it were possible.'

'It is possible,' she whispered. 'Come away with me. Let me live out the rest of my days with you.'

'I cannot. My sisters—'

'Do you truly think the king will free them?' she asked. 'Or will he use them to manipulate you?'

'Don't—' he shot back. 'My life is not my own. My choices are not my own.'

'Because you let them lead you by strings. You follow your commander's will blindly.' She reached down for his hands, knowing her words were cruel. 'But how do you even know your sisters are still alive?'

He jerked his hands away. 'I don't.'

She let the drying cloth fall away and rested her arms around his throat. 'Make your own choices, Raine. And live by them, whatever they are.'

His bare hands slid down her back to the curve of her bottom. 'You're asking me to make the wrong choice, Carice.'

She leaned in and rested her cheek against his armour. 'No, Raine. I'm asking you to make the right one.' She wanted him to turn away from his orders, to break the chains that bound him to duty.

'Give me a memory,' she answered. 'When I am dying, I want to know that I lived every day to its fullest. And when I think of you, I will smile.'

'I promise you, you won't smile. I am not the man you want.' His expression held the grim cast of a soldier who intended to betray her. He was tormented not only by the past, but by the choices ahead. There was no peace for him, and he was determined to push her away.

'Your past matters not to me,' she said quietly. 'But am I wrong to think that you care about me?'

Chapter Eight

When Carice stepped back, revealing her body once again, Raine was gripped by the undeniable urge to drink in the sight of her. He was held spellbound by her bare skin and the erect rose nipples that tightened in the cool air. His body grew rock hard at the sight of her, needing to touch the body she offered.

But God help him, she would despise him for doing this. The moment she realised that he planned to give her into the hands of her enemy, she would look upon him with hatred.

And yet, he was utterly lost. She held him beneath her spell, and when she took his hands, he touched that beautiful skin.

'No,' he breathed. He did care, a great deal. 'You weren't wrong. But I have no right to be with a woman like you.' He wanted her more than his next breath. Craved her until there were no words. He drew his hands down her silken skin, down to the base of her spine and over the curve of her hip.

'I don't care.' She took his hand and held it for a moment, her blue eyes holding him captive. 'Be with me now. Show me what you feel.'

His body was burning with need, and he hungered to give her pleasure. Yet this woman, who had suffered so much, should not lose her innocence to a man like him.

'I will never marry,' she said. 'I will never bear a child within this body. But before you leave me, I want to know what it would be like to have a lover.'

'Why?' His voice came out rough, revealing the caged frustration. 'Why would you offer yourself to a man like me?'

'Because you fought for me, protected me. Because I see the way you are looking at me now, as if you want to love me.'

Dieu, how he wanted that. What he wouldn't give to live the life of a normal man, to stay with this woman who raced along the ice and kissed him as if she needed him more than air.

Carice lifted her face to his. 'Or am I wrong?'

With that, he was lost. With his mouth, he

followed a trickle of water, as it outlined the curve of her breast. He tasted the wet skin, running his tongue to her nipple. And when he suckled her, her hands dug into his hair, holding him close. He ran his tongue over the hard nub, unable to stop himself from worshipping her. Then he kissed a path to the other breast, running his tongue along the curves until he captured the second nipple. He rolled the other with his thumb and forefinger, loving the taste of her.

'You aren't wrong, Carice.' He moved back, reaching for the fallen length of soft linen. Her hair had come loose from its knot and the dark waves spilled over her shoulders and down to her hips. 'I could spend hours touching you.'

'Then make me forget all else,' she whispered. 'Let me imagine that you love me enough to stay.'

Her words undid him, making him wish to God he could ignore his orders and take her away. But he knew better than to envision what could never be.

'Hold out your arms,' he ordered. He took the length of linen and drew it over her, gently drying her back. He used the cloth to caress her body, over her breasts and belly,

He knelt before her, drying her bottom and the back of her legs. Then down to her feet, where he moved the cloth over her calves and up her inner thighs. She was trembling from his touch, but he didn't care. He wanted her as aroused as he was.

As he continued to move the cloth over her skin, he realised that he could pleasure her without taking her virginity. The thought made his loins tighten, and he realised that this was the most honourable means of touching her.

There was a chair near the fire, and he guided her there, seating her in a wordless command. The fire warmed her naked skin, giving it a golden cast. Her hair had fallen over her shoulders, and he moved it away from her bare breasts, needing to see them. 'Open your legs for me,' he demanded.

Her blue eyes widened, and he didn't miss the fear in them. But although she hesitated, she parted her legs. He held her ankles in both hands, lowering his mouth to her calves. He kissed the delicate skin, moving up to her inner thighs. When she arched her back, he imprisoned her legs, not allowing her to pull away. Goose flesh prickled over her body, and he moved his attention to her other leg, kissing and licking the sensitive hidden places.

When he reached her intimate curls, with his mouth he breathed against her. A soft cry released from her lips. 'Raine, I don't know if you should—'

He cut off her words by kissing her opening, tasting the salt of her arousal. She tried to pull back, but he reached beneath her bottom and brought her legs to rest on his shoulders.

He was aching for her. The torment was rising higher, and he deserved all of the discomfort and more. But he was determined to pleasure her, to teach her how he could make her come apart. With his tongue, he worked the nodule of her flesh, suckling her and making her tremble.

But it wasn't enough. Carice was fighting against the feelings, refusing to let go. And so, he slowed down, pulling back. She was glistening wet, and this time, he kissed her nipple again, while he slid a finger inside her. She groaned at the sensation, and he caressed her from within while he used his thumb against her hooded flesh.

'Raine, I don't—oh, please,' she begged. She was nearly frantic for the release he could give her, and right now, all he wanted to do was fill her with his body, thrusting with his own needs.

He softened his touch, coaxing her towards the edge. Her body was trembling, and she met his gaze with her eyes. In them, he saw the yearning, and she whispered, 'Don't go back to the Normans. Promise me.'

He couldn't speak the words, for he was bound by duty. There was no answer he could give, so instead, he suckled hard against her nipple and she let out a shuddering breath, shattering as her body gave in to the overwhelming wave of release.

He revelled in her pleasure, holding her as she gripped his shoulders. Then, when she gathered her senses from the storm, she touched his face. 'Kiss me.' He did, and was dimly aware of her hands moving over his clothing, loosening the laces. 'Take off your armour and tunic.'

He paused a moment, but she said, 'I want to feel my bare skin against yours. Don't deny me that.'

He was so lost, he couldn't have refused her if he'd wanted to. When the barriers between them were gone, he groaned as she pressed her breasts against him. *Mon Dieu,* she felt so good.

He could spend all night loving her and never regret a moment of it.

Carice took his hand and led him towards the bed. He didn't protest, but she helped him remove his boots. Then her hands paused at his waist in a silent question.

'Will you let me touch you?' she asked. 'Please?'

He knew that she wanted more than he could give. But if he merely allowed her to touch him and caress him, there was no harm in it. So long as she held the power and he surrendered to her will, he could let go of the voices in his head.

She will hate you when she learns the truth.

If he dared to claim what he wanted most, *oui,* she would. But if he left her untouched, he could live with his decision.

And so he nodded, letting her do as she would.

Carice's heart was pounding as she touched her hands to Raine's chest. He stole her breath with a magnificent body she wanted to admire. His muscles were tight, like a figure carved of marble. And though she hadn't missed the troubled expression in his eyes, she wanted this night with him.

Her body was aching and wet, needing to complete the act of lovemaking. She was beyond all thoughts of shame or hesitation. All she knew was that she wanted this man, and she believed with all her heart that she could change his mind.

She ran her hands over his pectoral muscles, over his chest, and down his ribs. His manhood was erect and jutted out from his hips, and she imagined what it would be like to take him inside her. The very thought made her remember the intense pleasure Raine had given her earlier. She wanted to give the same back to him.

'Lie down,' she ordered, pressing him towards the bed. When he did, his erection rested against his stomach. It was so thick and hard, she couldn't resist touching it with her palm. The look of fire in his eyes made it clear that he liked what she was doing. She stroked him, marvelling at the velvety heat of his shaft.

As she continued to move her hand upon him, his face contorted as if she were tormenting him. 'Am I hurting you? Shall I stop?' She worried that she might be squeezing too hard.

'It will only hurt if you do stop,' he managed. As she stroked him, he began arching his hips in a rhythm. And she began to imagine how it would feel if he were thrusting within her.

I want this. So badly.

She paused a moment to straddle his body, then resumed what she was doing. He closed his eyes, and at that moment, she pressed his blunt head to her entrance. She was so aroused, the shallow invasion made her moan.

Raine seized her waist and his green eyes had turned to stone. 'Stop, Carice. You don't want this. Not from a man like me.'

In answer, she pushed herself lower, ignoring the slight pain as he breached her innocence. 'Yes. I do.' She surrendered her virginity to the man she wanted, binding him irrevocably to her.

When he was buried deep inside her, there was no going back. Slowly, he sat up, remaining embedded inside her. 'I never meant to claim you like this.'

It was a strange sensation to be joined so intimately, but as she relaxed around him, it began to feel good. 'I want this,' she reminded him. 'I want you.'

He grasped her hips and lifted her up, as if to withdraw from her. She began to protest, but then he lowered her. She let out a gasp at the sensation.

'Ride me,' he commanded. 'If this is what you want from me, then take it.' It was clear that he didn't want to force her into the love-making. But from the warmth in his voice, she understood that he wanted her, too.

She felt awkward at first, but it was easier when she closed her eyes. 'What should I do?'

'Lift up on your knees and then lower yourself,' he said. 'Any way that feels good to you.'

It went against everything she'd imagined, but she was making love to Raine, instead of the other way around. And slowly, she began to thrust upon him, shallow at first, and then deeper. Being in command made it easier to adjust to the soreness, and soon enough, she no longer cared. His hands moved up to cup her breasts, and he fingered her nipples as she moved up and down. When she sat upon him, leaning back slightly, he moved one hand down to her hooded flesh.

The moment he caressed her there, she clenched his length. 'Oh, Raine.' She could hardly breathe, and it took an effort to continue her movement. The delicious friction was guiding her towards another release, and she wanted it so badly. He started to move within her, but she held his hips back. 'Wait.'

He understood what she wanted, and while they were joined, he sat up, still fingering her while he suckled her nipple. The burgeoning feelings were gathering up like a thunderstorm inside her, and she arched against him.

'Let go,' he ordered, 'and let me feel you come apart. I want to be inside you when you feel your pleasure.'

The wildness was gathering momentum, building up until she could hardly hold back the moans of excitement. She arched hard, welcoming the rushing sensations as they crashed over her. Her body was a liquid heat, pulsing around his shaft, and she bit back a scream as he thrust forward.

This time, he rolled her onto her back, and she could only hold on as he drove himself inside her. The reckless fire was rising hotter, and she came apart once again as he plunged and withdrew. She scored his back with her fingernails, giving in to instinct, until at last, his breathing deepened, and he collapsed on top of her.

Carice welcomed the weight of him, feeling beloved. Their bodies were still joined, and she held him close to her heart, unable to hold back her smile.

'Thank you,' she whispered, revelling in the touch of his body upon hers.

She could feel his tension, but in answer, he leaned up and kissed her. The need to sleep overcame her, and she closed her eyes, letting go of all else but the welcome sanctuary of Raine's arms.

He awakened a few hours later with Carice nestled against him. Their legs were tangled together, and the sleep softened the features of her face. He supposed he ought to feel remorse for taking advantage of her. And yet, all he could feel was grateful. For these few moments, he was at peace.

She snuggled against him and opened her eyes. He waited to see if her expression would hold any regret. Instead, she sent him a quiet smile.

'Are you hungry?' he asked. 'I brought you food earlier.'

She nodded. 'I think I distracted you from it. Why don't you bring it here, and we'll eat together?'

He rose from the bed and fetched the tray.

Upon it was bread, meat and cheese. He offered it to Carice, and she chose a piece of cheese. 'There was a time when I ate nothing but bread.'

He lay beside her while she ate, wanting her to have her fill before he touched any of it. 'Why?'

'The healer thought it would keep my stomach from hurting so much.' She finished the cheese and reached for the meat. 'It never did. There was a time when I tried not to eat because it hurt so much. Or perhaps I wanted to die, rather than wed the High King.'

Raine reached out to touch her flat stomach, feeling his own tension tighten inside. He'd hated watching her be so ill, so weak. 'You were starving yourself.'

'It didn't hurt as much when I refused food.' She sent him a faint smile. 'It was only when I spent time with you that I was able to eat without pain. At least until we stayed at the village.'

He drew his hand over her skin, stroking it. It felt as if there was something he ought to understand, something that was causing her illness. 'Were you ever well when you ate at home?'

'Not often. And in the last year, I grew worse.'

He still couldn't let go of the suspicion that

she'd been poisoned. If she'd had enemies within her father's house, they might have tampered with her food to make her ill. There were many kinds of poison, some of which grew worse over time. Even if others had accidentally eaten her food, it might not have affected them with a smaller portion. Then, too, if she had lost a great deal of weight, even a slight amount of poison would be more potent.

Yet, it didn't explain why she had suddenly grown ill after they'd visited the village of Casheldrum. They had been alone, and there was no possible means of anyone poisoning her.

Raine gave her more cheese and reached for the bread. He was about to offer it to her, when suddenly he remembered what she'd said before—that she had only eaten bread in the past year. He frowned at the thought and then asked, 'Had you thought that it could be bread making you sick?'

She broke into a laugh. 'Don't be foolish. Why would bread make me ill? I've eaten it all my life.'

'You said your illness grew worse last year. And that was when you ate nothing but bread.' He stared at her, thinking for a moment. 'You ate no bread at the abbey, for we had none.'

'But I ate a little at Laochre on the night I arrived. I was fine then.'

'Until the next day,' he reminded her. 'And you had some at Casheldrum, didn't you?'

'The morning we left, yes.' Her expression grew thoughtful, and he wondered if it was possible. She leaned back and regarded him. 'But I cannot think that it has anything to do with my illness.' Her breasts were soft pebbles in the cool air, and she burrowed closer to him. It took only seconds for him to grow rock hard.

'Don't eat any bread for a few weeks,' he suggested. 'See if that helps.' There could be no harm in it. Her hands moved down to his hips as she pressed her body against his.

'I could try, though I'm not sure it would do any good.' Her hand wandered down his leg, and she brought her other arm around his neck. The posture brought her breasts into prominent view, and the distraction made him yearn to touch her again. He gave in to the urge and kissed one nipple, then the other.

She moved her leg over his hip and said, 'I'm cold, Raine.'

'I know. That's why I'm warming you.' He covered her body with his own, still paying homage to her breasts. 'I want you to be burning hot when I've finished.'

She sent him a secret smile. 'Have you decided to stay with me, then?'

He didn't answer her question, but drew her legs around his waist. His shaft was pressed against her intimately, and he rubbed against her. He didn't want to face the fate that lay before them, and yes, he did want to stay with this woman. But it meant abandoning not only his sisters, but his lands and his people. He had to atone for his parents' deaths, and he could not turn his back on them.

'Please,' she whispered, but he suspected she was not speaking of lovemaking. As he thrust inside her, she moaned, squeezing his length. Her blue eyes held his, and he slowed his pace, joining their bodies while he never took his gaze from her.

'You haven't answered my question,' she prompted, raising her knees to take him deeper. He plunged inside her, using his mouth and hands to guide her towards the edge of desire, his fingers digging into her hips as she drove him past the brink of reason.

No, he hadn't answered her question. For there was no answer to give.

* * *

Carice offered no conversation at all when they left on the following morning. She had tried everything to convince Raine to stay with her, but his silence was damning. He didn't bother hiding their pathway now, and she was well aware of the sun spearing her eyes as they rode eastward.

She would have to confront him soon. And though she knew he cared for her, by the way he'd made love to her and the way he kept glancing back to ensure she was all right, he didn't love her. Not enough to give up his purpose.

Her stomach ached again, but not because of food. It was from the knowledge that she couldn't change him. This man had stolen her heart, and now he was about to break it. Carice tried to tell herself that there was still time, but she knew the truth—it was over now. She had to stop Raine before they rode any further.

Halfway along their journey, she drew her horse to a stop. The sun was bright in the sky, gleaming across shadowed hills. 'I want to know why you won't speak to me, Raine.'

'I find that there is little I can say to you,' he said. 'Our time together grows short.'

'And you want to end it sooner by increasing the pace of our horses?'

His shoulders lowered, and he finally drew his own mount to a stop. 'Were it my choice, I would not leave you, Carice.' The weight of his guilt was evident in his tone. 'But I have wronged you. More than you know.'

Her face softened at that, for at least he seemed reluctant to betray her. 'Come and talk with me awhile, Raine.'

He glanced back at the path leading east and finally brought his horse closer to hers. His expression was shielded, though she saw a glimpse of emotion behind it. She beckoned for him to come nearer, and when their horses were alongside each other, she took his hand.

'I do not regret what happened between us last night. I remember every moment, and it makes me smile.' Her heart lay in her words, and she hoped he would feel the same.

Rainee squeezed her hand, and admitted, 'I will never forget you, Carice.'

His words were a physical blow, shattering her hopes. Her eyes welled up with tears, knowing that he really was giving up, and he intended to go through with this. With effort, she managed to speak. 'Somehow, I wanted to believe that you might change your mind.'

'About what?' Though his tone was questioning, she heard the wariness in his voice.

She pointed skyward, towards the sun. 'About taking me to Tara.'

The sudden transformation of his expression told her that she'd guessed correctly. His mouth tightened, and his eyes held a bleakness. When he didn't speak, she continued, 'We've been travelling east all day. And we've been going east since we left Laochre. Did you think I wouldn't notice?'

A thread of ice ran through her veins, but he made no denial. He looked at her squarely and said quietly, 'I hoped you wouldn't.'

Her heart ached, but she forced herself to continue. 'You knew those Norman soldiers,' she said softly. 'That is why they didn't attack us. Because they were your men all along, weren't they?'

'My commander was there,' he agreed. 'They've been following us.'

The coldness within her seemed to fill up every empty space. She was trying to keep from crying, but it took every effort to hold back her grief. 'And that was why you weren't at all afraid of disobeying orders,' she guessed. 'Because you were following their commands the entire time.'

He took a step forward. 'Carice, you—'

'I what? I wasn't supposed to know about what you were really doing?' She pressed her lips together. 'I suspected that something was wrong. But when you took care of me whilst I was ill, I wanted to believe differently. I wanted to imagine that you would keep your promises to me. But that was never a possibility, was it?'

He made no denial. 'You do not understand my reasons.'

'You're wrong. I understand quite well. You believe that the king will free your sisters if you obey their orders.' Her voice softened, and she gripped her hands together, wishing he would break free of the Normans.

'I don't believe they will let your sisters go,' she continued, 'for without that threat, they cannot control you.' A tear slid down her cheek, and he moved forward to wipe it away. The touch of his hand only brought more tears to her eyes. 'I suppose I deserve this. For I tried to manipulate you as well. I lay with you last night, hoping you would change your mind about delivering me into their hands.'

Raine caressed her cheek, and in his eyes, she saw his remorse. 'You never had to lower yourself in that way.'

'I didn't believe that was what it was,' she

confessed. 'For whether or not you believe it, I was falling in love with you. I gave myself to you because you were the only man I ever wanted. And before I die, I wanted a moment to be close to you.'

He drew her palm to his mouth. 'You deserve a better man than me, *chérie*. I should not have stolen your innocence. And I regret that I cannot change what happened.'

'You can change what *will* happen.' She remained motionless, praying that he would let her go. 'Don't give me over to Rory. Not if you care for me at all.'

He said nothing, and as time stretched on, her hopes sank. No matter how much she wanted to believe it, he would not put her above his orders. With sadness, she pulled back her hand. 'What do you plan to do with me now?'

The stoic look on his face only drove the invisible knife deeper into her heart. And she knew that there was no going back.

'Don't weep,' he said. 'I swear to you, Rory will never touch you.'

Then why was he bringing her to Tara? From the intensity on his face, it appeared that he was holding something back. She wanted to ask him his reasons, but the moment she began to speak, he moved in and kissed her hard.

His mouth moved over hers, reminding her of the hours they had spent in each other's arms. She surrendered to him, welcoming the affection and wishing to God he would turn away from this course.

Raine dried her tears, holding her face while he tried to tell her the words he couldn't speak. 'Trust in me, Carice. You will not wed him. Not while I am breathing.'

She didn't understand, but neither could she let go of her fears. He was indeed involved in something dangerous, and from the haunted look in his eyes, it did concern the High King.

'You could let me go,' she whispered. 'Ride away from me, and I'll return to Casheldrum until I can get another escort. No one would need to know what happened.'

'The Normans will find you. It's too late for that.' He took her hand in his and pointed towards the horizon. 'They are waiting for us, just over the rise of that hill.'

Her throat closed up with fear, but she tried one last time. 'And what would you do if I turned my horse and rode back? Would you hunt me down?'

The dark expression on his face sent a chill through her. 'Yes. I would.'

Chapter Nine

They reached the Norman camp at nightfall. The blaze of several fires lit up the darkness, and armed sentries stood all around. Several soldiers were working on setting up tents while others tended to the horses. Raine rode into the camp with Carice, and as they approached, her posture tightened. She looked back at him, and the sadness in her eyes only made him feel worse. He deserved this.

But what else could he have done? The men were too close, and even if he had tried to help her leave, the soldiers would have caught them. They would have treated Carice like a prisoner, and she wasn't strong enough to endure captivity. He, himself, might be sentenced to death for desertion. And it would only endanger his sisters more, if they were still alive.

The soldiers stood back to let them pass, and when Raine reached the centre of the camp, he saw her father waiting. The man's expression was a blend of relief and fury.

Raine helped Carice dismount and walked forward with her hand in his. Her demeanour was stiff, her expression holding resignation. He didn't like the way she was staring into the fire as if her entire body had gone numb.

'Are you feeling all right?' he murmured against her ear.

'I am feeling betrayed.' Her answer was dull, like she didn't care if she lived or died.

He could say nothing to her, for it was the truth. But he squeezed her hand in silent apology.

When they stood before her father, she said, 'Raine de Garenne, this is my father, Brian Faoilin, chief of our clan.'

Raine met the man's gaze evenly and gave a nod of acknowledgment. He offered no fealty, and perhaps it was best if he did not speak at all.

But Brian Faoilin moved forward to embrace his daughter. A smile broke through his expression, for a moment, before he said, 'I am glad you are safe, Carice. Go to the litter and lie down while I speak with this man.'

Her father addressed her as if she were a dog, which Raine didn't like at all. To Carice, he said, 'It is your choice whether you wish to stay or go.'

'I'll stay.' She drew in the edges of her cloak and regarded her father. 'I suppose I deserve to know the plans for my future.'

'The plans have not changed. You already know that the High King's men came to escort you to your wedding. And this man slaughtered half of them.' Brian's face turned thunderous when he turned to Raine, speaking in the Norman tongue. 'What right have you to interfere? I should have you slain, here and now.'

Raine stood his ground, taking Carice's hand. 'I would not try it, were I you.' He rested his hand upon his own sword in a silent warning.

The Normans closed in around them, and his commander signalled for him to come forward. Raine didn't want to leave Carice, but he saw no alternative. He squeezed her palm again and in a low voice asked, 'Will you be all right?'

Her expression held sadness. 'I would have been all right if you'd kept your promise. What does it matter now?'

He deserved that, he knew. But after he left

her side, he glanced back to ensure that she was protected by her father. When he reached Sir Darren's side, the knight ordered, 'Walk with me.'

The man's expression was unreadable, and Raine couldn't tell what he was thinking. Darren led him to the outskirts of the camp, and then dismissed the sentries at the boundaries. 'I am glad you kept your word.'

'Did you think I wouldn't?'

His commander stared out into the darkness. 'You have been too eager to give your own orders instead of following mine.'

'I brought her here, as you commanded. And now, we must bring her to Tara.'

'You could have brought her to us sooner, had you taken her as a prisoner.'

Raine shook his head. 'She was far weaker than I thought. I managed to help her rebuild her strength enough to make it this far. But she is still unwell.'

His commander didn't disagree. 'Nonetheless, the High King wants his bride. And you will accompany her father to Tara, to ensure that she arrives there.'

Raine made no argument, for he fully intended to accompany Carice to Tara. Although she was upset and angry with him, he intended to make matters right between them.

Yet, now that their arrival was imminent, he couldn't stop thinking of Carice's prediction, that King Henry would never let his sisters go. The man had a violent temper, and anything might set him off.

What if Elise and Nicole were already dead? His mood darkened at the thought. Was it right to murder the High King, for a sovereign he no longer respected?

Sir Darren paused a moment and said, 'Do not forget your task, Raine. You seem to be wavering in your orders.'

'I haven't forgotten.' But he was trying to decide whether or not to go through with it. Carice had made him realise that the Normans were indeed expecting blind obedience. And the truth was, he wasn't like the other soldiers. He held no true loyalty to King Henry—not any more.

'I saw the way you were looking at Lady Carice. I warned you not to get too close to her.' Darren turned to face him. He studied Raine a moment, his eyes narrowed. 'You swived her, didn't you?'

The crude words ignited a rage within him.

His hands clenched and he turned on the man. 'Don't speak about her in that way.'

'You *did*.' A smile curled across the Norman's mouth. 'What do you suppose her father will say when he learns what you've done?'

Raine seized Darren's tunic and twisted the fabric. 'Don't.'

'Don't what? Tell the High King that you've defiled his bride? Tell her father that his daughter is no longer a virgin?'

Raine swung his fist at the man's jaw and sent Darren staggering. Blood trickled from his commander's lip, and his thin smile stretched. 'Perhaps I'll sample her for myself. Or I'll let our men have her. Unless you do as you're told.'

'I will slit your throat if you touch her.'

Darren unsheathed his own blade. 'I could have you killed right now for such a threat.' In the firelight, the iron gleamed. 'Your life belongs to me, de Garenne. You have no freedom, no will of your own. I *own* you.'

Raine gritted his teeth, knowing that the knight was trying to provoke him. And he'd already fallen into the trap, admitting how much Carice meant to him. They would use that against him now.

From behind him, two soldiers seized him.

He could have fought them off, but when he saw the look in his commander's eyes, he knew that Carice would suffer if he dared to disobey. It didn't matter that her father was here with his men. Brian Faoilin could not protect her from the Norman soldiers.

'Take him to the centre of the camp,' Sir Darren commanded. 'He will receive fifteen lashes for defiance.' He moved in closer, crossing his arms over his chest. 'I would have thought you'd learned to hold your temper, Raine.'

He said nothing, but let the men lead him away. He knew the whipping was meant to punish him for striking his commander, to remind him of his place. To break him.

But no amount of physical punishment could eradicate the fires of rebellion brewing inside.

They bound him to a post at the centre of the camp, baring his back before Normans and Irish alike. In the firelight, Carice saw the reddened flesh that had healed from the night he'd been trapped in the fire.

'What is happening to Raine?' She turned to her father, but Brian gave no answer. It seemed that he was glad of the punishment. She approached a soldier nearby and asked, 'Why is he being whipped?'

'He disobeyed our commander,' the man answered. And when Carice searched for a glimpse of Sir Darren, she saw that the man's face was bruised and bleeding. Why had they fought?

Her questions died away when the first lash struck Raine's back. A line of red marred his flesh, and she bit her lip hard, to prevent herself from crying out. A few of her father's men roared with approval, but the Normans remained silent.

The look on her father's face revealed his own satisfaction. Brian was revelling in the whipping, as if he blamed the man for her abduction. And she knew that she could show no emotion at all. No one could know that it felt as if *she* were the one enduring each lash. It took every last bit of inner strength to watch the leather bite into his skin, knowing the pain he was suffering.

Not a sound did he make throughout the whipping. Were it not for the blood dripping down to the snow, no one would think the lashing had any effect.

'Disobedience will not be tolerated from

any soldier,' the commander said, when it was finished. 'We will uphold our laws from every man.' With a silent gesture, he ordered Raine to be cut down.

His hands fell to his sides, but he did not lower his head with subservience. Instead, he turned in a slow circle, his gaze searching until he found her. And when he met her stricken gaze, she saw the apology in his eyes.

I am sorry for what I did to you.

He had accepted this punishment as his due, not only because he had disobeyed orders, but because it was his penance for delivering her to them. She pressed her fingertips to her lips, hating the thought of his suffering. But she forced herself to look at him, even though it tore her apart to see his wounds.

He *cared*. She knew that now, and he held regret for all that he had done. She only wished that he would change it somehow.

'I am glad to know that the Normans mete out justice where it is due,' Brian continued. 'Though I still believe de Garenne should be held accountable for the men he killed.' He led Carice away from the crowd, towards his own tent. She allowed it, because she knew she could not reveal any sympathy towards

Raine. It would only cause greater retribution against him.

'He was escorting me to Laochre,' she told her father. 'We were attacked, and he defended me from the High King's men.'

'They were with *my* men,' Brian corrected. 'You had no right to leave King Rory's men or our travelling party. I know you were trying to escape the marriage by taking sanctuary with the MacEgans.'

'I was, yes. But none of that matters anymore, does it?' She saw no point in trying to hide it. He had captured her now, and Raine had aided them. The thought wounded her, and she wondered if he regretted what he had done. Or if he would find a way to help her escape.

'I don't understand why you ever wanted to avoid the marriage,' her father insisted. 'How could you not wish to be High Queen of Éireann?'

Carice met his gaze and admitted, 'Because I am dying, Father. What kind of a High Queen could I ever be?'

'You've been ill, yes. But you look better.' Her father guided her inside his tent. There were furs set up to serve for bedding, and he brought her a thick crust of bread. 'Try to eat more. You must be hungry.'

She thought of Raine's suggestion, that it might be bread causing her illness. And though it was unusual, she didn't want to spend the night in pain if that were true. 'I will take meat if you have it. No bread.'

Her father shook his head. 'No. The healer said you should eat only bread until you've regained your strength.'

'I only felt worse when he was treating me. Let me eat what I want, Father.'

But Brian would not yield. He set the bread down upon a cloth and said, 'When you grow hungry enough, you'll eat.'

That wasn't true. Whether or not bread had anything to do with her illness, she needed her strength now. 'I am tired,' she told him. 'I would rest now.'

Her father's stern expression softened. 'I must speak with the commander, but I agree. You should sleep.' He paused a moment and added, 'And you should welcome the idea of this marriage, Carice. You will have every comfort, everything you've ever desired. More wealth than you could dream of.'

'That was never what I wanted,' she whispered. But he hadn't heard her. Already he was leaving the tent, and she overheard his promise to return after he'd spoken to Sir Darren.

She sat up, holding her knees against her chest. In the solitude of the tent, she released her tears, wishing she had not let her heart lead her astray. She had given everything to him, but it wasn't enough to change his mind. And although she knew Raine regretted lying with her, his punishment had brought the memory of that night to the forefront.

He had never wanted to take her innocence, but she had driven him to it. Any guilt from that night was hers to bear, not his. She didn't know what had prompted the fight between his commander and him, but she didn't doubt it involved her.

Her eyes burned with grief as she wondered what to do now. They would force her to travel to Tara, where she would have to wed the High King. She would endure a wedding night and an existence that would surely kill her.

When she opened her eyes, she saw the bread lying before her. Although she was hungry, the thought of food sickened her. Or perhaps it was grief at the thought of facing a torturous future without Raine. When she was with him, he had made her want so much more. He'd made her want to live.

And now that he had delivered her back into this prison, she felt so foolish for wanting to believe him.

'Carice.' A low voice came from outside the tent, and she saw the shadowed form of a man. It was Raine. He sat near to her but did not enter. His shoulders were hunched over as if he were holding back the pain of the whipping. Her heart bled for what he had endured, but she didn't want to see him now. If she did, her resolution would crumble into dust. Did he know how much power he held over her?

'What is it?' she asked dully.

'Are you alone?'

'Yes.' She didn't know what he wanted from her, but words would not heal the bruised feelings.

'I was ordered to kill the High King.' His words hung in the space like a blade poised to strike. Before she could speak, he continued. 'That was why I came to you. My commander thought that escorting you to Tara would grant me a way to get close to him.'

She could hardly believe what she was hearing. 'And you agreed to this?'

'For my sisters' sake, *oui*.'

There were no words she could say that would make this right. 'Is that who you are, then? A murderer?'

'My soul is damned, Carice. There is no redemption for me. Not after all that I've done.' His voice was rough and emotionless. 'But the night in your arms was more than ever deserved. I am sorry that I hurt you.'

She pressed her hands to her cheeks, searching for an answer. 'It didn't have to be that way between us.'

'You gave me a priceless gift, one I will never forget. And I swear to you that, despite this journey, I will guard you with my life.'

'But you're still going to bring me to him, aren't you?'

He fell silent for a moment and admitted, 'I have no choice, Carice.'

And with that, he left her alone.

They arrived at Tara the following night, a day after the Feast of Imbolc. Sir Darren gave orders for his men to make camp half a mile away from the High King's lands while he ordered Raine to accompany him to the gates. They walked in silence through the darkness, but with each step, Raine felt as if it were a pathway to Hades.

The lash marks upon his back burned with the reminder that he was a slave to these orders. He had no freedom at all, and his commander would tolerate no disobedience. But he refused to apologise for striking at Sir Darren. He wasn't sorry at all for defending Carice's honour, and the knight knew it.

But he was sorry for having to use her to get close to the High King. With every hour that passed, he found himself questioning his orders. Even if he did bring down the Ard-Righ, he would likely be caught and killed. And then what would happen to his sisters? He hardly trusted the king to free them.

When they were close enough to see the torches surrounding Tara, it was clear that the number of guards had been doubled. Every man was on alert, and Darren turned grim. 'Something must have happened before we arrived. We were supposed to be here at Imbolc. I didn't think one day would matter, but I was wrong.' His commander's mood had darkened, and he appeared on edge.

'Why? What was meant to happen at Imbolc?' Raine didn't understand why the delay had any bearing upon their plans, but Darren appeared furious.

'We had men hidden among the High King's soldiers. One of the Irish kings was our ally, and he was going to help us infiltrate the fortress. If the Ard-Righ has increased his forces, then our allies must be dead or imprisoned.'

The knight began pacing, and he glared at Raine. 'We cannot take our soldiers anywhere near the fortress. They would be accused of plotting with the others. You must go alone with Lady Carice and her father's men. I will join you later, but you must pretend to be Irish.'

Which meant that his beliefs were indeed accurate—the Norman army would give Raine no support at all. He would have to kill the High King and escape captivity on his own.

Or he could attempt to get Carice out and disappear with her. His mind seized upon that hope, and he wondered if it was even possible. For so long, he had obeyed orders that had accomplished nothing. Was it not better to escape this life and go in search of his sisters?

'Well?' his commander prompted. 'Can you disguise yourself among them?'

Raine shrugged. 'It's possible. But what if

Brian Faoilin will not allow me to accompany them inside?'

'That choice is not his to make,' Darren answered. 'You brought his daughter back to her rightful place. I already spoke with him at length last night. He knows that there is unrest between both sides, but so long as his daughter becomes queen, he cares not what happens to Rory Ó Connor.'

'And is that your intention? That Lady Carice will become High Queen through her marriage?'

Sir Darren didn't answer. The stoic look on his face made it clear that he had little interest in Carice's welfare. 'The marriage will take place, as planned. You will attend the festivities in secret and kill the High King during the feast. Do it quickly and get out.'

'What about her?'

Darren sent him a sly look. 'If you move swiftly, they might accuse her of killing her husband. And then you'll be free.'

The man's utter lack of emotion revealed that all he cared about was ending the life of Rory Ó Connor. Nothing else mattered to him, and it didn't concern him if Carice was harmed in the attempt.

Raine held fast to his silence, for if he dared to voice his true feelings, he would strike Darren down. And if he laid a hand upon his commander, the man would try to kill him. He forced himself to remain cold as frost, to hold back his temper and concentrate on protecting Carice from this marriage.

She had accused him of becoming a murderer.

It's what you are, his inner voice reminded him. *You will never be forgiven for your past sins. But do this, and your sisters will be free.*

Would they? He was beginning to have his doubts. Darren had said it was possible, but that meant nothing without the king's approval.

They began the walk back towards the camp, but Raine wasn't listening to his commander's instructions. Something about him hiding among Brian Faoilin's men and then separating himself after the wedding.

His mind sharpened as he thought of stealing the bride from her own wedding and running away with her. Carice didn't want to wed the High King, and he'd shattered her hopes when he'd brought her here. But it wasn't over yet. He could change everything. The only remaining question was the fate of his sisters.

He didn't know where they were now, but he intended to find out.

They reached the Norman camp, and he stopped Darren, needing those answers. 'Where are Nicole and Elise now?'

Impatience crossed over the knight's face. 'They are not my concern. Your orders are to end Rory Ó Connor's reign. If you succeed in this, you may gain King Henry's favour, and ask him yourself.'

'Are they even alive?' he prompted.

Darren moved forward swiftly, unsheathing his dagger. 'You have your orders, and you must obey them if you want to live.' The man's voice grew agitated, filled with distrust.

'The High King's men may kill me during the attempt,' he pointed out.

'Have you changed your mind?' Sir Darren demanded. 'Tell me now if you intend to disobey orders, and I promise you, your sisters will pay the price for your cowardice. I can easily find someone else to complete the task. Rory Ó Connor will not live beyond another night.'

Raine gave no reaction, and no longer did he care. It was becoming more and more clear that he was meant to be nothing more than a killer. The Normans would do naught to protect him, and even if he succeeded, the king might punish him as an example.

He believed that with all his being. Instead of killing Rory Ó Connor, his time was better spent in trying to help Carice escape. He should have listened to her when she'd pleaded with him to take her west. But it wasn't too late—at least, not yet.

All he had to do was keep her from the wedding.

They rode through the gates of Tara the next morning. Her father led the way, and Carice followed behind him. She wore an emerald gown heavily embroidered with gold thread, and her father had given her golden rings and a ruby-studded torque for her throat. The tangible signs of wealth proclaimed her status, but the heavy jewellery only felt like chains to bind her to an unwanted marriage.

She could not run any longer. Instead, she planned to speak privately with the High King and seek an end to the betrothal. Perhaps he would listen, if she could make him see reason.

Raine had disguised himself as one of her father's men, and the Norman commander had done the same. Though she kept her posture straight, inwardly, she was terrified. She knew his true purpose here, and it bothered her deeply that he intended to go through with this. When she glanced behind at him, his face was masked like stone.

Inside the grounds of Tara, she searched for a glimpse of her brother Killian or Lady Taryn. Surely if they were here, they would come to greet her, but there was no sign of either of them. A grain of worry took hold inside her, and she hoped that they were all right.

The Rath-na-Rígh was a large fortification with two walls surrounding the structure and a deep ditch running between them. Several outbuildings were set up within the space, with hearth fires and armed soldiers everywhere. Carice didn't understand what had happened, but the tension within the Ard-Rígh's fortress was palpable. The men were pacing, some with their hands resting upon the hilts of their weapons, while others stared at her with open suspicion.

'Why are they staring at us?' she murmured to her father.

'I don't know. But I suspect there was an attack. Perhaps it involved Lady Taryn's father.'

She hoped not. But the absence of Killian

and Lady Taryn only heightened her anxiety. Carice continued riding through the grounds until they reached the banqueting hall. Raine helped her dismount from her horse, his touch gentle upon her waist. He squeezed her hands slightly, as if to reassure her, but she could not stop her fears. He kept back a slight distance and gave her horse over to one of the other men while he walked behind her. He was to act as her personal guard, it seemed.

Brian led her inside while Raine continued to shadow her. She felt his presence, and with every step, Carice worried for his sake. She wanted to beg Raine to abandon this task and leave Tara. But he wouldn't. He had sworn to do anything to free his sisters, and that meant obeying his orders. And God help her, she didn't want him to die.

The Ard-Righ was waiting for them at the far end of the banqueting hall. The High King was nearly the same age as her father, with dark hair tinted grey, a beard edging his jaw line, and silver eyes that were the same as Killian's. Rory Ó Connor didn't rise from his place, nor did he seem interested in her at all. Instead, he appeared annoyed with her father. 'I see you found my lost bride.'

The High King's gaze flickered over Carice for a moment, but there was no welcome in his eyes—only a cold resentment. She resisted the urge to take a step backwards.

'I am glad to present you with my daughter, Carice Faoilin,' Brian said, holding her hand and nudging her forward. 'She has been ill as of late, but now she is prepared to become your bride as we agreed.'

Carice wanted to argue, but knew that a public disagreement would not serve her purpose. It was better not to draw any attention yet.

The king's expression didn't shift at all. 'That is not what Killian told me.' He turned back to Brian. 'He claimed that Carice wanted no part of this marriage.'

She felt a sudden thread of hope. So her brother *had* intervened on her behalf.

Her father blanched. 'That isn't true at all. She was simply unable to travel. Why you would believe his lies is simply—'

'You dare to call my son a liar?' The High King moved forward, his gaze sharpened upon Brian. 'I understand that you treated Killian like a slave, all these years.'

Carice resisted the urge to smile. For the first time, she found herself approving of the High

King. At least *he* honoured her brother in the manner he deserved.

Her father's face turned crimson, and blurted out, 'Killian was one of your bastard sons, yes, but I never mistreated him.'

Carice crossed her arms and raised an eyebrow at her father. Now those were the true lies. He'd forced her brother to sleep in the stables among the dogs.

'Killian is not a bastard,' Rory corrected. 'He is my legitimate son.'

Her smile widened, and she beamed at the Ard-Righ, even as she delighted in her father's discomfort. Brian deserved it for his mistreatment of Killian. But even more wonderful was recognising that her brother now had the High King's support. 'Where is Killian now?'

Rory Ó Connor sent her a sharp look. 'You ought to keep a respectful silence, Lady Carice, about a conversation that does not concern you.'

His response irritated her, for he was treating her like a recalcitrant child. Even so, she bit back her annoyance, since she needed his cooperation in ending the betrothal. Carice murmured, 'Forgive me, Your Grace.' She lowered her head in deference and added, 'I was merely concerned for Killian, since we were friends as children. I thought of him as my brother.'

The Ard-Righ sent her an annoyed look. 'Killian has returned to Ossoria with the Lady Taryn, to bury her father.'

Carice touched her fingertips to her lips. Taryn had hoped to save her father's life, and she didn't dare ask what had happened. But clearly something had gone very wrong.

'Killian will return to Tara within a few days,' the High King finished. 'You may see him then.'

If I am still here, she thought. But Carice inclined her head in a nod of acknowledgment. 'Thank you, Your Grace.'

The Ard-Righ signalled for one of his servants to come forward. 'Take my bride back to our chambers. I will speak to her there later.'

'And what of the wedding, Your Grace?' Brian asked. 'Should I send Carice's ladies to help prepare her?'

'I have not yet decided whether she will become my queen. That is for me to determine, after I speak with her. But you may send her belongings.'

Carice breathed a little easier, for it did not seem that Rory was eager to wed her either. It might be her saving grace, a means of avoiding this union.

She picked up the hem of her gown, walking towards the waiting servant. And when she took one last look at Raine, his expression was unreadable. For all she knew, he might be ready to bury his sword in the Ard-Righ's heart.

Don't do this, she pleaded in silence. But he would not meet her gaze.

When the servant led her inside the king's private chambers, Carice sat down and stared at the wall. God help her, she didn't know what to do now. The Ard-Righ would decide whether or not to move forward with the marriage. She prayed he would change his mind.

If not, she could make herself physically ill, but it would only delay the inevitable. Publicly refusing the High King was unthinkable—he would never tolerate such defiance. She knew the stories of Rory's cruelty. He had ordered his own brother blinded in order to seize the throne of Connacht—she couldn't imagine what he would do to her if she denied him.

Her hands were shaking, and she heard the sound of movement behind her. Undoubtedly it was her ladies and a few servants who were bringing her belongings. But then she noticed the heavier sound of a man's footsteps. When she turned around, she saw the Norman commander, Sir Darren.

Though he was not wearing the chain mail and conical helm she was accustomed to seeing, he still moved like a soldier instead of a servant. He set down the tray he'd been holding, that contained wine and two silver goblets. The hardened glint in his eyes warned her to be careful of what she said.

'You think to dissuade Raine from his duty, but it will not happen.' He crossed his arms and regarded her. 'You might have been a diversion for him, but he cannot forget where his loyalties lie.'

'If that were true, you would not waste time speaking with me,' Carice countered. 'And I hope that he *is* reconsidering this task. It isn't right.'

'I would think you'd be grateful for our interference,' the knight said. 'Especially since you stand to benefit the most.'

He was wrong in that. Though she didn't want to wed the Ard-Righ, there were many ways to avoid her wedding without Raine becoming a murderer. 'I would not wish death upon any man. And I do not believe Raine would do such a thing.'

Darren smiled slowly. 'Do you remember the MacEgans who gave you shelter at Laochre?' She gave a nod before he continued. 'Raine was there when we attacked them on the peninsula. He killed their kinsmen in that battle, years ago.' At that revelation, he turned serious. 'Believe me when I say that Raine cares about nothing except his orders. He will fulfil them without question.'

Her heart grew cold at that, for Raine had never mentioned such a thing. He had accepted help from the MacEgans, and not once had he mentioned the battle. Unless that was another reason why he'd accepted the imprisonment— out of remorse?

Carice pushed back the questions, knowing that Sir Darren was planting doubts within her mind. 'I don't want to hear any more,' she whispered. 'Please leave.'

He didn't move. 'You should know that the Norman army attacked the High King, only a day ago. They failed in the attempt, and the Irish traitor, King Devlin of Ossoria, was killed.'

Her blood ran cold at the mention of Lady

Taryn's father. 'You had men already here, didn't you?' She was beginning to realise that the Normans would stop at nothing to achieve their goals.

'We did. And while they might be dead now, nothing has changed. Raine has his orders, and he must obey.' He crossed towards her and fingered a lock of her hair. 'Despite what you believe, he never intended to turn away from his duty.'

'Do not touch me,' she whispered, rising to her feet.

But Sir Darren only smiled. 'Interfere with Raine's orders, and you will get him killed. I came only to warn you.' He grazed his knuckles across her cheek, and the caress made her skin crawl.

Then he stepped back and walked towards a pitcher of wine and two goblets. He poured two cups of wine and sent her a faint smile. Lifting the silver goblet, he offered a mock salute. 'To your wedding, Lady Carice. You may want to offer wine to the High King when you speak with him. It will grant you courage.'

She closed her eyes and waited until he left. Her ladies came in afterwards, and from their expressions, she suspected that Darren had warned them to stay outside.

'Are you well, my lady?' one asked.

Carice gave a faint nod, though she was so afraid of what would happen now. Rory Ó Connor was coming to speak with her, and she wanted to be truthful with him. Were he any other man, she would simply admit that she had never wanted the marriage. Yet, it was not that easy.

Her ladies busied themselves with combing her hair and helping her wash off the dust of travelling. A few moments later, Raine entered her chamber. He was carrying one of her trunks, and he set it down in one corner. But instead of leaving, he remained standing.

The conversation of her ladies died down, and they waited for her to give orders. Carice couldn't bring herself to speak, for the sight of Raine filled her with such grief. She had given this man her heart, and yet she felt as if she didn't know him at all. He was a warrior, a man who struck down his enemies without mercy.

But he was also a man who had taken such care of her, holding her at night and warming her body with his own. She didn't want to believe that he could be a murderer.

'You shouldn't have come,' she said. 'The Ard-Righ will be here soon.'

'I know.' He sent a look towards her ladies, and they retreated to the far end of the room. A sudden tremor of apprehension crossed over her when she thought of the true reason why he might have come.

'Don't,' she warned. 'Don't even think of it.' She was so afraid he would kill Rory Ó Connor, the moment the High King entered her chamber.

Raine closed the distance between them. 'I've made many mistakes, Carice. But I will make this right again. I will free you from this marriage, I swear it.'

'No.' She took a step back from him. If she allowed him to interfere, he would try to fight this battle for her—and he would lose his life in the attempt. 'I will face the Ard-Righ myself and tell him. It's time for me to stop running.'

'He won't let you go.'

She knew that, but she was tired of behaving like a coward. 'I will be honest with him when we are alone and ask him to release me from the betrothal agreement.' The more she thought of it, the more she realised that this was the only solution. If she was forthright with the High King and gave him the chance to spurn her first, he might agree to end their arrangement. And if he insisted upon the marriage, she would have no choice but to face that battle when it came.

She was weary of living her life being afraid. It was time to stand up for what she wanted, no matter the consequences.

'And if he refuses to end it?' Raine asked. 'Do you think I'll allow him to force you into a wedding you don't want?' He dropped his voice low so that the maids would not overhear. 'Or a wedding night?'

A knot formed within her throat, but she met his green eyes with sadness. 'You gave me up when you brought me here, Raine. You already showed me that you believe in duty more than anything you might feel for me.'

There was no expression on his face at all, no sign of emotion. She wanted him to deny it, to say that he did love her. But his silence was the answer that hurt the most.

And though her pride was shattering into pieces, Carice moved across the room and opened the door. 'I will face my own demons without you.'

He didn't protest, but he stared into her eyes. 'Is that what you want? For me to let you go?'

With a heavy heart, she nodded. 'It is.'

Although her eyes burned from unshed tears, she forced herself to close the door behind him. Her fingers were shaking, and she reached for the silver goblet of wine to steady her nerves. The High King would be here soon, and she had to remain strong in her refusal. Even if he grew enraged, she would not waver.

Carice tasted the sweet wine, and took a swallow to fortify herself. Then another.

Her heartbeat seemed to quicken, and there was a rushing sound in her ears. She closed her eyes when the outside sunlight seemed to bother her. A strange sensation ran over her senses, and her throat grew dry, her stomach twisting with pain. But this was a very different pain, one she had never felt before. Her skin grew sensitive, prickling with the slightest touch. It was not the familiar illness at all.

And when the sharp stabbing pains caught her stomach, she realised the truth. This was poison.

The silver goblet fell from her fingertips, the wine spilling everywhere as she fought to remain conscious.

I don't want to die. She'd mistakenly believed that she was prepared for the worst, that she could face the end with dignity when it came. But it wasn't true at all.

She gasped for air, terrified of the darkness that beckoned.

Her last thought was of Raine and how she wished she could have told him the feelings she'd held in her heart. But now, he would never know.

Chapter Ten

Raine heard the sound of women screaming, and he hurried back to the chamber. A dark premonition passed over him, that something had happened to Carice. One of her maids bolted from the room and confirmed his fears, 'We need a healer. My lady is ill.'

But an ordinary illness wouldn't cause the women to scream. Something was terribly wrong.

'Go and fetch someone,' Raine commanded the maid. 'I will stay with Lady Carice.'

When he entered the bedchamber, he found the other maid sitting on the floor beside Carice's fallen body. She was so still, she looked as if death had already claimed her. His blood numbed within his veins, and Raine could hardly grasp what had happened.

'The wine,' the maid wept. 'I think the wine made her sick.'

He saw the silver goblet then, along with the pool of red wine. Outwardly, it didn't appear any different from other wine, but he couldn't know what was in it.

'Where did this wine come from?' he demanded.

The maid shrugged. 'One of the men who joined our travelling party this morning. He brought in the wine and the goblets. I thought he was your companion.'

The numbness turned from ice into hot rage. She had to be speaking of Sir Darren. And now their earlier conversation made sense. Somehow, the Norman commander had tampered with the wine, knowing that the High King would come to visit Carice. It was a means of ensuring the man's death if Raine failed in his duties.

And Darren wouldn't care if Carice drank it, too. The knight wanted Rory Ó Connor dead above all else.

Raine knelt beside Carice and lifted her into his arms. Her complexion was grey, and when he touched her throat, her pulse beat swiftly.

'Don't give up,' he pleaded. 'Stay with me, Carice.'

When the maid continued weeping loudly, Raine ordered her to go and find someone to help them. Crying wasn't going to save anyone, and he wasn't about to leave Carice's side.

He cradled her limp form in his arms, feeling as though someone were tearing his heart out of his chest. He didn't care that she had ordered him to go. Earlier, he had been so troubled about how to get her away from Tara, he'd not known how to answer her questions. Words weren't his strength—he far preferred actions. And regardless of what Carice had demanded, he would never leave her again.

Her breathing was laboured, and he stroked back her hair. For a brief moment, her eyelids flickered open, and her pupils were dilated. 'Fight for me, *chérie*. Don't leave.' Though he couldn't know if she understood his words, he pressed his face against hers. 'Would that I could take your place.'

It was true. If he had the choice to surrender his life and give hers back, he would do it without hesitation. Her eyes closed, and his chest constricted. If God was punishing him for his past sins, there could be no greater penance than to lose this woman. She had made him realise what it meant to live.

As he held her in his arms, he prayed that somehow she could be saved. He continued talking to her, stroking her hair and begging for her to keep breathing.

The chamber door opened, and he was dimly aware that the healer had arrived. 'Step back so I may look at her,' the old woman demanded.

But Raine couldn't bring himself to let go of Carice. It felt as if she were clinging to a fragile thread of life, and if he abandoned her now, she might surrender to death.

'We believe someone poisoned the wine,' the maid said.

The healer peered into the ewer and poured some of the liquid into another goblet. She held up a few crushed berries, and her face turned serious. 'Someone put deadly nightshade into the wine. I cannot tell if it was a root infusion or merely these crushed berries, but I may not be able to save her.'

'Try,' Raine insisted. He gently laid Carice upon the bed and held her hand while he urged the healer, 'Give her medicines or a tea—anything you have to stop the poison.'

The older woman gave orders for one of the

maids to fetch vinegar and boiling water. 'I will see what I can get her to drink, but she is in God's hands now.'

He sat beside Carice on the bed, gripping her hand as if he could hold her to him. His mind and body had gone numb while the healer steeped herbs he didn't recognise.

Anger was the only emotion that kept him from breaking down. Whether Sir Darren had intended the poison for the High King or for Carice didn't matter. If she did not survive, Raine wouldn't hesitate to kill Darren for what he had done.

Rage flooded through him, but he could not leave Carice. There would be time to enact vengeance against the Norman knight.

The healer brought over the tea to Carice, and Raine helped to hold her up. He caught the sharp tang of vinegar, and realised that she had steeped the herbs with vinegar and hot water. Most of it dribbled from Carice's mouth, but there was nothing else they could do.

'You must save her,' he commanded the healer. 'She cannot die.'

The older woman's face turned sympathetic. 'If she drinks this, there is a chance it might stop the poison. But I cannot force her to take it.'

'Give it to me.' He took the cup and coaxed Carice's lips open, slowly pouring it into her mouth. The strong potion made his eyes water, and he questioned whether this would work at all. Her colour had gone grey, and she was hardly responsive. But he continued talking to her, trying to get her to drink.

Never in his life had he felt so helpless. This woman meant everything to him, and if she died, there would be nothing left of his miserable soul.

'Stay with me,' he whispered to Carice, setting down the cup when it was empty. He pressed his face against hers, cradling her body in his arms.

Before long, several guards entered, along with the High King. Though Raine was well aware of how compromising it appeared, he wasn't about to let go of Carice. His pulse tightened within him, and when one of the men seized him, he swung out, his fist colliding with the man's jaw.

'Let go of the king's bride,' another insisted.

He ignored the command, shielding Carice's body with his own. Another tried to pull him off, but he twisted, shoving the man away. He fought like a man possessed, and none of the men succeeded in separating him from Carice.

Rory Ó Connor strode into the room behind them, and his face turned purple as he surveyed Raine holding her. 'What have you done to my bride?'

'I tried to save her,' he shot back. He tried to bring out the right Irish words, but despair tangled them up in his mind.

It was the healer who spoke to the High King and explained, 'Someone tried to poison both of you.'

'Sir Darren de Carleigh,' Raine added, hoping they would find the man and imprison him.

'That does not explain why you were holding my bride in such an intimate way,' the Ard-Righ said quietly. 'Or were you the reason why she tried to delay our wedding?'

Before he could answer, Brian Faoilin stormed in. 'What has happened to my daughter?' When he spied Carice, his face went white with fear. 'Let her go.'

Raine ignored the command, tightening his grip. At his refusal, Brian turned back to the High King. 'This man is not Irish. He tried to hide himself among my men, but he is one of the Normans.'

It didn't surprise him that Brian would cast blame upon him. But right now, Raine's mind was blurred with his own fear that Carice would not survive. He switched into his own language. 'I would die before harming your daughter. This was not my doing.'

The High King's men closed in on him, and this time, he could not fight them off. They dragged him away from Carice, and the Ard-Righ commanded, 'Question him. Find out what he knows.'

If he allowed them to take him captive, they would torture him for information. But if he ran, it would make him appear guilty. He could slip away and save his own life…but he would never see Carice again.

He couldn't leave Tara—not for any reason. Even if she died, he wanted to be the last man who held her. Carice had given him a reason to fight, and in her arms, he'd found the missing piece of himself. No longer would he punish himself, believing himself unworthy of love or happiness. She deserved better than this, and he would do whatever he could to bring her back to freedom. Even if it meant sacrificing his own life.

Raine struggled hard against the men who

held him, using every last ounce of strength he possessed. He slipped free of their grasp, but at the last moment, one of the soldiers struck a blow across his back. The agonising pain against his lash wounds was enough to bring him to his knees.

His last thought before they took him was a prayer for Carice: *Please, let her live.*

They chained him inside a prison built upon a hillside. Surrounded by earth and darkness, it felt like a grave. Every hour, Raine sank deeper into despondency. He wondered if Carice was still alive, and if the healer had managed to save her.

If she died, he no longer cared. He would not raise weapons against the High King, nor would he obey any orders at all. And if somehow, by the Grace of God, he managed to escape Tara, he would go back to England and find his sisters.

He had been in Ireland for two years, unable to leave these shores. The only leave he'd ever been granted was when he'd buried the monks. And now he realised that the Norman soldiers had followed him even then. His life had never been his own because he'd been imprisoned by empty promises.

No longer.

Raine steeled himself against a future he didn't want to face, but one truth was stronger than grief—he would break free of the Norman army or die in the effort.

He leaned against the cold dirt, drawing his knees up as he grieved for Carice. Her beauty haunted him, as did the memory of her smile. He gave himself over to the visions, letting them pull him back from the horrors of the present.

But then the door swung open, and moonlight filled up the small space. Raine didn't move, but he stilled at the sight of Sir Darren. Instead of the familiar violent rage, a slow burn of fury filled him up from within. No longer did he feel the frigid cold. An inner fire of hatred filled every part of him, and he had no doubt that Darren would no longer be breathing when this night was over.

Neither spoke, and Raine waited, like a predator stalking its prey. At last, the knight said, 'Well? Aren't you wondering if she's still alive?'

If he dared to speak, the man would only taunt him. And so, he held his silence, knowing that it would anger the knight.

'If you'd rather not know, then I will take my leave. You can stay here until they return to question you.'

Raine didn't rise to the bait. *Come closer,* he bade the knight. He clenched the loose chains, willing the man to obey.

'Or am I wrong?' Darren moved inside the space. 'Is it tormenting you as you wonder what happened? The way you've been tormented about your sisters all these years.'

The embers of rage burned hotter, but Raine forced himself to wait. 'They're dead, aren't they? Nicole and Elise.'

'You'd like to know, wouldn't you?'

The taunt ignited his fury. Raine lunged at the man and bound the chains around Darren's throat, shutting off the man's air.

'You're going to die for what you did,' he said, tightening his grip while Darren clawed to escape. 'Not only for poisoning Carice, but for taking my sisters captive.' He squeezed tighter, shoving the man to the ground. 'I hope you burn in hell.'

He felt no remorse, nothing except fiery vengeance. And when the Irish soldiers invaded the space, a blow struck him across the head. Raine dropped to his knees, blood running down into his eyes.

Dizziness roared through him, and as they dragged Darren's fallen body, he could only hope that he'd succeeded in killing his commander.

Her entire body ached. Carice couldn't move, but she managed to open her eyes. The healer was sitting beside her, and the old woman's face held a warm smile. 'There now. Drink this, and it will help.'

She couldn't even lift her head. When she tried to speak, no words came out, but the healer supported her and helped her sit. 'You've had quite a day, haven't you? But you survived. It's lucky you didn't drink more of the wine. If you'd finished the goblet, you would be dead.'

She winced as the woman placed a hot cup of tea to her lips. But instead of the horrid brew that had made her retch, this was chamomile, sweetened with honey. It soothed her raw throat, and she sipped it slowly.

Where is Raine? she wanted to ask, but her voice wouldn't speak. She tried again but could only mouth the words.

The old woman's expression turned serious.

'I suppose you're asking about the man who was holding you.'

She managed a nod. But when the healer answered, there was no only resignation in her tone. 'I fear they've taken him in chains. The High King was very angry to find him in your chamber.'

Undoubtedly the king blamed Raine for what had happened. And if she didn't rise from this bed and face the Ard-Righ, he might die.

'Rest now,' the healer urged her. 'Sleep will do you the most good in regaining your strength.'

But there was no time for that. She needed to confront the High King and explain who was truly at fault. They needed to find Sir Darren, though she suspected the man had hidden himself somewhere.

When she tried to swing her legs to the side of the bed, the weakness in her body overcame her. Even the effort to raise her head was more than she could manage. How was it even possible to help Raine? Walking was beyond her abilities.

With great effort, she tried again to speak. 'I need…'

The words came out more of a rough growl

than her natural voice, but she pressed on. 'I must speak with the Ard-Righ. Will he…come and listen to what I have to say?'

The older woman's face turned grim. 'I fear not. He knows that the poison was meant for him. The brehons will hold a trial and determine if you or the other man are guilty of plotting against him.'

'Guilty of what? I've done nothing wrong.' She had never even considered trying to harm the High King.

'We know you were not responsible for the poison, for you drank it. But as for the other man…' The healer's voice trailed off as she shook her head. 'Too many people saw him embracing you. They might accuse you of infidelity to the Ard-Righ.'

Carice was about to argue again, but the old woman cut her off. 'If they were to examine you, would you still be a virgin?'

The rising fear took hold, and Carice gave no answer. No, she was not. But the healer offered her more tea and reassured her, 'You may be found innocent, Lady Carice. After all, many could also say that you did not ask to be in the man's embrace. You were hardly awake while you were suffering from the poisoning.' She held the cup and added, 'If you deny knowing him, no one would lay the blame at your feet.'

But Carice knew that if she denied it, Raine would suffer tenfold. Even if it was proven that he'd played no part in the poison, they had both betrayed the High King. She had broken her betrothal, giving her innocence to a man who was not her husband. For that alone, the Ard-Righ had the right to punish her. A betrothal was nearly a marriage though the vows were not yet given.

Carice didn't know if it was possible to save both of their lives, but she had to try. No matter what her body had suffered, she could not lie here and wait for decisions to be made. She took a deep swallow of the honey chamomile tea, finishing the cup. If it would help her voice return, she would continue drinking. The heat seemed to soothe her throat.

'Will you send my father to me?' she managed.

The healer nodded. 'Of course. He has been keeping vigil outside your door. I will bring him inside now, if you feel you have the strength.'

Carice lay back against the pillow, wondering if it was possible to ally with Brian. Her father's ambitions had led him this far, and she knew he would do nothing to help end her betrothal. But perhaps there was a way to save Raine's life.

When Brian entered the room, he appeared pale. He crossed over to her bedside and sat down, taking her hand. 'Thank God you're alive.'

In his tone, she heard the relief, and the affection. Despite everything, her father did love her. He squeezed her palm and admitted, 'I didn't know if you would survive.'

'Neither did I.' Carice held his hand and braved a smile. 'I am glad you are here.' And she was. Although she and Brian had never been close, she saw a break in his tight composure. His blue eyes held worry and traces of fear.

'Will you be all right?' He leaned over to stroke her hair. The gentle caress warmed her heart, and in his shadowed sorrow, she found herself wanting to mend the differences between them.

'I think so.' She caught his hand again and said quietly, 'But I do need your help. Now, more than ever.'

At that, Brian's expression turned guarded. 'What is it you want?'

She chose her words carefully. 'I need to

speak with the Ard-Righ. Can you bring me to him? I haven't the strength to walk.'

Her father started to refuse. 'Rory is very angry right now. This is not a good time to interfere.'

She knew that. But she would face the strongest storm if it meant saving Raine's life. 'I know. But I need the High King to know the truth about what happened.'

'Believe me when I say it is best if you remain here. Let them hold their trial and stay away. The Norman will bear whatever punishment you might have had.'

She knew he was only trying to protect her, but letting Raine take all the blame was unthinkable. 'No. There should be no punishment, for we did nothing wrong.'

'Didn't you?' The knowing tone in her father's voice made her wary. She didn't want to meet his stare, afraid he would guess the truth.

Instead, she changed the subject. 'When you married my mother, did you love her?'

The question caught Brian unawares, and he frowned. 'Not at first. She was beautiful, and the union brought our two clans together.' He studied her and added, 'You look very much like her. Especially now.'

'I don't remember her any more.' She had only been three years old when her mother had died in childbirth. 'Sometimes I wish I had even one memory.'

'She wanted sons,' her father said. 'She miscarried several children, and because of it, you were her treasure.'

She risked a smile at him. 'And yours?'

'And mine,' he agreed. 'But I did love your mother in the end. I thought of remarrying, but I couldn't quite bring myself to do so.'

With that, Carice pressed, 'When you love someone, you give away a piece of your heart. And you can never quite get it back.'

He understood, then, what she was saying. 'Carice, don't endanger yourself by asking for something you cannot have.' His gaze turned troubled, and he added, 'For your sake, the High King must never know. I saw the way the Norman was embracing you. If Rory learned of it—'

'Raine cares about me,' Carice said. 'And I have grown to love him.' Though she had nearly succumbed to the hand of Death, Raine's pleading words had bound her to him. He'd given her a reason to fight, and she had battled for each breath. 'But that is not why I wish to speak with the High King.'

Brian waited for her to continue, and she said, 'I know I sought to end this betrothal. I never wanted to wed the High King, though you went to a lot of trouble to arrange it.' She steadied herself and said, 'But I am willing to consider it now.'

His eyes softened, and he questioned, 'And why is that?'

'Because I want to save Raine's life. And I will agree to wed the High King if they let him go.' Inwardly, her heart was bruised and broken. She wanted to be with Raine, to love him freely and enjoy whatever time they had together. But she also knew that Rory Ó Connor was not about to forgive the insult of another man coveting his bride. He would have Raine killed or maimed as an example. And she would do anything to stop that from happening. Even if it meant giving him up to save his life.

At that, her father turned solemn. 'The Ard Rígh is not going to forgive a Norman soldier. Especially when others saw him embracing you.'

'Raine was only trying to help me when I was poisoned,' Carice interrupted. 'And only a few people saw it. I can meet with the High

King in private to explain what happened, but it must be done before Raine is harmed.'

Brian let out a sigh and shook his head. 'All your life, you have been a strong-willed daughter. What makes you believe you can convince the High King to obey your wishes?' But despite his words, he lifted her into his arms.

She sent him a grateful smile, though. 'He may not. But I will do what I can.'

Her father began walking from the chamber, carrying her outside towards the banqueting hall. 'Carice, why would you give your heart to a man unworthy of it? You could wed any man in Éireann that you wanted. Why a Norman soldier?'

'Because he saw me as a woman to be loved, not a possession to own. He took care of me and made me feel beloved. And that is all I ever wanted.'

Her father's mood darkened. 'Do not tell the High King any of this, Carice. He is not a forgiving man. And if he believes you betrayed him with a Norman, it is not only Raine's life that is in danger. It is also yours.'

The flare of torches hurt his eyes after being imprisoned in darkness. Raine squinted as he was led forward into a meadow clearing. The High King, Rory O'Connor, sat upon a raised platform, while the chief poet remained beside him. Several men were seated in a row nearby, and he realised that these were the brehons, the men who would place judgment upon him.

Because he was Norman, he could sense their hatred and distrust. And while he knew that it was common for men to receive an advocate to speak on their behalf, no one volunteered to defend him.

The first witness was brought forth, and Raine recognised the maid who had attended Carice. They questioned her about the poison, and she shook her head, denying that he was involved. The second maid agreed, and both admitted that the wine had been brought in by another man.

The advocate changed the questioning and asked, 'Do you deny that Raine de Garenne was seen embracing the High King's bride?'

The maid paled but shook her head. 'I do not deny it.'

The first maid agreed, as well, though a flush came over her face. They had witnessed him holding on to Carice, begging for her to stay with him.

Raine kept his face impassive, uncertain of why these questions were being raised. He did not know the Irish system of justice, but he understood the tenuous nature of his freedom.

'Would you agree that de Garenne had prior knowledge of the High King's betrothed?' the advocate pressed.

Before the maids could answer, there was a rippling of conversation through the crowd. Raine turned and saw Brian Faoilin carrying Carice towards the High King. Her eyes were open, and though her complexion held a deep pallor, she was alive and breathing.

Thank God. It took an effort not to fall to his knees. The sight of her filled him with such hope, Raine could not speak a single word. Only prayers of thanks came to his lips, and he lowered his head.

The High King looked irritated at Carice's arrival. 'Why did you bring your daughter to this trial?' he demanded of Brian.

'I brought her because she wishes to speak to you, Your Grace. And because she lacks the strength to walk.'

A sudden apprehension gripped Raine, for whatever had brought Carice here went beyond curiosity or the desire for conversation. This was dangerous in a way she could not possibly understand.

The High King's expression remained cool. 'Can it not wait?'

Brian helped lower Carice to stand, and he stood behind her for support. She lifted her gaze to Rory's and said, 'I came to warn you, Your Grace. You already know that someone tried to poison you, and I drank it by mistake. But there is another Norman in your midst, one who brought the poison with him. And he is the one who should be on trial now, not Raine de Garenne.'

'We already know that de Garenne did not put the poison into the wine. That is not why he is here.'

Don't, Raine wanted to warn her. He looked to her father and said, 'Take her away from here, Brian.'

The Irish chief saw the warning and nodded his agreement. But the High King intervened. 'No. If she chose to come this far, I would know why she delayed our wedding.'

Carice lifted her chin and replied, 'Because I was ill.'

'Killian told me that you had no desire to go through with a wedding.' The High King leaned forward in his chair, and there was no mistaking the venom within his voice. 'And when you did arrive, this Norman was among your servants. You brought a traitor in our midst—two, if what you say is true about the other.'

Raine wanted to move in to protect Carice, but if he did, the High King would only grow angrier. He needed to diffuse the man's rage, to somehow make him see the truth.

'I will fulfil our betrothal agreement,' Carice said softly. 'I will wed you to join my father's lands with yours.'

Her decision stopped Raine cold. Why would she do this? She had fought so hard to escape this marriage…and now she was surrendering? He didn't know what to believe, especially when her blue eyes avoided his.

But she wasn't finished. 'In return, I ask that you end this "*trial*" for a man who was not involved with my poisoning, and instead find the Norman soldier who tried to kill us both.'

Although Carice kept her voice steady, he saw the slight tremor in her hands. And he understood that she was doing this to save him. She had pulled upon the last of her strength to plead for his life, though she could not show the High King the truth about her feelings.

He wasn't going to let her go through with this. She would not sacrifice her own happiness to spare his life—he would fight his own battles.

The Ard-Righ stood and motioned for his men to draw closer to Carice. In a low voice, he said, 'This Norman was holding you as a lover would. He never left your side when you were poisoned. What is he to you?'

Don't speak, Raine wanted to warn her. Lies or truth would not matter to the High King. But Carice met his gaze and said, 'I was unconscious, Your Grace. I can hardly be blamed for someone attempting to save my life.'

'Do you know what the ancient law requires of a woman who is guilty of infidelity?' the High King asked. His voice hardened and he said quietly, 'Years ago, we used to burn them alive.'

At that, Raine moved behind her. He wasn't going to allow any man to lay a hand upon her. 'She is innocent.'

To Carice, he spoke beneath his breath in the Norman tongue. 'Tell the High King that if I am guilty of admiring a beautiful woman, of not wanting her to die, then let that punishment fall upon me.'

But her face turned sad and she shook her head. In a whisper, she answered, 'I will not translate words that will bring you suffering. Not when I can set you free.' There was bittersweet love within her words, and he wondered whether the High King had overheard their quiet conversation.

She stepped away from him and knelt before Rory Ó Connor. 'Your Grace, I am yours to command, whether you want me to wed you or return to Carrickmeath.'

Raine wanted to go to her, to pull her from her knees and take her away from this place. The lines of her face were drawn, as if every movement took an effort. To Brian, he said beneath his breath, 'If he lets her go, take her away from here. She's about to fall, she's so weak.'

The chief gave a slight nod to show he'd heard him. But before he could move towards his daughter, Rory asked, 'Did you know de Garenne was a Norman?'

Carice raised her face and nodded. 'I did, yes. Raine heard there was a plot against you, and he warned us about it. We believed that he could find the culprit and stop him.' The lies contained enough truth to be believable, and

her swift thinking seemed to make the king re-
consider. 'We never realised that the guilty man
was his comrade in arms.' She lowered her face
again, and asked, 'Please, Your Grace, search
for Sir Darren de Carleigh. He is the man you
seek, the one who wanted you dead.'

The High King descended from the platform
and came forward. 'Why should I believe a
word from either of you?'

'You may not believe them,' came a woman's
voice, 'but perhaps you will believe me.'

The crowd parted, revealing Aoife, the heavily pregnant woman whom they had saved. She
was dressed in silks, her hands resting upon her
swollen womb. A rope of pearls rested upon her
forehead and a veil covered her red hair.

'Lady Aoife.' The High King inclined his
head in greeting. Raine noted a slight tension
within the man. 'You did not send word that
you were stopping at Tara.'

She continued to walk slowly towards the
Ard-Righ, and when she reached Rory's side,
she sent him a smile. 'No. I came because my
husband is journeying here. He received word
that Norman soldiers attacked Tara, and several died.'

Again, Raine saw the flare of uncertainty

cross the High King's face. 'The Normans were traitors who disguised themselves among my people. But we resolved the matter, and there is no need for Strongbow to travel here.'

'Since Norman soldiers died in the battle,' Aoife continued, 'my husband will have to notify King Henry of those men who were involved.'

There was a thread of steel beneath her voice, of a woman unafraid of the High King. She was far more than a noblewoman—she spoke to him as an equal.

Raine put the connection together, suddenly realising her identity. Aoife was the daughter of Diarmuid MacMurrough, the King of Leinster. It meant that her husband was the notorious Richard de Clare, known to all as Strongbow. A dawning hope broke within him, for she might speak on their behalf. But he worried that she also could endanger Carice, by her knowledge of their relationship.

'I will have rooms prepared for you and your servants while I await him, then,' Rory said, signalling one of his stewards to come forward. 'You will want to rest after your travels.'

Aoife nodded, her expression serene. 'You are very kind. I am certain we can renew the peace between the Irish and the Normans. But that is not the only reason I am here.'

Her glance fastened upon Raine, and she beckoned for him to come forward. 'My husband will want to reward the Norman who saved my life from soldiers who attacked our travelling party. This man protected me, as well as my unborn child.'

She sent a slight smile towards the Ard-Right. 'Strongbow would not be pleased if you harmed the man who saved the life of his wife and heir. I have heard the witnesses, and I can tell you that Raine de Garenne is innocent of any attempt upon your life.'

Her gaze passed over him, and in Aoife's eyes, Raine saw the trace of warning. She knew what Carice meant to him, but it also appeared that she also recognised the consequences of revealing the truth.

Lady Aoife extended her hands to the High King and added, 'Will you release him so that my husband and I may reward him for his service to us?'

Chapter Eleven

Carice forced herself to look downward to avoid revealing any joy. Though she knew the High King was furious at being interrupted, he had no valid reason to hold Raine prisoner. To do so would only threaten the peace with Strongbow.

'He may be innocent of trying to poison me,' the Ard-Righ hedged, 'but his demeanour towards my bride was not innocent.'

'Let him leave, and you will not have to see him again,' Aoife suggested. 'There is no reason to keep him as your prisoner.'

She sent the Ard-Righ a kindly smile and continued. 'Sometimes I grow weary of the tensions between our people. You and I both know that we are fighting to keep our country from becoming part of Henry's kingdom.

I wed Strongbow to protect my people from the Normans. Both of us would do anything to guard what is ours.' She gave a light shrug. 'One man who happened to take an interest in your beautiful bride is hardly worth the effort. Send him away.'

Despite Aoife's insistence, the High King didn't appear at all interested in letting Raine go. It seemed that he was bent upon further punishment to satisfy his bruised pride.

But then, Carice spied a hint of movement in the shadows. Discreetly, she turned to see what was happening. Someone was pushing past the Irishmen and women gathered together.

To her surprise, she saw Trahern MacEgan. She hadn't realised that he'd followed them to Tara. Surrounding him were the other MacEgan soldiers who had accompanied Killian earlier. The Irish giant held Sir Darren in a fierce grip, and there was an expression of satisfaction upon his face. 'I believe you were looking for this man, Your Grace.'

The Ard-Righ leaned forward in his chair. 'Was this the Norman who brought the poison?'

'He was.' Carice faced him openly and said, 'My maids will bear witness to that.' She took a step towards the Norman, and her expression was grave. 'I demand that he be punished for attempting to kill us both.' She didn't know if this would save Raine's life, but it was her best hope.

The brehons began to speak quietly amongst themselves. The Ard-Righ went to join them, along with his advisor, the chief poet. When he returned, before he could speak, Raine dropped to one knee. 'Your Grace, I would like to ask for a trial by combat. Grant me the right to kill him on your behalf.'

Carice's heartbeat quickened at Raine's suggestion. Though she knew he loathed his commander and wanted vengeance, she worried that he might die in the battle. It was a risk she didn't want him to face.

The High King's expression remained guarded. 'And if you are killed?'

'Then judge him based upon your laws. But first, he should be tried by ours.'

Carice tried to catch Raine's expression, wanting so badly to plead with him not to do this. But if she dared to speak to him, it would only prove her own guilt. She could only hold her silence, terrified by what was to come.

Raine stepped back, awaiting the High King's response. The Ard-Righ consulted with the brehons and his chief poet, before he raised his hand to indicate that he had made a decision.

'I will let you fight Sir Darren, according to your laws. If you succeed, then you may have your freedom as compensation. But you will not return to Tara.'

The Ard-Righ gave a nod to his servants, who pushed back the onlookers to form a circle. Raine was given a blade, and the same was given to Sir Darren. A moment later, Aoife moved to her side. The young woman squeezed her hand in silent support, while Brian stood on Carice's opposite side. Her fingers were trembling with fear as she watched the man she loved.

Both stripped their armour and were bare from the waist up. The red lash marks upon Raine's back were evident for all to see. Sir Darren had a powerful build, with broad shoulders and a few scars. He, too, was given a blade.

Carice gripped her father's arm, praying that Raine would succeed. The two men circled one another, and she had no doubt that Darren would attack Raine's wounded back.

'Shall I tell them about you and the king's bride?' the Norman commander taunted. 'How you shared her bed and took her innocence.'

Raine slashed his blade towards the man's throat, but Darren dodged it, ploughing his fist into his gut. The air exploded from his lungs, but he countered with his own blow. 'Keep your lies to yourself. No one here will believe your attempts to dishonour the lady.'

Carice's blood ran cold with fear that the High King would believe it, but she didn't dare meet Rory Ó Connor's gaze. Instead, she watched the two men battling, stricken at the thought of Raine being hurt.

He moved with swiftness, striking blows with his left hand while slicing with the right. Although Darren tried to reach his wounded back, Raine was careful to guard it.

Until his commander lunged and caught a handful of dirt, tossing it into Raine's eyes. Carice bit her tongue to avoid crying out a warning. It was killing her to feign an impassive expression.

You cannot let the king know your feelings. You must behave as if Darren lied. But inwardly, she was dying.

Raine rolled over, and she watched in horror as Darren's blade cut his shoulder. Blood welled up from the skin, and the two men grappled on the ground.

Carice closed her eyes, as if to will him to stay alive. Only the tightening of Aoife's hand made her open them once more.

She saw the man she loved pinned beneath Sir Darren, the blade inching towards his throat. *No.* Tears burned in her eyes, her silent scream caught in her lungs. Raine's fallen weapon lay only inches from his hands.

At the last second, Raine smashed his head against Darren's and reached for the blade, burying it in the knight's throat. The knight's breath choked with blood before he lay still.

Carice gripped her hands to her mouth, her heart pounding. Aoife looked at her, and the young woman's gaze was knowing. She prayed Strongbow's wife would say nothing.

Raine stood up from his commander's body and cleaned his blade. Then he lowered to one knee before the High King, waiting for judgment.

The Ard-Righ studied him for a long moment before he said, 'The trial by combat is finished. Go with the Lady Aoife, and leave Tara. I will grant you your freedom as promised, but do not return.'

The threat within his voice was unmistakable. Carice desperately wanted to turn to

Raine, for one last farewell. But if she dared to do so, it would further arouse the High King's suspicions. Though she was so relieved that Raine was free to go, she was well aware that she did not have her own freedom.

Instead, she kept her face lowered, trying to hold back her emotions. The man she loved was leaving, and she would not see him again.

Inside, her heart ached with the loss. Though she desperately wanted to be with him, she would pay any price for his life. Raine would accompany Lady Aoife back to her husband, and Strongbow's position with the Normans was well-respected. If anyone could free Raine from King Henry's forces, it was he.

She heard Raine murmur his thanks to the High King, and then the crowds dissipated. Carice remained where she was, and her father came up behind her. 'Let me take you back to your chamber.'

She glanced up for the High King's permission, and he gave a nod. Her father picked her up, and she allowed him to carry her back. As she rested her face against his tunic, she felt a sense of the world closing in. She was indebted to the Ard-Righ, and if he demanded marriage, she could not refuse.

Her father slowed his pace and stopped for
a moment. Carice could not tell why, but when
she lifted her head, she saw Raine standing
there. His green eyes met hers with the intensity of a man who loved her. The sight of him
cut off any words she might have spoken. Tears
gleamed in her eyes, but she sent him a silent
message.

I love you.

He touched his fingers briefly to his lips before he turned away.

'The chief of Carrickmeath is here to see
you, Your Grace,' the servant announced.

Brian Faoilin raised a knee in deference to
the High King. Rory Ó Connor was standing
at the top of a wooden raised platform to ob-
serve the land surrounding them. The winter air was warmer, and sun gleamed over the
green hills of Tara. Brian awaited permission to approach, and when it was given, he
climbed the ladder up to the top of the platform. From here, they could see the grassy
knolls covered with melting snow.

Ever since he'd left Carice's side, his daughter hadn't spoken. She had stared at the wall,

curled up as if she wanted to die. Never had he seen such desolation on her face.

Although she had promised to go through with the marriage, it was clear that she didn't want to live without the Norman soldier.

'Are you certain this is what you want?' he'd asked her.

'I would do anything to save Raine's life. Even give him up.'

Brian had tried to convince himself that she would get over the heartbreak, that she would learn to care for the High King. But the truth was, he knew her feelings too well. When he'd lost his wife in childbirth, he'd felt the same cold emptiness. And he'd have given his own life in her place, if it would have brought Saoirse back.

When an hour passed and his daughter hadn't spoken, Brian had spent time reconsidering the choices he'd made. Carice was all he had left, and he didn't know how many years she had remaining. If he forced her to go through with this marriage, she would wither away and die of grief. And he didn't want to lose her, too.

For that reason, he had decided to take matters into his own hands.

'I have come to offer compensation for my

daughter,' Brian began. 'I will send a hundred cattle and fifty horses.'

Rory Ó Connor turned to face him. The man's steel eyes were hard, as if he couldn't bring himself to answer.

Brian moved to stand beside the High King. 'It is not only to apologise for my daughter's actions…but also for the way I treated your son Killian.'

'I will expect you to give the cattle and horses to him, then,' Rory answered. 'If your apology is real.'

The High King wasn't going to make this any easier. But though Brian had made many mistakes over the years, he believed it was possible to put them to rights. 'If that is your wish.'

'You want me to let your daughter go, don't you?' Rory said at last.

Brian moved to stand by a railing and rested his hands upon it. 'There was a time when I would have done anything to arrange a marriage between the two of you. What father would not want his daughter to be High Queen of Éireann?' He looked away towards the landscape. 'But that is not what she wants.'

'She wants the Norman soldier, doesn't she?'

The High King's voice was grim, and Brian knew he had to tread carefully.

'I want to make amends, Your Grace. For everything.'

For a time, the Ard-Righ remained silent. It was all Brian could do not to fill the space with pleading or offers for more. But this negotiation was for his daughter's happiness.

'She would not have made a suitable bride for me,' Rory conceded at last. 'I will put an end to the betrothal, and you will take her home. But—' He turned and levelled a stare at Brian. '—you will tell her that it was Killian's intervention. Let her believe that *he* caused me to change my mind.'

The smug air upon the High King's face was difficult to face, so Brian turned his attention to the wooden platform. 'So be it.'

Raine entered Carice's chamber silently and saw her sitting in a chair facing the wall. Her back was to the door, and she didn't seem to care that anyone had come inside.

The emerald gown she wore had slid against one shoulder, and Raine longed to touch his mouth to the bared spot. He could hardly move for fear that all of this would disappear, like awakening from a dream.

'Am I being summoned?' she asked, without turning around. 'Has the High King ordered me to wed him?'

'He let you go.' The moment Raine spoke, Carice turned around. Her expression held such joy and bewilderment, he couldn't stop himself from kneeling at her feet. 'You do not have to wed him.'

She embraced him hard, her tears mingling with a laugh of relief. 'But why are you here, Raine? I thought he ordered you to leave.'

'I am taking you with me first.' He didn't ask permission, but lifted her into his arms. 'That is, if you want to go.'

'Yes. Yes, I do.' Carice wound her arms around his neck and lifted her mouth to his. It was a kiss of wonder that held all the hopes of a new beginning. He kissed her like a starving man, so grateful for this day when he could claim her as his own.

'I love you,' she blurted out against his mouth. The words warmed his heart, and he could not resist stealing another kiss. This fragile woman had become his very reason for life, and he could not imagine being without her.

'I love you, Carice.' He pressed back a lock of her hair, still disbelieving what had happened. Though he knew she was still fighting back illness, he wanted this woman for whatever time remained between them.

She drew back and asked, 'What of my father?' Worry creased her face and she added, 'He will forbid us to leave.'

Raine sent her a reassuring look. 'Brian is waiting for us. It was arranged earlier this morn, and he sent me to fetch you.'

'I don't understand.' She shook her head with confusion. 'Did you speak with the High King? Was this your doing?'

He wasn't certain how to answer that, for he'd had no intention of negotiating—he'd planned to steal Carice away from Tara.

'I was already planning to return and capture you,' Raine admitted. 'I spoke with Lady Aoife and asked for her help in saving you.' He sent her a grave look. 'I would have cut down any man who stood in my way. She knew I was going back, and that I would never let you go. But it was your father who stopped me, only an hour ago.'

Never had he imagined he would find an ally in Brian Faoilin. But the man had surprised

him, blocking Raine's path before he could shed
any blood.

*'If you try to take her by force, they will kill
both of you. Is that what you want? Especially
after all I risked, to save you?'*

He hadn't understood at the time what Brian
was talking about. But given the choice between
fighting for Carice or accepting a father's sacrifice, he'd known which was the better course.
'He told me that your brother Killian used his
influence to end the betrothal.'

'But Killian isn't here,' she mused. With a
discerning look, she said, 'This was Brian's
doing.' She touched a hand to her throat, her
face softening. 'He spoke with Rory and ended
the betrothal. I am certain of it.'

'I believe so. But he won't admit it.' He kept
her in his arms and touched her mouth with his.
'I would have torn down these walls before I'd
have allowed you to wed Rory Ó Connor. Nothing and no one would have stopped me.'

'I know that,' she murmured. 'But my father
made it so you didn't have to. I am glad.'

Although Raine didn't like being in Brian's
debt, he agreed with her. But more than that,
it bridged the way to forgiveness between fa-

ther and daughter. He would not stand in the way of that.

He brought Carice from the chamber, and as they departed, he gave orders to her maids to pack Carice's belongings. Only when they reached the door to the outside did he let her down to walk. 'Have you the strength to ride?'

Her face broke into a smile. 'Yes.'

He knew that it would not be wise to display affection towards her when they were within the boundaries of Tara. Once he opened the door, he let her lead the way, following several paces behind.

Her father was waiting for them with horses near the gates. And though Brian appeared uncertain about Raine's presence, he softened at the sight of his daughter's joyous smile.

They rode out of the gates of Tara, through the melting snow and down the hillside. Raine only breathed easier when they were nearly a mile away from the High King's men. He spurred his horse and moved to ride beside Carice. The moment she saw him, she reached for his hand. 'I suppose Lady Aoife will be grateful that you didn't have to storm through Tara's defences to rescue me. Especially after she tried to save your life.'

'She did invite me to visit her fortress at Leinster,' he told Carice, 'and she knew I could not let you go.' He gripped her palm and asked the question that had been troubling him. 'If the Ard-Righ had demanded it, would you truly have wed him?'

She met his gaze and said, 'I would have wed the devil himself if it meant setting you free.' With a sheepish smile, she added, 'But I am glad I don't have to.'

'And what of us?' He kept her hand in his, studying those sea blue eyes. 'Will you wed me now?'

Carice sent him a sidelong glance. 'I might. If you can convince me to say yes.'

A shot of heat rippled through him at the thought. 'Your father is watching.' But he reached over and pulled her onto his horse.

'Raine, what are you doing?' Her eyes widened as he held her in front of him. He tethered her horse loosely to his, and the two animals walked alongside one another.

'Convincing you.' He kept one arm around her waist and adjusted the folds of her cloak to hide her gown from view. A moment later, his hand found her soft breast. The moment he touched her, his body grew aroused.

'Don't you dare,' she warned. In answer, he stroked at her erect nipple, tempting her. With his thumb, he reshaped it, drawing it between his fingertips until she squirmed against him. Her backside pressed hard and the movement made him wish he could lift her skirts right now.

'Say yes,' he commanded. Her breathing grew hitched as he continued to stroke her. 'Unless you want me to stop.'

Her breathless moan made him laugh softly against her hair. But she tilted her face back to look at him. 'Raine, I love you.'

'Then you'll wed me?'

'Yes,' she whispered. 'But you had better put me back on my own horse, or my father will have you flayed alive.'

He didn't care that her father was watching but took her mouth in a long kiss. She touched his face with her hand, leaning back as he claimed her. The heat of her lips kindled a fire that could only be quenched by her. He gave in to the desire, invading her mouth with his tongue, promising her everything.

'I love you, *chérie*. And I promise that I'll take care of you always. For as long as that might be.'

She stared up at him, and in her eyes, he caught a glimpse of heaven. 'It will be forever.'

It was silent within the camp, and Carice stirred from her bed furs. Her maids awakened instantly, but she raised her finger to her lips, insisting that they stay behind and not follow her. She slipped outside the tent, pulling the heavy woollen cloak tightly around her.

Although she was weak and tired, she wanted to spend her first night of freedom with Raine. Quietly, she tiptoed past the rows of tents, keeping to the shadows, until she reached his.

When she peered inside the flap, an oil lamp was lit, illuminating the space. Raine was not asleep, but he had set aside his armour and wore only his braies and chausses. The moment he saw her, his eyes grew heated.

'Did you need something, Carice?' he murmured, rising to his feet.

'Yes.' She untied her cloak and let it fall to the ground. Tracing her palm over his cheek, she said, 'I needed to see you.'

The dim light from the lamp illuminated his blond hair, and he looked as if he wanted to run his mouth over her skin. The thought was shockingly sensual.

'I needed to know that this is real,' she continued. 'That I won't suddenly awaken and find myself trapped in a life I don't want.'

Raine stared at her for a moment, a faint smile upon his face. 'This is real, Carice. As am I.'

She brought his hands to her shoulders, wanting so badly to have this moment with him. Restlessness had flowed over her body until she'd had no choice but to seek him out.

The anticipation was so strong, she needed his arms around her. Even if she did nothing but sleep beside him, she wanted to feel his touch.

'How are you feeling?' he asked gently, his hands grazing her spine. Her skin grew sensitive, tightening with desire.

'Better with each moment,' she admitted. Though she'd had to fight to survive, she could think of nowhere else she wanted to be.

'I don't think you should be standing,' he said. 'Lie down.'

It did feel easier when she lay back against the furs. 'I didn't want to be alone tonight. Not without you.'

He lay beside her and pulled her into his arms. She twined her legs with his, resting her cheek against his heart. 'Did you ever imagine, when I wandered into the abbey, that it would end up like this between us?'

'No.' He stroked her hair back, holding her close. 'I never thought I deserved happiness.'

She leaned over to kiss him. 'I want that for you. For us.' But she knew that the thought of his sisters was still preying upon him. She hadn't pressed him, but if they were still alive somewhere, she intended to reunite him with them.

'Kiss me,' she murmured. 'Be with me to-night.'

His mouth moved upon hers, as if he were trying to be gentle. She licked the seam of his lips and felt the answering heat of his arousal against the juncture of her thighs.

She touched his bare chest, feeling his heart-beat beneath her palm. The rapid pulse was like her own, and she moved her fingers over his bare nipples. He sucked in a breath of air, his eyes smouldering.

'Do you know what it did to me when I thought you were dying?' he asked, catching her fingers.

She shook her head, stilling her hands upon him. He sat up, pulling her onto his lap. 'When I saw you fighting to breathe, I couldn't breathe myself. I didn't even care that they took me prisoner—all I cared about was your life.'

'I'm going to live, Raine.' She believed that now, with all her heart. With each day, she grew stronger, and her stomach no longer hurt. And whether that was from embracing a new life with him or whether she had to be careful of the food she ate, she believed she would spend the rest of her life with this man. 'Besides, I have you to live for.'

He kissed her as if she was his reason for being alive. In his embrace, she felt whole and beloved. He laid her back, helping her undress until she lay naked before him. He removed his own clothing and ran his hands over her flesh. 'You are beautiful to me, Carice.'

She smiled and brought him down to her. His body was warm, the hardness of his muscles pressing against her softness. For a moment, he simply lay on top of her, skin to skin. Then he adjusted his weight, moving his hands along the sides of her body, caressing her curves. His callused palms evoked a strong reaction, and though she was already anticipating his body inside hers, she recognised his desire to slow down, to savour.

He nipped at her earlobe, and a shudder

passed over her. But when his mouth lowered to her throat, she jolted at the sensitive place, biting back a shriek.

'That wasn't the reaction I was hoping for, *chérie*.' But there was amusement in his voice.

She couldn't stop herself from laughing. 'I was ticklish, Raine. When you put your mouth on my neck, I couldn't stand it.'

He started to move in, and she put both hands on her neck. 'If you dare, I'll scream so loudly, my father and his men will descend upon us.'

Instead, he moved his hands to cup her breasts. 'I don't mind if you scream loudly, Carice. So long as I bring you pleasure.'

Her laughter died away, and she gasped as he stroked her nipples. He bent and suckled one, pressing her back against the furs. Her fingers dug into his hair, and she arched beneath him. While he worked her with his mouth, he brought both hands down her hips, parting her legs. She surrendered, and he worshipped at the altar of her body, before his fingers touched her intimately.

She could hardly catch her breath when he found her damp opening and slid two fingers inside. 'Raine.' His name was a prayer upon her lips, and he began invading and withdrawing with his fingers. All the while, he continued tormenting her nipple with his tongue, but when he began to circle his thumb against her hooded flesh, she raked her fingers against his spine.

'Come inside me,' she pleaded. 'I need you.'

In answer, he put only the head of his shaft at her opening. She tried to bring him inside, but he held her down. 'Not yet.'

He turned his attention to her other breast, and she grew even wetter, seeking a full joining with the man she loved.

He found a rhythm that she delighted in, pressing and circling her intimate flesh, until she felt herself beginning to tremble. Her body ached to be filled, and she dug her hands into his shoulders. She was quaking, straining to meet him, when suddenly a white hot shuddering release unfurled within her. The wave of ecstasy pulsed through her, and when he slid deep inside, she bit back her cry of relief.

He moved slowly, caressing her with his shaft, while she tried to urge him faster. Her entire body was pliant against him, and when he began to thrust, she squeezed him from within.

'Do that again,' he commanded, as he entered and withdrew. She locked her leg around his waist, meeting him as he plunged deep.

As he continued to drive his body within hers, she heard him murmur words of love in the Norman tongue, words that praised her beauty.

And when he hastened his thrusts, reaching for his own release, she tightened around him, startled when her body bucked and another ripple of pleasure caught her in its grasp.

'I love you, Raine,' she cried out, as he thrust hard and pulsed against her, his body finding its own fulfilment.

He leaned down to kiss her, his lips softened and swollen from their lovemaking. With their bodies joined, he held her close. 'Know that I will always love you, Carice.'

She fell asleep with his body against hers, feeling blessed beyond words.

They returned to Carrickmeath, but Carice made him promise to wait until the summer before they wed. Although Raine had wanted to wed her the moment they reached her father's estate, she had insisted on delaying the marriage for a few months while they attempted to find out the fate of his sisters.

Raine had sent over a dozen men to search England, but there was no sign of them. He'd wanted to travel there himself, but he was wary of leaving Carice. Although her health had continued to improve with each day, he was still afraid of her declining again.

Lady Aoife and Strongbow had agreed to intervene with King Henry on his behalf. They had made it possible for him to end his service as a soldier, and Raine had come to live at Carrickmeath with Carice. In time, King Henry hardly seemed to care what became of him. With the Irish Sea to separate them, the man was disinterested in stirring up conflict among the Irish chiefs—especially when he wanted to rule over them all.

Even so, it was the longest three months of his life. For Carice had also demanded celibacy until their wedding night.

Although Raine guessed that she wanted to be strong enough to fully enjoy their wedding celebration, it didn't make it any easier. The one consolation was that each day she grew stronger. Now, he could no longer see her ribs, and her body held a softness with curves that tempted him beyond reason.

He stood outside, anxious for the wedding to be finished so he could be with his wife. The summer sunlight shone over them, and it took an effort not to pace.

Her brother Killian came to stand beside him. 'You do realise,' he remarked, 'that if you hurt my sister in any way, I will peel the skin from your body.'

'She's not really your sister.' He grinned at the man who had come to be a good friend over the past few months. As the High King's son, Killian had taken over the province of Ossoria, along with his new wife, Lady Taryn.

'Not by blood, perhaps. But in all the ways that count.' Killian fingered the knife at his side. 'You had best make her happy, or I will make you wish you'd never been born.'

'That I will. But I do not know why she insisted on waiting so long for our wedding.'

'Like as not, she wanted it to be summer. Carice despises the winter.' Killian shrugged and accompanied him down the stone stairs. Below, in the inner bailey, several wagons had arrived, bearing gifts from the MacEgans and from the Connelly clan. 'She also commissioned a special wedding present for you and went to a lot of trouble.' With that, he withdrew a blindfold. 'I'm going to put this on you, and when Carice arrives, she will reveal her gift.'

The secrecy intrigued him, but Raine saw no reason to protest. Once the blindfold was in place, Killian took him by the arm and guided him towards the stone chapel. 'Walk forward six paces,' the man ordered, and Raine counted as he did. He felt the warmth of the summer sunlight transforming into shadows against his skin as he approached the doorway. Then he heard the voice of Lady Taryn as they drew closer.

Feminine hands touched his face, and when the blindfold was removed, he saw his bride standing before him. Carice's long brown hair hung below her waist in waving curls. She stood just outside the chapel, and the sun illuminated her hair like a halo. Her sky blue eyes held love and anticipation. 'Are you ready, Raine?'

'I was ready to wed you three months ago,' he reminded her.

'Not for the wedding.' She smiled at him. 'Something else. I know I should wait to give you your gift until after we are wed. But I find I cannot stand it any longer.' Carice clutched her hands together with excitement, and her smile held such joy, it echoed the feelings in his heart.

'Go on, then.' He let her take him by the hand, and they entered the stone chapel. Inside, it was darker, and when his eyes adjusted, he saw his sisters standing inside. Elise and Nicole both ran forward, and he caught them in his arms, unable to believe they were alive.

'Raine, I've missed you so much—'

'I cannot believe you're here—'

'—I'm so glad to see you.'

Their voices jumbled together, and he couldn't stop from crushing them close, so thankful they were here. 'You found them.'

'With Queen Isabel's help,' she agreed. 'Her father is Norman, living near the border of Wales. He learned where they were and arranged for them to travel to Carrickmeath. That was why I delayed our wedding.' In her face, he saw the quiet joy. 'I wanted them to be here for you, after all you endured. King Henry never harmed them—he only sent them far away.'

Raine let go of his sisters briefly to lift Carice up, kissing her hard before he let her slide down. 'I love you. You could not have given me a greater gift, Carice.'

She sent him a gentle smile, touching his face. 'Perhaps in the next year, you might give *me* a greater gift. Like a child.'

'It would be my pleasure.' He leaned in and kissed her neck, only to have her squeal again at the sensitive place. 'Raine, stop! I cannot bear it.' But her protests were mingled with laughter.

He took her by the hand, and they gathered together among friends and family. They spoke their vows before the priest to be faithful to one another for the rest of their lives.

But for Raine, even an eternity would never be enough.

Epilogue

Two years later

They rode through the gates, and Carice held their son Guy before her in the saddle. Raine's mood was quiet as they approached, for he had not set foot upon his father's lands in many years. King Henry had granted the land to Richard de Clare and his wife Aoife, but now Richard was dead. Lady Aoife had offered Raine the chance to visit his family holdings, and she had hinted that they might one day govern them on her behalf.

It should have been a blessing. Although Carice knew that her father would want their son to eventually become the chief of the Faoilin clan, she wanted Guy to know his Norman lineage as well.

Raine hadn't been eager to return to England.

Carice knew that there were many ghosts who haunted him here, and the small estate held an air of neglect. But on the far side of the tower, a few fragile roses struggled to climb the stone walls.

Several servants came forward, their eyes wide as a few recognised Raine.

'Do you want a moment to walk around?' Carice asked. 'I could wait here with Guy.'

'I would rather have both of you with me,' he answered. He helped her down, and she balanced their son on her hip.

'My lord.' An older man hurried forward, bowing before them. His beard was grey and he was bald, but there was no mistaking the excitement in his demeanour. 'We have waited so long for your return.'

'Bertrand, it is good to see you as well,' Raine answered. The older man led them up the stairs and inside the main gathering space. But the moment they entered the Hall, Carice saw a change come over her husband. He grew pensive and quiet. Instinctively, she reached for his hand.

'My mother died here,' he said quietly. 'She took her own life in this place, after my father was killed by King Henry's men.'

Carice rested her forehead against his shoulder, trying to offer her own comfort. She let him spill out the details of their deaths, and when Guy began to fuss, she handed their son to Raine. The moment the boy wrapped his arms around his father's neck, he calmed. The presence of their son seemed to bring a different peace to Raine.

'They loved each other, didn't they?' She rubbed her son's back, still remaining close to Raine. 'The way I love you.'

He turned to her. 'I never understood, at the time, why she killed herself. Why she didn't want to live for her children.' He touched Guy's baby curls and kissed the boy's head. 'And then they buried her on unconsecrated ground.'

'Can you show me where?'

He gave a nod, but before he could lead her outside the gates, Carice stopped near the climbing roses. She took her knife and cut part of the cane, digging up some of the roots. With the rose cutting in her hands, she followed him towards the woods. There, near the edge of the trees, was a bare space of earth without anything to mark the place, save a small oak sapling.

Carice knelt by the grave and spoke a silent

prayer for the woman who had given life to Raine. Then she planted the rose cutting within the earth. It would take root and grow, a living promise of beauty to the woman she had never met.

In the meantime, Raine took their son towards a small brook that ran through the woods. He scooped up a handful of water in his palms and showed Guy how to do the same. Both of them walked back to the grave, letting the droplets spill over the planted rose.

'My mother would have loved you, Carice,' Raine said, when they stood beside the grave. 'She simply wasn't strong enough to live without my father.'

'I don't want to live without you, either,' she said. 'But however long we live, a part of us will always live on in our son. And in other children we may have.' She brought his hand to her womb. Though it was early yet, she was certain that another child grew within her.

The words had their intended effect, and Raine's sadness transformed into wonder. 'When?'

'In the winter, I think,' she answered. 'But you will have to decide whether we stay here or return to Éireann. It is your choice.'

He thought a moment and studied the grave. 'There has been too much grief within this place. Before we go back to Carrickmeath, we ought to rebuild it and make it a place of better memories. Then, perhaps our son might wed Lady Aoife's daughter and bring the lands back into our family.'

'I agree.' Carice took his hand and started to lead him back towards the tower. 'And since Guy is eager to take a nap, we should let him rest within our chamber. Then we can start making better memories while he is asleep.' She sent him a sensual smile and touched his chest. 'If you will show me the way.'

His green eyes grew heated at her suggestion, and he kissed her fingertips. 'You are a very wise woman, my wife.'

'I am, aren't I?' But, in answer to her teasing smile, he bent again to kiss her throat. Her screech of laughter broke through the darker memories, leaving room for new ones to fill their place.

And when he led the way to their chamber, she was only too willing to follow.

* * * * *

Author Note

The mysterious illness that Carice Faoilin suffered from is known by modern readers as celiac disease. It was present in Ireland, though medieval healers would not have known the cause. Thank you to Dr Katherine Roberts for the story suggestion and to Dana Rollins for your insights on the symptoms. You both have my deepest appreciation.

I took a bit of literary licence by not fully describing the digestive results of celiac disease—let's face it: diarrhoea isn't exactly romantic—but her stomach pains, overall fatigue, and weakness would have been true to the illness.

While symptoms can often remain dormant for years, they can also emerge at a time of great personal stress—such as an arranged marriage to the High King—making gluten intolerable. Carice's stomach ailments were caused by eating bread and grains. The healer's advice to eat only bread would have essentially caused her to weaken and die, for her digestive system would not have tolerated the gluten. She also could not have gained any nourishment from food, especially if she consumed bread at a meal. Eliminating it from her diet would have caused a complete recovery.

And thus, she was able to live a long and fulfilling life with Raine de Garenne.

Thank you for reading *Warrior of Fire*, and if you would like to read Killian and Taryn's story, look for *Warrior of Ice,* book one in the *Warriors of Ireland series.*

If you have time, please consider leaving a review online. You can find a complete list of my titles at *www.michellewillingham.com*.

If you'd like me to email you when I have a new book out, please sign up for my newsletter at *http://www.michellewillingham.com/cgi-bin/dada/mail.cgi*. Your email address will never be shared or sold, and you may unsubscribe at any time.

MILLS & BOON®

HISTORICAL

AWAKEN THE ROMANCE OF THE PAST

A sneak peek at next month's titles...

In stores from 1st January 2016:

- **In Debt to the Earl** – Elizabeth Rolls
- **Rake Most Likely to Seduce** – Bronwyn Scott
- **The Captain and His Innocent** – Lucy Ashford
- **Scoundrel of Dunborough** – Margaret Moore
- **One Night with the Viking** – Harper St. George
- **Familiar Stranger in Clear Springs** – Kathryn Albright

Available at WHSmith, Tesco, Asda, Eason, Amazon and Apple

Just can't wait?
Buy our books online a month before they hit the shops!
visit www.millsandboon.co.uk

These books are also available in eBook format!

1215/04

MILLS & BOON®

If you enjoyed this story,
you'll love the the full *Revenge Collection!*

**Enjoy the misdemeanours and the sinful world
of revenge with this six-book collection.
Indulge in these riveting 3-in-1 romances
from top Modern Romance authors.**

Order your complete collection today at
www.millsandboon.co.uk/revengecollection

1115_MB517

'The perfect Christmas read!' - Julia Williams

Jewellery designer Skylar loves living London, but when a surprise proposal goes wrong, she finds herself fleeing home to remote Puffin Island.

Burned by a terrible divorce, TV historian Alec is dazzled by Sky's beauty and so cynical that he assumes that's a bad thing! Luckily she's on the verge of getting engaged to someone else, so she won't be a constant source of temptation... but this Christmas, can Alec and Sky realise that they are what each other was looking for all along?

Order yours today at
www.millsandboon.co.uk

MILLS & BOON®

The Billionaires Collection!

This fabulous 6 book collection features stories from some of our talented writers. Feel the temperature rise with our ultra-sexy and powerful billionaires. Don't miss this great offer – buy the collection today to get two books free!

2 FREE BOOKS!

Order yours at
**www.millsandboon.co.uk
/billionaires**

1215_MB16

MILLS & BOON®

Why shop at millsandboon.co.uk?

Each year, thousands of romance readers find their perfect read at millsandboon.co.uk. That's because we're passionate about bringing you the very best romantic fiction. Here are some of the advantages of shopping at www.millsandboon.co.uk:

* **Get new books first**—you'll be able to buy your favourite books one month before they hit the shops

* **Get exclusive discounts**—you'll also be able to buy our specially created monthly collections, with up to 50% off the RRP

* **Find your favourite authors**—latest news, interviews and new releases for all your favourite authors and series on our website, plus ideas for what to try next

* **Join in**—once you've bought your favourite books, don't forget to register with us to rate, review and join in the discussions

Visit **www.millsandboon.co.uk**
for all this and more today!

MILLS_WEB